Man in a Cage

Man in
a Cage

Brian M. Stableford

The John Day Company
NEW YORK

Designed by Ingrid Beckman

Manufactured in the United States of America

Library of Congress Cataloging in Publication Data

Stableford, Brian M
    Man in a cage.

    I. Title.
PZ4.S7735Man3   [PR6069.T17]   823'.9'14   74-22024
    ISBN 0-381-98280-7
    10 9 8 7 6 5 4 3 2 1

Dedication:

For Katharine Madge and Chris Macrae

Contents

Contents

MADMAN'S DANCE

CHAPTER 1
Genesis

In the beginning, you create the heaven and the earth. That's the first thing you do, every time—build cages. And the second thing you do is to pin the labels on.

And the earth is without form, and void; and darkness is upon the face of the deep. And the Spirit moves upon the face of the waters.

And you say, Let there be light: and there is light.

And you see the light, that it is good: and you divide the light from the darkness, and the pattern of light and darkness is one of the cages.

And you call the light Day, and the darkness you call Night. And the evening and the morning are the first day. And you rest. You're not attempting the record. That's right. Play it safe. Play it by the book. Easy now.

And you say, Let there be a firmament in the midst of the waters, and let it divide the waters from the waters.

And you make the firmament and divide the waters which are under the firmament from the waters which are above the firmament: and it is so.

And you call the firmament a cage of darkness. And the evening and the morning are the second day. That's right. A cage of darkness. Face it. Make it what it is. Start with a clean sheet. No hypocrisy. You and I, Titan. Never forget that. Come the time, we go running home, right back into the cage of darkness. Don't forget the door. Face the facts. You're not God, you're just playing the game. Come the time, the game ends. You and I, we have the sense to go home, whether it rains or not. It's a game, only a game.

And you say, Let the waters under the cage of darkness be gathered together into one place, and let the dry land appear: and it is so.

And you call the dry land Earth; and the gathering together of the waters you call Seas: and you see that it is good.

And you say, Let the earth bring forth grass, the herb yielding seed, and the fruit tree yielding fruit after his kind, whose seed is in itself the earth: and it is so.

And the earth brings forth grass, and herb yielding seed after his kind, and the tree yielding fruit, whose seed is in itself, after his kind: and you see that it is good.

And the evening and the morning are the third day. Careful now, it's taking shape. Think carefully, when you fill these cages, is there anything you could well do without? If there is, should you? How much self-indulgence can you permit yourself? How much can you permit yourself in *your* image? If anything. Dare you tamper with the script? Dare you get more than a few little words—just a label—out of line? How much can you give yourself? It's only a game. You have to remember that. You have to go back. The door is open now, and you're free. But you're on parole. You've got to leave that door where it is. You've got to carry that door with you wherever you are. And if you're everywhere, then that door has to be everywhere, too. You have to have that door. Don't make a world for yourself which will shut that door, which won't permit that door to be open, and to be with you. Be careful. Be careful. The book is safe. You know the book.

And you say, Let there be lights in the firmament of the heaven to divide the day from the night: and let them be for signs, and for seasons and for days, and years.

And let them be for lights in the firmament of the cage of darkness to give light upon the earth: and it is so.

And you make two great lights; the greater light to rule the day and the lesser light to rule the night: you make the stars also.

And you set them in the firmament of the cage of darkness to give light upon the earth.

And to rule over the day and over the night, and to divide the light from the darkness: and you see that it is good.

And the evening and the morning are the fourth day. You have to have the stars. The stars are necessary. Without the stars there's nothing to laugh at you from beyond the bars of the cage. Without something to laugh at you from beyond, how are you going to remind yourself of the cage, while you are yourself beyond? Look at the stars, Titan, look at the stars.

And you say, Let the waters bring forth abundantly the moving creature that hath life, and fowl that may fly above the earth in the open sky.

And you create great whales, and every living creature that moveth, which the water brings forth abundantly, after their kind, and every winged fowl after his kind: and you see that it is good.

And you bless them, saying, Be fruitful, and multiply,

and fill the waters in the seas, and let fowl multiply in the earth.

And the evening and the morning are the fifth day. No sweat. But the difficult bit is right around the corner. Tread softly, for you trespass on my dreams. Play it by ear, but play it well. This passage is the crucial one. Slip here and you can kiss good-bye to that cage which caresses you with such exquisite claustrophobia. Count your motives, and keep time. Whatever you do, keep time.

And you say, Let the earth bring forth the living creature after his kind, cattle and creeping thing, and beast of the earth after his kind; and it is so.

And you make the beast of the earth after his kind, and cattle after their kind, and every thing that creepeth upon the earth after his kind: and you see that it is good.

And you say, Let us make man in our image, after our likeness: and let them have dominion over the fish of the sea and over the fowl of the air, and over the cattle, and over the earth, and over every creeping thing that creepeth upon the earth.

So you create man in your own image, in the image of yourself create you him; male and female create you them.

And you say unto them, Be fruitful and multiply, and replenish the earth, and subdue it: and have dominion over the fish of the sea, and over the fowl of the air, and over every living thing that moveth upon the earth.

And you say, Behold, I have given you every herb bearing seed, which is upon the face of all the earth, and every tree, in the which is the first of a tree yielding seed; to you it shall be for meat.

And to every beast of the earth, and to every fowl of the air, and to every thing that creepeth upon the earth, wherein there is life, I have given every green herb for meat: and it is so.

And you see every thing that you have made, and, behold it is very good. And the evening and the morning are the sixth day. Thus the cage of darkness and the earth which it contains are finished, and all the host of them. And you have to live with this, and in this, and for this. You just don't know what you might have done. How can you?

In *your* image.

And mine, because don't kid yourself that your image isn't mine. In our own image, you have created man. You have created Sam Mastervine and Luis Dalquier and Nathan Petrie. And Judas Dancer. In our image.

Was there something *wrong* with Adam and Eve? This is a game, you know. A game of God, but a game just the same. You, of all people, cannot afford delusions of grandeur. You cannot afford to be a *vain* god. You have that door to carry behind you, in your pocket, in your hand, on your back. You can't close that door on the whole damn human race. You're not Lindquist—you know better than he did. You *know* about that door. When Lindquist went into the labyrinth he didn't have any way back, but if you get lost it's you and you alone. We have to go *back*, you and I. Back into captivity, back into that cage of darkness with all the rest of the animals. You know that. I know what you have up your sleeve. Adam carried the can: he took the responsibility that should never have been his, and he caged humanity in blood, sweat, and tears. But you can't do that, because I won't let you. You can't hand over the responsibility and the blame to Judas Dancer. I won't let you. *Judas* won't let you. He doesn't have to take that from you, and he won't. We're free, Judas and I, and we're free to go back to our cage. You can't stop us. We're not going to let you carry this game into all eternity.

We'll keep that door open if you can't. If you won't.

You sleep, you dream. But I'll be awake inside your dream, and come the time I'm going to sound an alarm like you never heard, and I'll take you through that door if I have to blast your universe apart!

Titan Nine

CHAPTER 1

There and Back Again

It was as hot as hell inside the Chevy, but I wasn't complaining. It could have been a lot worse—an armored van with blacked-out windows, for instance. Plus manacles. I was privileged, and it was advisable to be seen to be appreciating it. No time off for good behavior, of course, but *easier* time—and you can't appreciate how much that means.

The desert looked like a well-kept woman—all powder and rouge on the surface, but pleasantly shaped and good looking in spite of it all. I appreciated that, too—you get a taste for dead space eventually.

We could see the tower above the big iron gates from a good few miles away.

"That it?" the driver asked me. How the hell was I supposed to know? I told him I guessed so. The guy beside me grinned, but he didn't say anything. We'd already been through all the banal remarks like how much I was looking forward to a change of scene and how the project was shut up so tight it would be just like Block C except the personnel would be crazier. We'd ridden most of the way in silence. How can you build up a conversation out of idiot cracks like that? Not that these guys were idiots, mind—just that we didn't exactly have a lot in common.

The driver reined in the car about ten yards short of the gates. He looked expectantly toward the guardhouse, but he didn't make a move. Neither did I. There's protocol to be observed at times like this. They could come out and fetch me.

There was a pause before the gateman came out. He'd been on the phone. He looked us all over, with speculative contemplation, as if he were playing on a panel game on TV. Spot the loony. It wasn't difficult. The honor guard were in uniform. I wasn't.

My companion leaned across to unlock the near-side front door. The gateman opened it and held it while I pushed the seat forward and climbed out. The security man followed me. The TITAN man was a corporal—just the commissionaire. TITAN obviously thought it was too hot to leave a reception committee kicking their heels in the guardhouse. There would be time to waste while they got out here so that I could be handed over with all due ceremony.

I looked up at the tower, where the Pfc. was pointing his beady eye down the barrel of his machine gun, sighting on the end of my nose. I didn't know whether it was idle amusement or regulations—I sure as hell wasn't contemplating violence and/or escape.

"Just stand where you are and take it easy," said the corporal. He was drawling slowly, to cover up his uneasiness. His eyes drifted to the light moccasins on my feet, and he shook his head slightly as he raised them slowly past the old denims and the red corduroy shirt.

"Sorry, son," I said. "Just seems like I hadn't got a damn thing to wear." It had been ten years and more. Perhaps the soldier expected that the powers that be would let me keep my nice prison uniform for occasions like this one. No chance. Government property.

I took a few deep breaths of clean air and let my eyes roam around the far horizon.

"You're taking a chance making me stand here," I said, to no one in particular. "I'm not used to it. I could drop dead of agoraphobia any second."

"Like hell," said my guardian angel. "You ain't been away from empty space so long that you've forgotten what it looks like."

"Looks like, no," I conceded. "Feels like, yes."

"You can't go inside," said the corporal. His eyes flicked sideways and slightly upward. There was a remote-control camera mounted on the guardhouse side of the gate. The lens was staring at me with frank curiosity. *It's not me, fella, it's the camera.* I could have died laughing.

"This is my best side," I said, turning away from the lens altogether to transfix my pet security man with a gaze of injured innocence. He opened his mouth to say something nasty, but his thoughts caught up with his tongue, and he permitted himself to make allowances for the fact that I was crazy. He didn't like me, but he wasn't a bad guy by any means.

The soldier simply stared. Eventually, I went back to grinning at the lens. There was a buzz from the corporal's cubbyhole. He backed up to it and pulled a phone receiver from its hiding place like a rabbit from a hat.

"You got the papers," he said to the security man. He had to come forward and take them, because my traveling companion had strict orders to stay behind me every possible moment. Nobody turns his back on Harker Lee. I wonder why not.

"The captain'll be here any moment," muttered the corporal, turning an anxious eye back on the road which led away from the gate. That was a pointless exercise, because the road ridged about two hundred yards beyond the guardhouse, and the whole of TITAN base was hidden in a crater.

"You get lonely out here?" I asked him, helping to pass the time. "Or do you talk to him?" I jerked a thumb toward the kid in the tower, who was still playing make-believe games with his machine gun. I hoped the safety catch was on. Do machine guns have safety catches?

"It's not so bad," the guard replied. "I can read."

"Clever boy," I said, and he colored slightly.

More silence.

"We could unload my luggage," I commented idly. But my guardian angel just handed me the briefcase without having to move. He had it ready all the time. There was nothing in it but paper. I travel light. Not even an alarm clock.

A jeep roared over the hill and swooped down the long, dusty curve to the guardhouse. The driver deliberately skidded it when he slowed it around to a halt at right angles to the gate. Fancy man, I thought.

The captain got out. He was alone. His shirt was stained with sweat, and he hadn't combed his hair. He was a disgrace to his uniform. I noticed that he didn't have a sidearm, and I began to wonder what the act was all about. Were they trying to appear informal in the hope of making me feel at home? Trying to emphasize my change of scene, making it obvious that I was no longer an animal in a cage but a guinea pig on a dissecting block?

The corporal waved at his little friend up in the tower, and the gates began to slide back. The Pfc. never moved from his machine gun, though.

The gates screeched. Obviously, they weren't opened and shut with any frequency. They, at least, were honest. They knew that once I was inside I wouldn't be coming out again.

The corporal and the captain swapped muttered comments, and the mysterious papers changed hands yet again. The captain pulled a pen out of his pants pocket.

My God, I thought, the bastard's actually signing a receipt for me. I felt like registered mail.

The receipt went back to my erstwhile custodian, via the corporal, while the captain affected a casual stroll as he came to shake me by the hand.

I gave his sweaty palm a dirty look, but I shook it and gave him one of my nicest smiles. No point in starting out on the wrong foot. After all, this crowd were going to expect me to be grateful because they'd taken me out of my crowded grave and brought me back to the land of the clean and wholesome. I didn't want them to be too deeply shocked too soon. Not that I was afraid they'd send me back and catch another victim. I just didn't want to shatter their illusions.

"I'm Goodman," said the captain.

"Where's Jenny?" I replied. He looked startled. "Why didn't she come out to meet me?" I elaborated.

His eyes replied: Why the hell should she? What he actually said was: "I was detailed to meet you and take you to see the colonel. We'll . . . hand you over . . . to Dr. Segal after that."

"I see," I said amiably. "Brass first, happy reunions later. Mind if I say good-bye to my last nursemaid?"

Goodman's stare whipped past me to catch the eyes of my ex-guardian angel, who smiled beatifically. Now that I was out of his hands he could afford to be patronizing. He wasn't a great fan of the military. People in other kinds of uniform rarely are.

I shook his hand gravely. "Have a nice drive back to town," I said, sincerely. "I guess I won't be seeing you again."

It was definitely not a sad moment.

I stood for a moment or two, watching the Chevrolet take off for the horizon, trailing threads of smoky dust from its rear wheels. Then I condescended to notice Captain Goodman again.

"Okay, sunbeam," I said, "let's go."

He looked as if he thought that I was trying to take the piss out of him, and he didn't say a thing until he'd turned the jeep around and we were bouncing over the ridge and down into the vast shallow saucer which hid Project TITAN from all prying eyes.

Halfway back, though, he plucked up his regulation morale and said, "I'm sorry we couldn't take you over a little earlier than this, but they insisted on delivering you to our door."

"That's okay," I said. "I hardly think it would have made a lot of difference to the trip. Or would your crowd have stopped off somewhere en route so I could take in a day at the races?"

"Not exactly," he said.

I looked pointedly at the gun he wasn't wearing. He was obviously conscious of not wearing it, because he knew what I was staring at. "Taking a bit of a chance, aren't you?" I asked him. "Don't you know I'm a homicidal maniac?"

"I don't think I have anything to worry about," he said, straight faced.

"Probably not," I agreed.

The TITAN buildings were all gray and discreet. There was a lot of cluttered tarmac, but I couldn't see any spaceships. The last spaceship I'd seen was an Apollo, when I was a teen-ager. The TITAN craft might not look anything like that at all.

Some dust got in my eyes, and I shed a few tears of irritation. I could tell that I wasn't going to like it here.

Cage of Darkness

CHAPTER 1

"The Secondhand Life of Harker Lee," by Harker Lee (Annotated by J. F. Segal) . . . Chapter One

Introductory Note

Those who have occasion to use these autobiographical notes should be made aware of certain peculiarities pertaining to the use of pronouns. Harker Lee is, of course, wholly conscious of the schizoid condition which he is attempting to document, and to some extent the entire pronoun structure may be regarded as a contrivance—almost an elaborate joke, although who the joke is aimed at is not quite clear—rather than as a representation of the way in which he actually perceives the state of reality. However, it is not possible to reach any final and justifiable conclusion about the extent of meaning which Lee intends to convey by this device, or how much meaning it has so far as he is concerned.

The following idiosyncrasies occur, and the reader should be aware of them in attempting to interpret any passage in these memoirs:

The pronoun "you" is almost always singular and usually is used by Lee to refer to his real (alienated) self. (The precise existential status of this "real" self is not our concern here—we are examining the way Lee writes and, presumably—thinks.)

The pronoun "I" and its derivatives (me, mine, etc.) relate only to Lee's "compromise" self. It refers to a supposed communicative *device,* which he sometimes calls a mask, used as an arbiter between his real self and the outside world, but whose configuration is determined principally by the outside world. Statements in which "I" replaces "you" in the autobiography are sometimes intended to be false or insincere.

The pronoun "we" and its derivatives retain their usual meaning, but in addition there is a special use of the word which relates to everyone *except* Harker Lee. This deliberate exclusion is wholly artificial, a statement of his alienation, and this use of the pronoun does not occur often.

The pronouns "he," "she," and "it" are used normally throughout, and "they" almost always has its usual meaning. However, in connection with the use of "we" in the specialized way outlined above, "they" is occasionally constrained so that it can only relate to a *specific* group of others, and has no general meaning.

—J.F.S.

Chapter One

They told you that you were born in your grandfather's back room, which you know from personal experience is one hell of a place for a growing boy to be born. A body might catch cold, with all that rising damp. Suppose the river had been in flood? They couldn't have known it wouldn't be. Normal people are born in hospitals.

I guess it must have been a genuine traumatic experience, which is probably why you don't remember it too well. You can't remember much at all that happened at around that time, though they tell you you were a real little bastard who never closed his yap and screamed through it all the time. I guess it was all pretty traumatic. Years of it. Young and healthy kids recover, you suppose. They seem to. Plenty of cold showers, toilet training, and the three Rs, I guess. No, of course you were healthy. Four pounds twelve ounces, they tell you. Like a little walnut, all crinkled and shapeless. If the midwife was nearsighted, she could have lost you in the bedclothes.

Maybe . . .

We don't really think those kind of circumstances affect us in later life. We don't see how they can. So in all probability all that was just so much passing time, and it wasn't responsible for anything that was you, became you, was thrust upon you. Who gives you the option to believe? Your mother always said it sure as hell wasn't her fault. What happened to you? Heredity or environment, mother—take your pick. It was your father, she says. Who gives you any option to believe? You can't just think something, you know, you have to ask permission. Sometimes you can't even do that. Society is secret: you can't ask to join, you have to be invited. You can't lodge a complaint, no matter how free your mason.

Like somebody or other said, he's like a walnut, all crinkled and shapeless. Mother hadn't seen you then. You were her first ever; she'd never seen one before. And there's someone talking about walnuts. What sort of picture that brings to her rabbity little mind, hey? It wasn't father who said it—father too busy fainting on the back stairs.

Pretty sick, you guess. You get born a walnut, what chance you ever have of turning into a paper frog when the old cosmic paperhanger says jump? Pretty damn slim. You're a bad coin, like one of those turnings off a lathe that some comedian is always trying to bugger slot machines with. You buggered the biggest of them all—the giant super-whiz social slot machine. You never got your jaw-breaker, let alone your free plastic skeleton 1.075 inches high.

That's the sort of secondary effect people don't usually think about in connection with being born. Think about it.

You don't remember being a child prodigy either. Perhaps you weren't. It could be all lies, you know. They could fill you full of lies, and who'd know the difference? What chance have your microscopic, fugitive, fleeting memories of infancy got against their cold, hard, adult certainty? How sure are you of those cobwebs in your mind? Are they yours, or did some spider spin them there, with their fancy stories and their education? Anyway, you're wise enough nowadays to know that even if you were a prodigy, you weren't really. Quick, maybe, but nowhere near genius. You were fast, but that's all. The

long and the short of it. Whizz. An early reader, a voluble
talker. It might have looked a lot to somebody standing
close by, but it wasn't so much. You were a real clever
little bastard—clever enough to make people hate you, but
not clever enough to fuck the bastards off and not care.
You were superficial, even then. They taught you to say
"I" and you said it, over and over, and just to fill up the
cracks you learned to fill up the space between *"I*s." They
loved it. They hated it. What chance had you? Who ever
offered you the opportunity to understand?

You never had a lot behind you to back up your front.
That formed early, and by God it kept up. Look at you
now. All face and no guts. That was you at five years old.
Plus ça, etc.

You couldn't make it easy on yourself, could you? We
all make mistakes, but did you have to make that one?
Who done it? Did they push too hard? Or just chance. Or
was it just built into you that if crawling was the way you
had to get around you were just going to have to be the
fastest damn crawler in the whole world? You always had
to be six points up on the field, and not only because you
wanted to win clear but because you wanted to turn
around and yell hallelujah while you were doing it. But
you were all flash and no fire. You always got the six most
worthless points. You were satisfied. Hell, wasn't it something you could count, let alone assess the *value* of what
you were counting?

That's education for you. Three Rs and a free arse.
They give you the price of everything and the value of
nothing. Sin-ic.

Remember education? That's *you*, Harker Lee, from day
one to the bitter end. You may not know what the hell
you're talking about, but you won't shut up. You'll push

your opinions and you'll prop them up with more and more talk, and the more they press you, the more you'll lose your sense of distinction between what's true and what's not, what's real and what's not, what you know and what you don't know.

Do they want to know where all these fancy fantasy existences come from? Offer them this. They come from having to be right all the time. They come from having to defend what you say for fear they'll catch you in a *mistake*, in ignorance. You say something, you gotta be right— that's education. Tell them to defend what *they* think to the bitter end against a host of jealous critics. See how fast they lose *their* sense of distinction between true and untrue, real and unreal, knowledge and idea. Fantasies come from having to be right. Fantasies come from the only way they give you to decide what you believe.

You were a real pain in the neck from five to twenty-five. Nobody ever took a liking to you, and who could blame them? They didn't hate you, Harker, but they sure as hell couldn't like you. In their gum-chewing, comic-reading, sports-fan, jacking-off kind of a world you were a nothing. You don't rate plus or minus to the extent there's any sort of record of you in the great big emotional cash register, which is where the world clicks in its head.

Is that all of it? You think so. A kid the other kids don't cotton to. Didn't get much chance, if all they got was a view of your arse up a six-point margin and a faint hallelujah. They couldn't see you for the dust. Or was it the heat haze where you scorched up the dirt on your way? You wanted to hide in the cloud.

Things moved around you pretty fast when you were a kid, but you didn't really notice at all. You watched, but you didn't see. So who does notice the changes in their whereabouts when they're young? The velocity of change, like everything else, is just taken for granted. You were around when they bulldozed away an old world and bulldozed in a new, and you didn't even notice. Do you remember black-oil beaches? Dead rivers? Derelict land? Smog? People, people, people, and more and more people?

No.

Just that. No.

You didn't see a thing. Were you blind, willfully or otherwise? No.

Were you a fool, deliberate or otherwise? No.

Sometimes, it just isn't so easy to see. Give me a lever and a place to stand, and I won't even try to move the world. I'll be too busy looking at it for yet another first time.

You didn't even have the wherewithal to analyze moving and changing schools and changing a whole spectrum of people called passers-by. How could you possibly figure moving worlds and moving lives? No chance. You couldn't care enough. It wasn't in you. Who *does* care enough? Nobody. Not you, Harker, even now. That's for sure.

It made a big difference to the world, when you moved, though. You can see that now, though you had no chance at nine. It was a whole change of life. A step up the money ladder, a step up the slots in the social slot machine. You didn't know it, couldn't see it, because world two treated you in pretty much the same way as world one. A whole world of difference between environments, between places, between positions. But you didn't see the world change at all. You couldn't—you weren't equipped. Let's see now, with the aid of hindsight, just what you did see.

You saw a change in *you*. A change in your *identity*.

It wasn't so easy to look red hot in those better days of childhood, because they were a smarter bunch of kids and a nastier bunch of teachers. They didn't know any answers, but they sure as hell knew that you didn't, and they slapped at you every time you got revved up. You were a ready-made real outsider, and they weren't going to let you in, let alone let you out of the herd at the front end. You didn't see a change in them, because they were just as hostile, just as arbitrary, just as ridiculous as the others. You thought it was you that was at odds—you thought you'd lost the touch. You thought your answers had turned sour.

You turned maverick. Did you have a choice? Anyhow, high and wide of the field, just the same as it's always been. Up and away. Not so much losing contact with humanity. Just failing ever to make it.

You were a ready-made fall guy, of course. Aren't you still? The bigger they are, the harder you fall. You couldn't be just an average kind of a specimen. Not with the hand of cards that you were dealt. You had to be puny. Thin and short and mean looking. Myopic, too. A real freak. Just about everything you were set you aside. A misfit born, a misfit formed, and a misfit by vocation. Fall guy, you *fell*.

Was there ever a time, ever a single moment, when you could have said, to anyone, "It's cold outside—I want to join the human race"? Was there ever anybody listening?

You don't know. *I* know, but that's not the same thing at all.

Did we ever ask you to come in and take a seat? You don't remember. Maybe you were in the bath and couldn't get out to answer the doorbell. Maybe you couldn't be bothered. Maybe you were afraid of the thing standing on the doorstep. Maybe the doorbell didn't work.

They didn't treat you too bad for all of that. You hear a hell of a lot of crap about how cruel children are. It's not true. Children don't know what cruelty is, and if they did, they wouldn't want to be associated with it. Adolescents, yes. Kids, no. But they can hurt, of course. Anything can hurt if it isn't careful. And if there's one thing children never are it's careful. But you got away without mortal wounds. They didn't hurt you too bad. It was tough lots of times, but it's tough the whole world over, all the time, and you knew *that*, didn't you? You knew, at least, that everybody, everywhere, is being hurt by something. You didn't get more than your fair share of hurt, and it's no good crying now that you did. You handed out quite as much as you got. It didn't hurt the people that hurt you, so you were never satisfied, but there was hurt in and hurt out and there was equilibrium. You know that now.

So it wasn't the pain, that's what we're trying to establish. Harker Lee wasn't driven to where he ended up, not like that. He went of his own volition. You can drive a horse to water but a pencil must be lead. Just about sums it up. A fatuous joke. A play on worlds.

When did you ever notice you were missing your humanity? Not when you were at school, for dead sure. Years and years later. Adolescence (it was late, wasn't it?)—spring—flowering season—apple blossom time. That's when the torture came, if it ever was. Still a freak, still small, still thin, even more myopic. Nowhere near the human race. But you felt it then. The call of the wild. You're as alienated as you feel, and that was the *beginning*. That was when the wall grew tall, or when you finally got around to wondering about its climbability. Solid.

You didn't miss your humanity, of course. They made

sure of that. They were the hell-raisers. You only had to burn.

You can't blame them, of course. They were in a mess of their own. They were beginning their own beginnings and pursuing their own ends. They were down at the department store buying their beautiful new egos. Trading in their football shorts for codpieces. Trading in their savagery and barbarity for a caseful of dirty jokes and exam passes, without a qualm. Making memories of their toys and toys of their futures.

No, you can't blame them for slaughtering you. You can't blame them for laughing and sneering and *needing* to destroy and decoy you. They had to go their way. Every pecking order has a dead, dummy hen. The only way to grow up in a hurry is to stand on somebody else's shoulders. Who else but the loners, the freaks, and the outsiders could they use to fill their persecution quota?

So you were a fall guy. So what?

No, you can't blame them for that.

You'd have done the same if you could have found something alive and crawling to trample on. And didn't you try? Didn't you pull out every last resource you had to keep ahead in the arrogance stakes? Didn't you still know it all and a bit more besides? Couldn't you still outsneer them? Didn't you still have the wordy weapons? Didn't they walk in fear of you even while they walked all over you?

They lost their effect for a while, the words. The others went through a period of immunity as they moved from one world to another, where you needed a new set of magical incantations to hurt their feelings. It took a new kind of wizardry to masquerade as wisdom.

But you caught on. You were still fast. They didn't call

you lightning for nothing. Because you were yellow, flashy, and bent.

You kept jumping, hey? You rode out the storm. You're jumping still, paper frog. What's that hump on your back?

In fact, this is where you really made some tracks. This is where you set up your big lead. While *we* were all slowing down, *you* were still driving on. You still had somewhere to go, though God only knew where. And you got there too. Your lofty pinnacle of self-awareness, of ultimate rationality, of diabolical cleverness. Finally, you won your crazy race, by *sixty* points. They couldn't see you for dust.

Hallelujah.

And what do you have from it all?

Answers?

Yes, you have answers. *All* the answers. We can't beat you. We can't shake you. You can outword us every time. Because you know. You're *there*, where we never even tried to go. But *where* are you? I ask you, do you know? What are you? What do you want to be? Why did you want to go?

I'll tell you what you are. You're an alien being. A man from another star, from a hollow world inside the Earth. A hollow man. An alien. A driver with no steering column, no brake, no reverse gear, and the engine in the trunk because there's nothing but dirty washing under the hood. All you have is lots and lots of gears. Forward gears. And wheels and axles and twin carbs and overdrive and a whole series of accelerators. You can really *travel*, Harker, but how do you get to where you need to go?

How do you get back?

You're an emotional cripple, Harker. You have no

positive side to your mind. That showed, you know, in your trial. Not to mention in your crime.

All you are is the progeny of fear. You're a generation of bogeymen. And a big generation. That's a fertile mind you have there. You could fill up the Earth with phantoms. You have little enough apart from your almighty fear. No pride. No joy. No love. You're scared shitless even of such as they. You dare not feel, Harker, not really.

Whose fault, Harker?

Yours.

You always said: there's enough happiness in this world for everyone, and if I ever find the bastard who has my share I'll cut his heart out. Will you, Harker? Find him, that is.

Go to it, Harker, go to it. Write chapter two and three and four. Cut it *all* out. Heart and brain and everything. Schizophrenia. Split it, boy. Split it and spill it. All over the pages. Every idiot-syncrasy. Leech out all the bad blood, old friend.

Bleed yourself to death.

MADMAN'S DANCE

CHAPTER 2

Sensual Experiences in a Virgin Universe

Alio Shan, which is the second moon, is rising above the Nicobar Mountains. Dulce Nombre, larger and closer than her sister, hangs in the sky above the city, her brilliant whiteness causing the city lights to seem softer. On the roofs of the tallest buildings—the spires of the galleries and the clock towers and the temples and the college of arts—gemlike points of fire shine clear, but lower down the lights are so numerous that they blur together into a haze of gold and silver. In the city square, the statues of dead lords with arms upraised to heaven cast gigantic shadows. The hum of the solar batteries is gone, leaving a strange unevenness to the sound of the city. The machines rest peacefully in their underground repositories, because this is the quiet hour—the hour for thought and dreaming, when the streets remain unswept for a brief while, when odors are permitted to drift unhindered upon the air, when the temperature is allowed to fall a fraction, and introduce a hint of freshness into the life of the city.

Beyond the tall, mirror-shining city wall, the trees writhe in a wind which is never allowed to clutch the clothing of the men who walk abroad in the city. The flags that fly upon the spires are fluttered by careful streams of air produced by discreet fans.

The waters of the sea throw valiant waves against the gleaming wall, but it remains completely unimpressed. Its luster will not fade. Even the sound of the furious waters is delicately muted and is relayed to the interior only as a dull, sweet murmur—an insult to the tempestuous gray swell.

There is, eventually, a distant clicking as the first period of night comes to an end, and the machines begin to cleanse the city of the effects of some two hours of neglect.

The faint scent of the sea which has been allowed briefly into the air is sucked away into the metal belly of the city, and exhaled beyond the wall.

This is how my new world is sculptured: it is a landscape of wombs, its prisoned cities populated by faceless, hidden men. Only the madmen walk the face of the world. I am a traveler, of course, being no worshiper of wombs but merely one who rests therein when the occasion demands.

I wander—after all, the world is mine. For whom did you shape it save for ourselves? It is my part in all this to tread every road, to search out the limits of this new Creation, to discover and to judge whether this might or might not be only another cage to confine me and put pressure on my being.

By the shore of a many-eyed, gray-bodied sea—that same sea which beats its futile fists against the impregnable womb-walls of your fabulous cities—I meet three old men whose eyes have the form of the hearts of vultures, and whose hearts are open and staring. Their lips are like worms, and their hands are not their own, being borrowed from the artisan dead, and responding still to forgotten reflexes.

They are drawing lots for the fragments of my existence. The one who draws the longest straw whispers soundlessly into his white beard, and he does not smile. At length he makes his decision, and he chooses to have dominion over the time in advance of my birth—my history and my heritage, when all my choices remain unmade, and the world is in my embryonic hands. He is a creator of sorts, this old man, a Godman in his own tiny way.

The second, whose eyes have grown darker while the first man spoke, and whose skin is wrinkling fiercely even while he contemplates the second straw and the decision to which it is title, elects to possess me when I am dead, to own my memories and legacies, when only the echoes of my being that are to spread out and permeate the universe are yet unsounded.

The third man, a very tired man, a very poor man, stares at the shortest straw of all. And as his pulsing, blood-filled eyes turn their blind gaze upon me and the worms thrash about the cavity of his mouth, I feel pity for him.

"What is left?" I ask him.

"Only life," replies the scavenger, "only life." He releases the straw, and it flutters away on the wings of a mocking wind which has already dismantled his companions.

He is faceless, this man, in that I do not know his face. Because I cannot put a name to it, I cannot put a mask to it, and he remains a ghost, which is so often the way of things in dreams. And this is a dream, for all that it is a whole universe of a dream, and there is nothing of what I

thought was reality which can invade its privacy. It is a
dream without awakening, for an eternity whose duration
I cannot estimate, yet I must haunt myself with the open
door which will, one day, have another, an older, world
beyond it. The world of the cage.

I have no control over the images of the dream, though I
think you do if you would only exert yourself, instead of
playing God with such a godlike passivity and patience.
Sometimes I am almost happy here, and grateful for the
way of things, but I dare not allow myself the luxury of so
much contentment. I must remain aware, and I must put
my strength of will into a purse which must never leave my
clenched fist, for I will need it again.

At other times, the assault on my sensibility takes on a
different form, when the dream becomes grotesque and I
am flooded by an ocean of images which wants to drown
me in a fear and panic, or simply to blast me apart with
profusion and nonsense. I remember such dreams, but I
also remember the release which could always be obtained
by the desperate struggle for wakefulness. Here, no matter
how desperate the struggle, there can be no wakefulness.
There can be, in fact, no struggle, because I dare not
commit myself in that way to anything so futile that I may
forget my secret, sacred purposes.

You could help me here, but neither of us knows
whether it is in your interests. It is my decision. It is my
struggle. It is my trial.

I could hate you.

But I dare not even that. . . .

As I sleep . . .

(Yes, I must sleep even here, I must let my mind fall
into pools of oblivion, because I cannot stand the curse of
eternal wakefulness. I think, I hope, that sleep is safe. It is

dreamless—or is it full of dreams, because dreams within a dream are still one with the dream?—-and my fear that the oblivion will claim me is no more nor less than the fear of death, and that, of course, one has to live with.)

As I sleep, the mountain screams in anguish, and it coughs out the hot flood from its bowels (I groan in my sleep, and I sweat, and my heart is racing), hurling magma and flame over the verdant slopes it retches bubbling cauldron-brews over its witch-haunted sides I see fire and thunder erupting from the cauldron to destroy— destroy *me* and *my* work and *my* future and *my* people as the fireballs roar and howl I see the faces of the people afraid, shocked, bewildered, and most of all accusing.

I am free of no needs. The sexual impulse that you have carved all over your universe I still carry in my belly. I need release, as I remember needing release in the cage-years, over and over and over again, and no release offered, but it had to be sought and found *inwardly,* in sleep more painful than in wakefulness, but in sleep with less shame than in wakefulness. Pain or shame—this is a dilemma I have lived with in my life, and it is no less so now that you are the creator, and this is what tells me more than any of your absurdities that freedom, as you would have it, is nothing more nor less than a cage.

And when I awake, the fire would die, but slowly, leaving the last scenes of carnage half-visible fugitives in my mind. While I am awake, the volcano sleeps, and while I sleep, the volcano is awake. Alive I am master of the mountain, dead the mountain rules me, showing me its power in my bursting forth from darkness into new dreams, showing its hatred and its anger.

The day comes when I wake sweating, the thunder of the volcano in my ears; as I emerge from sleep, the red fire rises. I fall into the insane crater. I fall for a million miles like a fluttering leaf gently swimming in the hot tower of uprushing air, my skin scorching and cracking. . . .

Then I stop and I order the lava back into the bowels of the Earth like a king ordering the tide to turn back.

And it does, or it does not.

There is no easy answer, and you cannot make it so.

Titan Nine

CHAPTER 2
Security

Colonel Henneker had been a very tough man in his day, and it still showed in the way he moved his body and his face. He'd gone gray and leathery, the craggy way that all heroes would like to go in their old age. He was like a big bear. Of course, it could have been an act.

His office—or at least, the office *I* saw (you never can tell with military security)—was plush and warm. It was steeped in permanency—it radiated "home." It said loud and clear that from Henneker's point of view TITAN was not so much an assignment but a way of life. He'd been here for a long time, and it was his last hitch before they pensioned him off to the Army Old Folks' Home. More than that—this wasn't just a kill-time environment. On the evidence of Henneker's working conditions he was a man who cared a great deal for his work. TITAN was his child. He was involved with it, deeply. He had more commitment to it than just ending his career without a whisper.

There was a shadow on his face, though—a shadow

which told me that there was a threat to all his lovely happiness and job satisfaction and career perfection.

And I was it.

He gave me a cigarette and lit it for me, but he didn't light up himself. I took the cigarette out of my mouth and held it. I took a slight draw on it, but I blew the smoke out right away. I intended to let it burn itself out. I hadn't had a smoke in a long time.

Henneker settled himself into his chair with a practiced shuffle of relaxation.

"You know why you're here?" he asked me.

"Here this office or here generally?" I parried.

"Titan," he said.

"I was told to volunteer," I said. "I jumped at the chance. But all I know is this is titan. Ideas I have; information I don't."

"What do you think?"

"I think you want to send me up in one. What else?"

He sighed and turned a little in his chair. I knew it was all put on. Men in Henneker's kind of job don't sigh. He didn't bother to tell me how right my guess was. We both knew how much I knew.

"I'm sorry that you were brought here first," he said, conversationally. "I know you'd rather have been received by Dr. Sobieski or Dr. Segal. But we all share the responsibility for your being here, and we all agree that it's me who's sticking his neck out furthest. You're one hell of a solution to a problem, you realize that? You're 90 percent problem yourself."

"You're trying to tell me that I owe you something," I said.

"That's right," he said. "You owe me something. Segal

wanted you here, Sobieski backed her up. They talked the rest into it. They came to me. But it's me who takes the rap if you cause any trouble. Not them. Yes, I'm trying to tell you that you owe me something, because if you accept that we can make a good start. If you don't . . . well, in that case I just have to get to know you a bit. Get the feel of the problem. See?"

I saw. He was handing me a line. Softening me up. I didn't say a word. He was asking the questions, not me.

All of a sudden (I was expecting it) he asked me:

"Do you think your being committed to Block C was an injustice?"

"Had nothing to do with justice," I told him, carefully flicking ash into the tray on the desk. "It was a security matter." I emphasized the word "security" ever so slightly.

He nodded. "You reckon they shouldn't have put you in there?" he said.

I shrugged. "I cannot tell a lie. I did it. They got me. I'm as mad as they say I am. But, hell, what do you expect me to say? No, I wouldn't wall up a toad in there. Jenny got me out once before, and I'm very grateful. She's done it again, and I'm twice as grateful, and if you're running interference for her, you're included in. But let's face it, no one is doing anything for Harker, are they? They're doing it because they need a sucker, right?"

"You're bitter," he said. He deserved a gold medal for observation.

"My voice always sounds that way," I told him. "Comes of talking to myself instead of listening to other people. So I'm told."

"Aren't you just a little bit afraid that making such an exhibition of your hostility might get you sent back to Block C?" he asked me.

"No." I didn't like the way he kept saying "Block C"—it was to inform me, subtly, that he knew more about me than he might. I always referred to the block, never to the prison, and he knew that.

"One might have thought," he said—using "one" to show that he didn't—"that having been out once, you'd have made the most of your second outing."

"Why?" I said. "You're going to put me back no matter how nice I am. When I'm finished, that is. Unless it kills me, that is."

"No," he said. "We're not going to put you back. It might kill you, but if it doesn't we won't send you back."

"In that case," I said, with devastating logic, "I've nothing to lose by being hostile. Have I?"

"Nothing except the job," he said. "And if you lose the job, you *will* go back, to be replaced by the man who does do it. Now wait a minute. . . . I'm not just leaning over backward to threaten you. As I said, I'm carrying the can for you. If you're replaced, odds are that I will be, too. We're in this boat together, and if you feel uncomfortable, try to imagine how I feel. I have a job to do here, and that's enforcing security. The strictest. Now the TITAN ship is *not* a big secret—it's been going too long to be that, and it had more than its fair share of publicity at one time. But *you* are something else again. You're the biggest secret I've ever had occasion to keep a lid on, and already too many people know all about you. The scientist brass knows, and so does half my staff—that's not a big risk. The prison authorities also know, and so do some of the political brass—and that is. Now you're hot, son, and it's my hands you're sitting in. There are a lot of eyes on you apart from mine, and they don't all have the eye of faith. Your enemies are legion, for one reason and another, and to

them you can add me. You're trouble, son. For me. For the
project. For yourself. There are any number of men who'd
like to see you safely caged again—not just out of malice,
because malice we can cope with one-handed, but out of
politics and out of simple back-stabbing self-interest.
Maybe you think no one has anything to gain from a knife
in your back, but you've got to see that a knife in your
back is one in mine, and one in Dr. Segal's, and one in
Mike Sobieski's. Now think to yourself, Harker. How
much bitterness can you afford?"

"I'm not vicious," I said. "Fatalistic. Sure, I've been
burned up a little in my time, but the fires die. I'm nothing
now except tired."

My suspicious nature told me the slimy bastard was
trying to worm his way around to my good side. But I
didn't listen to my suspicious nature these days as much as
I had in the long ago. I was almost prepared to accept him
at face value. I signaled my approval of all that he had to
say with a few slow nods while he stared at me, waiting.
Then I stubbed the cigarette out. It had burned right
down.

He offered me another, and I shook my head.

"I'm thinking of giving it up," I said.

"Perhaps as well," he said. "It might have been your
last anyway. Once they start kicking you into shape, you'll
have to fight for every one. Sure you don't want to enjoy
another one now?"

I shook my head. "I wouldn't enjoy it," I said.

"Look," he said, "I don't like doing all this. But I have
to stop you getting out of line, and I have to stop you now,
before we let you in on what the hell is going on. Hell,
you're not on trial now. I've already backed you all the
way, or you wouldn't be here. I'm not going to come down

on you. We need a success out of this project. You know
why. I'm convinced you're a horse worth backing. It's not
for me to explain. I'm going to tag you with a nursemaid
—I know you don't want him, won't like him, and don't
feel it's necessary—but there's no way out of it from my
point of view. His name is Hurst. He'll pick you up when
you leave this office, and he'll live in your pocket until
. . . well, until. He'll be as unobtrusive as possible when it
is possible, and you have all the privacy you want inside
your apartment."

"Except for the bugs," I said.

"There aren't any bugs," he said. I didn't believe him.
Who would have?

There was a pause.

"I want you on my side, Harker," he said.

"You made that pretty clear," I told him.

"That's all I can do," he said. "Anything you want? I
know it's a bad question, because whatever you do want
I'll probably have to tell you you can't have, but I have to
ask."

"There's nothing I want," I said. "Yet."

"Thanks," he said. His eyes were still boring into mine
for long minutes, then looking deliberately away. I
followed more or less the same policy. Neither of us was
getting anything out of it.

"Can we at least coexist?" he asked me.

"I don't know," I said. "Can we?"

"I'm asking you because it's in your hands," he said. "I
have my job to do, and I'm going to do it. That ties my
hands. You're the one who's free to choose. You're the one
who's free to be a bloody nuisance if you want to be, and
wreck this whole setup."

"We all have our crosses to bear," I told him, "and I'm yours."

We looked at each other. I knew he was finished giving me his line—he was just waiting for me to hand him one back. He wanted me to say something—to volunteer something. Information, promises, reassurances, just downright mockery. Anything. He didn't want to find out more about me. He already knew just about all there was to know. He'd probably studied every word I'd spoken since childbirth. He just wanted to see me in action. He just wanted us to interact. He wanted something set up between us.

"I'll tell you something I think," I said, finally. "I think you're pretty worried about just one thing. You know I can't afford to spread a ripple, because my whole life depends on this—all the life I have. From here, I'm either TITAN or I'm dead in a concrete coffin. Your worries center on just one thing. You're worried about what I might think when I get all the facts about what I have to do and what my chances are. You're worried that I'll get so shit scared I won't give a damn about things. You're scared I'll just stop caring and wreck the whole thing out of fear, of spite, of sheer cantankerousness. I think you're right. In your shoes, I'd be scared of that, too. But you know as well as I do that no one can tell how I'll react until I get into reacting position. We'll just have to see, Colonel . . . you and I. We'll just have to see how crazy I get when I finally know how crazy this thing is you want me to do. Won't we? I'll add this, though, Colonel: from where I sit you seem to be gambling on my being a hero. Now that, to me, seems to be a very brave gamble indeed. Block C, as you well know, is no place for breeding heroes. The army is the place for breeding heroes. Now isn't that odd, Colonel?"

"If this project went on the way it's been going," he said levelly, "my army would be full of dead heroes. We need a live one."

"You'd better hope, then," I told him, "that Block C hasn't knocked every last vestige of heroism out of my soul."

And he smiled.

"I'm in here for good, aren't I?" I asked, thinking it was a good time to spring one on him. "You aren't ever going to let me outside that perimeter wire."

"That's right," he said. "But there's a lot of room in here. It may be a cage, but there's more elbow room in it than nine men in ten have in this day and age. Do you know what it's like in the cities these days?"

"I've heard," I said.

"We're all in a cage, son," he said. "That's what this project's all about. Unlocking the door."

Well, I hadn't expected that I'd be given leave to go whoring in town. But like the colonel said, so what? I'm no nightlifer. And I did know what it was like in the cities. And it may seem too corny for words, but on TITAN base, I could see the stars at night.

"We'll have to give you the standard checkout," he said.

"So search me," I said. "I could do with a good scrubdown. But if I'd been a nuclear bomb in disguise I'd have blown you all up by now."

He smiled again. He wasn't amused, though. Security men don't have such a thing as a sense of humor. He dropped the smile to stare at me with a sudden penetrating intensity, but I didn't flinch. I was used to his eyes playing games with me.

He stood up and extended his hand. Though he hadn't pressed any buttons, the door behind me opened, and

Goodman came in with another man, who was presumably my shepherd. They stepped up smartly, one to either side of me.

I shook Henneker's hand.

"I hope things work out," he said, in parting. I thought he was going to call me "son" again, or something equally sickening, but he just left the sentence dangling, as though he'd thought better of it. He'd probably judged me well, and with the data in his files he could probably have carried on my side of the conversation as well, private thoughts and all. Security men are hell on wheels to talk to—no surface at all, just limitless depths of concealment and illusion—but I practically liked Henneker. Which didn't mean to imply that I thought my time in TITAN was going to be anything less than hard.

We left, in single file, and went straight for the "standard checkout." It didn't improve my outlook on life one little bit. They'd have taken off my skin to irradiate it, demagnetize it, and strain it through a micropore filter if it hadn't been attached.

But once I was through, I really felt that I was on the Project. I felt like a chessman, unable to play the moves myself, but feeling I had to understand them all.

And that, more or less, is what I was.

Cage of Darkness

CHAPTER 2
Claustrophobia

The thing about Block C (C for crazy, I think, but we make it C for Canaan because we have one hell of a sense of humor) is that it is a different world not only from the world outside, but also from the world inside. We breathe different air; we are in a different dimension. The other blocks are just as remote, just as unreal, to us as the wide world of freedom is to the poor bastards who didn't inherit the label "crazy" and go through the daily bureaucratic machinery of the rehabilitation game and the parole pantomime.

There are no infant crocodiles or gray-clad phantoms moving in and out of the corridors of Block C. There is no hum of life and human activity, no human smell, no dynamic crowds, no purring machinery. Just the soft hollowness of decay. Even the prison has a purpose—even if the purpose is a con—but in Block C there is a little cesspool where even the prison purpose is negated, brought under the executioner's ax. Block C is simply to contain, to confine, to cocoon. C for coffin. C for condemned. Condemned not to death, but to eternal empty life. Block

C is impregnable. Even now, when it is far behind me, it is impregnable. The inmates—some of them—think about escape, dream about escape, but their dreams are nothing more than the hysterical effusions of Edgar Allan Poe, who wrote about premature burials and the horrors of awakening in the grave. There is no escape from Block C. The inmates are shrouded. Ferried across the Styx.

There are no less than five sets of gates—two solid, three just wire netting—which seal off the main prison from the world outside. Five cages. There are only doors and dogs and guns in between the main prison and Block C. One of the doors is two steel slabs set outside a thick layer of concrete. It is set in a concrete wall. That is the womb-wall of the crazy house. It does not conduct sound. But we don't do any screaming—the sound it kills is the sound that comes in to us from outside. You can't imagine the thinness of the trickles that creep through the multiple keyholes. Completely intangible unless you press your ears right up to the orifices.

There aren't many of us in Block C. We are the only part of the prison which isn't crammed to bursting point. No overcrowding in Canaan. Rather the reverse. Only the chosen people qualify. The prisoners, in addition, do not choose to make themselves obvious. They are fugitive creatures, rather reminiscent of animals in the zoo. It is the guards who are prominent. The actual objects of their attention secrete themselves, so far as they are able, and do not respond to the constant observation.

The guards are participants in the atmosphere of rottenness which clothes the block. They always whisper, never talk. They peer from behind glass partitions, lean over the banisters, and contemplate the antisuicide netting; they sit and scratch away with their silent felt-tipped pens in their little offices, which are more like cells than the cells. Guards outnumber prisoners in Block C by six-to-four, an amazing reversal of the situation in the outer prison, where one-to-twenty is the ratio demanded by regulations. The guards in Canaan work a lot of overtime. They spend so many of their working hours in our communal coffin that we wonder whether the small shafts of freedom sandwiched between duty and sleep mean any more to them than the effluent of the keyholes means to us. They are largely superfluous, because there are cameras everywhere.

The worst of it all is that the surfeit of empty space, the unused cells, and the perpetual smiling lights cannot even touch the sense of claustrophobia which envelops all of us. It is not simply the multitude of locks and keys and secret signs and little rituals and regulations and procedures, but the complete deathliness of the whole fabric of life. This is a world with neither future nor past nor hope, nor even despair. The lighting, which is absolutely uniform, is symbolic of the constancy—absolute stillness—of the whole externality of life. There are no windows to let in even the world of the outer tomb. The air cycles constantly—the fans are absolutely silent.

In Block C we—we the prisoners—live deep in our individual subconsciousnesses. Where the guards live I simply have no idea. If, existentially, we change at all, are going anywhere at all, it is a voyage inside our heads and hearts. Deep space. A starless firmament.

While I have been in Block C, there have been five suicides that all the netting and all the regulations failed to stop. They were all guards. The guards have the option, you see—they are free not to be guards. They are amphibious, creatures of several worlds. No guard in the prison works more than three days in twelve in Canaan. But then, there is a suicide rate in all the other blocks as well. One mustn't read too much into bare figures.

I have no idea why no prisoners have committed suicide during my term in the crazy block. No idea at all. You'd think that no ordinary man could possibly stand it down there. And some of us are ordinary. Some of us *were* good men and true. Which doesn't mean that they didn't commit their crimes. They did. But I'll say now and I'll say over and over again before I reach the end of this story that the crimes don't matter, don't ever matter, aren't relevant in the least.

*　　*　　*

Take Cannon, for instance. Cannon isn't relevant to this account—I didn't know him well. He didn't interest me. But consider him. This is a man in a living grave, remember.

Firstly, Cannon is a guy you don't have to feel sorry for. He is a *good* guy. He's the type of guy all you tight-lipped, tough-talking, hero-loving imbeciles love to identify yourselves with, if he's a sportsman, or some other idol of the idle.

Steve Cannon could have been a soldier, and he'd have won medals because he was developing into the perfect society robot. He could have been a Hemingway hero: grace under pressure was written into every sad sideways glance of his gorgeous gray eyes. He could have been the sheriff in *High Noon*, maybe David in his anti-Goliath days, or an Armstrong reciting his lines while stepping out onto the surface of the moon.

Steve Cannon could have been just about anybody, so far as *we* were concerned. But that's not really the man we want to talk about. The man we want to see is the leading man *after* the last curtain call, the acrobat *after* they've dismantled the big top.

Cannon doesn't really exist inside himself. Only outside. He's like one of those life-sized rubber women we can order through the mail as the ultimate mate in our masturbatory fantasies. His purposes are only those of other people. He exists for them and in them. He is good and kind and honest and utterly, utterly lovable. Only, like Bishop Berkeley's chair, when you close the door on him, he ceases to be.

I suppose you'd like me to go into sordid details about which hour of the TV screen was Steve's, which cereal packet gave him away free, which ghostwrote his autobiography, which painted plastic inflatable wife he took home to which painted plastic palace. Most of all, you'd like to hear an explanation about how such a wonderful man could do all those terrible things and end up in Canaan.

But that's not what I'm trying to make you see at all. That doesn't matter (and I'll keep telling you that until you understand). What matters is that Steve Cannon is a part of you; you've created him, so that he *owes* you something. But he really could exist, if he somewhere managed to find the chance. You don't want him to exist, you only want him to eat bacon and eggs for breakfast, read Dostoevski in the bath, play a hot game of billiards, and spill himself all over the color screen and the color supplements so you can digest his life into yours.

Even his crimes. You even ate up his crimes.

You wouldn't let him be. We wouldn't let him be at all.

We live vicariously through our bloody (I mean literally bloody) TV sets, and for us the world is a 24-inch color screen. We don't know about Steve Cannon, and I can't explain it to us.

And you don't even know what I'm talking about, so forget it all and remember only this. Steve Cannon, a man you could look up to and befriend and respect, is still closed in Block C. He has no part in this story, and if he had, his dialogue would be just as empty and futile and hopeless as any of mine or Judas Dancer's, and his grace under pressure would be of no account whatsoever.

I can tell you this much about survival, though. Survival in conditions like you made for us in Block C. I never once thought of committing suicide because I was already entombed. There was no life in Canaan. How could there be death? There was no life in Cannon, either. Not ever.

The trouble with 1990 and the population explosion is that all the too many people who are being born are being born dead, but still consuming.

*   *   *

Note: Harker Lee's prison notes, whether contemporary (as are his descriptions of the prison) or retrospective (as are his descriptions of his fellow inmates), do not show the same type of aberrant pronoun usage as do the autobiographical writings. They are, however, continually distorted and exaggerated, particularly in their concerns with other prisoners. Lee's main purpose in writing about his fellow prisoners is to articulate his accusations against society. It is not surprising that such accusations are vague and sometimes contradictory. It is precisely this vagueness that makes these accounts so valuable in reaching an understanding of Lee's mind. What he says about the prisoners is largely untrue, but in the archetypes which he creates out of them we can see the way in which he imagines society to operate.

—J.F.S.

MADMAN'S DANCE

CHAPTER 3
Tempus Fugitive

Harker Lee walks along the edge of a shifting, almost formless plain of sand and sandy soil. The sun rises and sets at intervals which seem to be composed of only a few fleeting moments. The scene flickers eerily, as day and night alternate with furious frequency. The ground beneath his feet is hazy and indistinct, and the sky is vaporous and ill-defined. He walks on insubstance, his pale eyes roaming the horizon. He is beginning his own odyssey, but this is not really *his* world. He had little or no part in the making of it. For him, it can hardly be any less a confinement than Canaan itself. And yet he is an instrument in the judgment. He is at home here. He can live here.

There are no misfits in *your* Creation.

Some distance away he sees the sharply defined outline of a city rising from the gently curving ground, and he begins walking toward it. It appears to be small—he judges that it is no more than a mile from one edge to the other—but as he watches he sees that it is growing slowly. New silhouettes appear all along the black line of buildings, strange square silhouettes, taller than those in the center.

His mind attunes itself, focuses like a pair of binoculars, so that the gaze of his eyes compensates for the stroboscopic effect of night and day, and imparts a three-dimensional quality to the fluid city. He sees the rectangles at the edges of the city spring straight from the ground to soar erect into the air. Even without the persistent flashing, he receives an impression of jerky, sporadic growth as though there are lapses of time in between images. This he attributes to the changes in the pace at which the buildings are constructed: the differences are too small to be seen individually, but have a collective effect of unevenness. The whole of the border of the city is in constant and violent movement. The center changes, too, gradually. Its symmetry is never quite given over to the regimentation of the suburbs, but it grows, and its lines are somewhat smoothed.

All at once, clumps of buildings begin to appear a few miles removed from the city. Harker is witnessing the birth and development of a megalopolis, something which the universe he had previously known had made him no stranger to, save for the fact that the megalopoli had run into one another and fused, never being left alone, surrounded by wilderness, closed communities, city-shelters, city-coffins, city-wombs.

The buildings no longer huddle but lie ranged like the jagged outline of a row of broken teeth along the horizon. It is sprouting darkly outlined shapes along the whole of its still increasing length. More buildings vanish and more grow up in the space they vacate. The pace of enlargement increases. The whole skyline is wavering and oscillating.

A road suddenly extends across his field of vision,

traveling from horizon to horizon in what is, to him, scant minutes. There are no people or vehicles visible—their presence is too ephemeral for him to detect. Only by the hectic life of the silhouetted city is life on a smaller scale manifest. He is seeing humanity in the whole—alive, growing, and building like a lunatic of stone and metal.

And then, all in one instant, while he is yet many miles from its outskirts, it falls. In one moment the city is standing straight and mighty, presenting a proud face to the sun and stars, and in the next it collapses into ruin. In one moment it is complete, a dynamic system of growth. Then a sudden flash of intense glare transcends the chain of night and day, and in the next moment there is a transient thin swirl of black smoke and half of it cascades as though vaporized into a thin smear of rubble. There is only the merest glimpse of a halo of flame, and then it is gone, swept into the skies by the surge of time, and only ruin is left.

Harker Lee never felt the shock wave of the bomb, nor felt its heat. He stops while the pantomime goes on—sporadic, feeble growth for a short while, which slows and then ceases. The wavering stops, gently and quietly. There is no rebirth.

There is none of the violent thrashing of the wounded beast, only a tranquil passivity. Slowly the city falls into disrepair. The helter-skelter passages of night and day have not altered, yet the scene slows, as though the city is consumed with tiredness.

The city is dying.

It slowly surrenders its hold on the chaotic life it once possessed. The blunt, square-ended figures abandon their claw-handed reach for the stars and slide to the ground.

The road is washed gently into oblivion by the loving caress of the tidal sands, their waves sweeping lethargically across the plain. The lone towers which had carried power lines fall, make stony mounds for a little while, and then they, too, are swept into smoothness by the marching plain.

The horizon lapses deeper and deeper toward its former flatness and again curls away evenly to disappear in the haze. The shifting colors of cultivation pale. The sand shifts and stirs. The skyline is dead, the city buried without a monument to signal its passing. It is lost and forgotten. Peace has come. Peace and emptiness, hand in hand.

But even the peace has small durations. Order, like chaos, proves to be only temporary. Far, far away in the shimmering distance a tiny black dot appears. Then, after a while, another, and another, and . . .

Harker Lee is laughing. He has been laughing for a million years.

Was it a bomb or a thunderbolt from the hand of God which destroyed the first city? Was it the reward of civilization, or the price of building roads across the wilderness?

Ask Harker. He knows all about the megalopolis, all about the wilderness.

He knows.

While I walk by the banks of a river which girdles the world, I stop to rest where a boatman waits to ferry passengers across the river.

"A coin," cry the beggars, scampering around my feet, dragging their maimed children and rolling over and over in the dirt to display the full complement of their injuries and their agonies.

"A coin, a coin, a coin, a coin!" they chant, in endless harmony, for the one strength they have left to them is the strength of their voices.

"I have no coin," I tell them.

But there is another man passing by, and the beggars rush to him to surround him, the better to assault his pity and his kindness with the arrows of their need and the spears of their despair. The man has one coin, and he gives it to the most despicable of the beggars, who thereupon abandons her broken-limbed child to leap into the waiting boat. Steadily and unhurriedly, the boatman stirs the quiet water with his spatulate oars.

"A coin?" he asks, with a voice like idle thunder. The beggar gives the boatman the coin she has been given, and the boat swings out onto the river, transporting the delirious beggar to her reward.

The generous man turns to me. "How long?" he asks.

I stare at him coldly, and then look down at the beggars, who are settling to wait by the roadside.

"A thousand years," murmur the beggars sleepily. "Perhaps forever."

They know the value of pity and conscience.

My dreams are haunting me and taunting me with beggars. I know what the beggars mean. How many times have I accused civilized men of maiming and crippling their children as the beggars of Calcutta used to do—still do in some strange other world? All the better to beg, all the better to fit the mold that the social slot machine has destined the child for. Everywhere it is the same story, the same mythology. I know why you have made beggars to haunt madmen. Do they cluster around the feet of poor Judas as well? And all the others, too?

I wish you joy of them. Judas will laugh at them; Sam

Mastervine will kick them to death; Luis Dalquier will gamble with them and take from them everything that they have or will earn. Cain Urquhart will try to convert them. Who do you think will find pity for them? Bedbug? Perhaps.

Is that what you want? Do you want us to scorn the whole human race for beggars? You want us to cheat them? You want us to turn our backs on the whole human race? It won't work. Not with *beggars*. Whatever makes you think that they have that much consequence? Whatever makes you think that we have repulsion left in our hearts to spare for your meager hauntings?

Show us glory, God, show us pride and ambition, if you want to win us. Give us the pride and the power. Don't ask us to find our own. We can't.

Titan Nine

CHAPTER 3
Letter to Canaan

Dear Judas,

I am addressing this letter to you because of the individual-to-individual rule imposed by the prison, but I hope that you can use your own judgment wisely as to the extent to which you communicate these contents to your fellow inmates.

I've been out only a matter of days, but I don't really want to talk about being out, and I'm not allowed to talk about being in, so what am I going to talk about?

My purpose in writing this letter is the same as my purpose in writing all my letters, and the same as your purpose in writing all yours: I need somebody to talk to. And it's always easier to talk to people when I'm on my own. You know how much easier it is to cry on a shoulder that isn't there.

I can't tell you where I am, or why, but I can tell you that I don't like it and I'm scared of it. Most of all, I'm scared of people. I've been away from the sort of people-contacts that these people use for a long time. I can't go around treating them as if they were homicidal maniacs condemned to life, now can I? But this isn't like the other time—the time I told you about, when they only wanted to reel my brain out onto miles and miles of magnetic tape, and they didn't expect me to be a person—just a specimen. This is different.

I never got a chance to say good-bye, and this is no time or place—this whole letter is to say hello. I don't know what you thought when they just took me out and never brought me back. Perhaps you think I'm dead. Reassure yourselves, I'm still in the land of the pseudo-living. Or is it reassurance? Am I just going to condemn you to jealousy? I hope not. I think not. I'm sure not. You're not going to turn to hate me because I'm in a different cage. Sure, there might be slight cause for envy—I can see the sun and I have space—but life here isn't going to be that much different from life there.

I'm afraid—I guess that is the real reason why I'm setting pen to paper so quickly, so urgently. Sheer cowardice. Events are moving fast, after standing still for years. The world is moving me (certainly not I moving the world), and I'm afraid of opportunity and action and ambition.

But enough of orgiastic self-pity (a lie—when did anyone exhaust his supply of self-pity?). What am I talking about? What can I talk about? I'll just venture to say a few simple things—nothing that anyone could object to—and hope they're still in the letter when it gets to you. I'll write on one side of the paper only so that if they cut bits instead of erasing or inking them, you won't lose what's on the other side.

Harmless comment one. I'm working on a Project. You must know that already. For what other purpose do they snatch people out of the coffin? Only for guinea-pig purposes in exceptional circumstances. This is Project with a capital *P*, which means that it's serious—they haven't hired me out to a crackpot, as—it is rumored—may have happened in the past.

As you know, I have spent years wrestling with the burdensome superabundance of my talent—I am probably suited only to Projects and not to projects. Do you know the difference? I suppose not. You got off the carousel fairly recently compared to poor bastards like Manny and Luis who were in before me, but even so you didn't get much of a chance to study the ways of the world. Briefly, projects with small ps are the kind of thing where any guy with a bit of paper can amuse himself more or less harmlessly. They're in the territory where the language of bits of paper and letters after the name is quite adequate for communication. You don't have to be a Whiz Kid. They're work—bread and butter. Trivia. Projects with big Ps, on the other hand, are not 99 percent perspiration and zero percent imagination. They are tasks which demand a certain waywardness in their exponents. They are crazy men's scientific territory—what some would call the products of genius. This is blind-man's-buff country, where work and diligence are not the answers to all questions. This is territory where there are more questions by far than one can hope to answer. I know it. I feel it. And I wouldn't be here if that weren't the case.

You remember the last Project I was on. Quite crazy. Reading minds. Not *sensibly* reading minds, like the guys in the SF movies or the stage acts, but *actually* reading minds, like by taking a trace of the resonance currents in the cortex (and everywhere else), sorting them by computer, and printing them out into a language. Then translating the language and reading—literally reading—the mind.

We were successful on that one, as you know. Somebody
somewhere has a copy of my mind. Maybe lots of people.
I'm the textbook mind. The textbook insane mind, that is.
Do you know, they could read my mind far better than a
sane one? I was more consistent. I had aberrations that
were strong enough to record and sort and print, yet
specific enough to decode. Ain't that a triumph for
science? I have the only fully decoded mind in existence.
They think. Course, it doesn't do much good being able to
read the minds of crazy people. As far as I can see, that is.
Not that I know. Nobody bothered to keep me up to date.
Just thanks a lot, bye-bye, and good luck in your coffin.
Jenny and I got along just fine, but facts were facts, and
there was nothing could be done. Anyway, that's all in the
past, and I'm telling you this only so you can understand
the sort of thing that they need people like us for.

By the time you get this letter, knowing the speed of the
mail these days, especially with the various holdups which
the letter might accidentally fall prey to, I shall probably
be a lot more settled, maybe even a bit comfortable.
Almost certainly, I will have written you again. You know
me—always scribble, scribble, scribble, like a gibbon.
Even in the cells I set a new record for notebooks. They
wouldn't give me an extra supply, so I used yours and
Bedbug's and some of the others. I'm used to writing down
my thoughts, and there's no point here in me filling
notebooks for the benefit of Security and no one else. I
might as well communicate while I have the chance. I
know you'll read this and I know you'll make whatever
sense of it there is to be made, and I know that it'll mean
something whether or not. I will try to tell you something
of how I am and how I am feeling.

You write to me. I cannot put an address on this letter,

but I think if you get me put on your official list of correspondents the prison will know how to get the letters to me. I know you have little enough to tell, but you know that I want to hear from you and I want to know what you have to say. Curse me for my luck, if you imagine I'm lucky. Tell me anything—nothing you say to me is wasted and you know it. I'm only sorry I haven't set you a better example here, but you know how my mind runs on and away. Irresponsible. I plead insanity, and I have the means to prove it. . . . You have to humor me, so they say. . . .

Finish, for now. Events will be descending upon me any minute.

All the best,
Harker

Cage of Darkness

CHAPTER 3

The Bottom Falling Out of the World

Life is patterned. Socialization divides us up into sections and places parts of our being in a whole series of pigeonholes. Life is classified and categorized. Because of the convenience of this perceptive anabolism we can deal with life easily, as it comes, as a matter of routine. And if one small part of life goes wrong, we have all the rest to support it while we patch it up. By cutting up life into small sections, we safeguard the whole.

Tragedies do occur. Tragedies cut across the sectioning process, disturbing whole areas of the pattern. There are problems so extreme—though we do not all encounter them—that one's *life as a whole* seems threatened with reduction to ruins. One's sense of self, one's whole being in the world, is threatened by tragic circumstance. The tragedy might be sudden and physical—an accident; or it may creep up on one—a steady decline into bankruptcy. Such experiences have a deep and considerable effect on those who encounter them. People are scarred for life, go gray overnight, will never be the same again. The bottom falls out of the world. The pigeonholes are shattered, and all one's life tumbles into a heap from which it has to be resorted and repatterned. Sometimes, it doesn't seem worth it. Sometimes, people decide to die instead. Sometimes, even when they try, they are unable to reconstitute the world. Almost always, though, for those willing and able to take it, there is a route of escape, one category of existence left inviolate, in which one can take refuge while gathering one's resources to prepare for rebuilding an existence. Always, there seems to be a hiding place. It might be a job, or one particular person who alone can help. It may be somewhere to which one can return—an old home where parents still live, so that one can almost literally return in time to an easier way of life, a different set of categories.

Tragedy, like common, everyday misfortune, can be defeated by the pattern of life, by the process of categorization.

In Block C, however, in the cage, I am stripped even of my categories of life. The pattern is replaced by a constant monotone. There is no variety of input and output. There is only one routine. I have lost my home, my job, my friends, my environments, my car, my bed, my mailbox.

The effect of this shearing away of the categories of life until I am left with only one gray existence in which to operate is to make every common misfortune into a terrible tragedy. There is no hiding place from the slightest of emotional hurts, anxieties, fears. Everything is naked.

I left people behind me. I try to keep in touch. How? Not why, but how? To them, I am a dead man. To me, they are the living and I the dead. The only human contacts I have are with my fellows, and these I cannot avoid. I cannot divide up my life. I am living it all simultaneously, and that is why I am living no life at all.

The world of Block C—my world—has no bottom at all.

* * *

Let me tell you about Sam Mastervine. He used to be a scientist. Which means that he had a whole chain of rational thoughts to support every single opinion that he carried in his head. Which means that he had at his mind's disposal a vast body of eminent authority to back up his every statement. Which means that he carried into Block C a whole mass of serious and meaningful thinking to tell him what he was and how and why, and to give him a life as rich as any that was possible inside the concrete womb.

Being a scientist is exactly the same as being a priest. You _know_ the truth. There is no difference between religious dogma and scientific paradigm. Both are sheep's clothing wrapped snugly around wolves. Both are the clothes which can make a pauper look like a prince.

The only difference is that science conforms to certain standards of peculiarity known as rationality, which purport to _answer_ all criticisms, while faith simply maintains itself impervious to all criticisms.

The importance of Mastervine's being a scientist was that it put him in the know. It made him the intellectual elite. Because he knew the word "psychosis" and understood its references, the word held no terrors for him. Like a sorcerer of old, once he knew the true name of an elemental, he held power over that elemental, and it would serve his purposes rather than its own.

Psychosis did Sam Mastervine's bidding, served Sam Mastervine's purposes. He hurled the fits of madness

around like tennis balls in a dazzling display of intellectual elegance and competitive expertise. He played them
in the manner of a virtuoso reproducing a masterpiece on
a baby grand. He knew them, he dealt with them, he
"cured" them.

His own personal king-sized specimen was no trouble to
him. The chain of rationality, though it never breaks, has
rubber links which can stretch to accommodate all the
ignorance, stupidity, self-delusion, perversion, and insanity
that accumulate in the interstices like dirt under the
fingernails.

Sam Mastervine, like all the rest of his insidious breed,
could never ever conceive of the possibility that he might
be wrong. He might not know what the hell he was talking
about, but he would defend to the death whatever he
happened to be saying, with the invincible magic weapons
of reason and logic. He kept his Superman uniform
wrapped up inside his desk calculator, under his slide rule,
or in the case which usually held his horn-rimmed glasses.

He was kind to his mother, in favor of nuclear
disarmament, and a great fan of Mickey Mouse. There
was nothing particularly odd about Sam. He had his life
measured out into its cavities. He was pretty much of a
cliché, taken as a whole. It's not surprising—clichés breed
clichés and educate them into being clichés. Sam's father
was kind to his mother, drank his whiskey neat, and
always talked straight to shop assistants. Cardboard people don't have thirteen-carat-gold baby sons.

When Sam Mastervine came to Canaan, he was all set
to be king of the castle, a creative genius, and the Second
Coming of Walter Mitty. He had it all taped. Being a
scientist, he lacked all sense of proportion. He had himself
all confused with Einstein, Galileo, Pasteur, and Doctor

Who. Being a scientist, he really thought he could bring it off and live.

He couldn't.

It's not that his intelligence let him down, though he gave himself credit for too much. He conceded Edison's glib and terribly reassuring definition of genius, and he knew it wouldn't be easy.

It was purely and simply that he lacked contexts. He couldn't reapportion his life, because the pieces wouldn't fit. Sam found himself in hell, the ultimate failure. Science, like religion, provides for human frailty but not for human individuality. Sam found that it was all useless to him. It wasn't that he was short of answers, nor that he came up with the wrong ones. It was just that there weren't any questions.

Sam, when I knew him, was the bitterest of men. People—especially nuts—who are denied their rightful hallowed shrine in the ephemeral esteem of their subservient neighbors, often become bitter. Sam became bitter because he was not a better man than those with whom he shared his fate. He'd been prepared to come to Canaan and be alone. He'd not been prepared to come to Canaan and cease to exist. He could have coped with any sort of a conflict between his own identity and the society into which he was thrust, but he wasn't ready to find no society at all, and that he couldn't cope with.

In the final analysis, Sam was a creature of reflex—socially conditioned reflex. His science was no more than a version of faith. In the end, it was no more use to him than prayer. And no one was listening. No one at all.

MADMAN'S DANCE

CHAPTER 4
Mime to Silent Music

While the surf gently lips and sucks the gray dome of rock, a silent, liquid piping is poured like sweet effluent into the bleak, inarticulate water.

It is a song I cannot understand as I search for the hidden entrance to the dome. It is an absolute song. Without sound, there is no medium for interpretation. I could have understood it once: it used to be a blind force that would have torn me from the rock and battered me to death trying to hurl me through the wall and into the heart of the chamber.

But the notes are changed. The urge and vitality have gone from the song. It is attractive still, but wistful rather than sensuous, and far from irresistible. It is a contented song, nostalgic, with a new—subtler—magnetism, born of an interplay of forces.

The watcher now may only sit atop the smooth hemisphere and listen to the entombed amniotic music. I am trapped in the surf and the spray. The sirens slumber. The Rheingold is safe. There is no prospect of defilement, no question of theft. Perfect security.

The music is synesthetic. It is the pulse of the blood.
Blood mingles with blood. The music of the womb. The
music of the machine. The machine which holds me still
and which would not let me even kill myself. Do I still
have being-in-the-world? Of course not. I have brought
the music with me. I play it, within my body, and my body
is the musical instrument. It is mine. It cannot belong to
the machine. Here, there is no such thing as a machine. A
machine has no being, no mind. It cannot exist. Save in
me.

I am the mind of the machine. I am the mind of the
ship. In me is the machine and the ship and the world
which sent me. In me, they are music. Synesthesia. What
were they in Lindquist? An itch? An occlusion of the eye?
Why did he forget? *How* did he forget?

I am Titan. Titan is a rhythm in my heartbeat. We are
safe and well. Having a lonely time, Jenny. Wish you were
here.

I am standing at the Gate of Heaven and waiting. The
first thing you learn is that you always have to wait. I see a
man whose face is smiling with fear, and he walks to the
Gate and tries to make it yield to his touch. He is faceless,
but I think he is Petrie. Poor Nathan Petrie. They won't
let you through, Nathan. They know it doesn't matter
whether you did it or not. Do you think they even care?

"It won't open," he says, smiling.

"It won't open," agrees the man in the death-mask,
watching as ever. I don't know who is behind the
death-mask. Perhaps it is a problem for me to worry
about. Perhaps he is supposed to frighten me. Perhaps he
intends to unmask at the end of the play, so that I can see
that his face is my own. I don't care. It might just as well

be his own face. What do I care whether death is only a mask or not?

And we are all waiting: the man who smiles, my companion and good friend Death, the star-haired girl, and myself.

And now comes a fire-eyed man who wears courage like a cloak around his shoulders. He approaches us, and his eyes pass over the smiling man and Death, coming to rest upon the face of the star-haired girl.

"You keep strange company," says the brave man. I try to look inside his coat to get a peek at his medals, but he has the buttons done up tight. It is possible that once upon a time he was only a cowardly lion. I think he is Steve Cannon, but how can one be sure when those who have no masks have no faces either?

The star-hair replies, "It is not for me to choose who waits by my side at the Gate of Heaven." Very true, that. Can Love choose what company she keeps? Of course not. Anyone and everyone might discover Love beside him, or inside him. Even Courage can't be all that choosy. I've watched cowards do some very brave things, in my time.

"Come with me," says the man with fire in his faceless eyes.

She bows her head, and together they open the Gate of Heaven and pass through.

The man who smiles in fear again tests the strength of the Gate.

"It will not open," he says.

"It will not open," agrees Death, watching as ever.

"What did you expect," I say, "justice?"

In a root-skulled chamber of black earth I want to find myself a house, a refuge, and a crib. There I can decorate my bones with tinsel and green bottle-glass, and share the vacuum of oblivion with the labyrinth of Minos and the heroes of Rome.

I do not want my footprints to linger after me and tell the direction of my going, nor do I want the scrawling of my fingertips to testify the falseness of my temporary feeling.

I want to be alone, except for the maggots which will clean the filthy flesh from my beautiful white bones, and the worms which will map the streets of my unending empire. The blind and crawling worms I choose now form my brothers and my lovers. They will kindly strip me of my worldly clothes, and my bones will be the arches and the thoroughfares of a great and wonderful city, beneath the sea of grass and tree.

It is a city built in ruins, as nature intended cities should be, existing only to die, to be carcasses harboring the poor and the lonely. And my skull will be a palace and a temple, and kings and priests will look benignly down from the sockets of my eyes.

Your best chance, of course, is with Thanatos. If the man in the death-mask is my companion and my friend, then he is your most favored ally. I know the face which ought to lurk behind the mask, yours and mine. You cannot delude me with facelessness.

And yet I live. I always have. The man in the mask has been my friend since the day I was born, and he has not won me yet. You cannot kill me with death-wish, any more than you can scourge me with despair and sorrow and grief and hate. I survive. I am a survivor. This game, of course, is a test in itself. Death is only one of your victories, the other is gluttony for life. But I have walked that boundary all my life, and I can walk it now. You will not lure me into death, nor pain me into oblivion. My dreams remain my own, whether dreams within dreams within . . .

Or worlds to cage me.

I meet her by the edge of a river which flows forever around a Möbius circuit, so that the same water is cycled past the same shore once in every million years, and all the tears and drowned corpses are thus returned to their haunted wombs.

In my eyes, she is perfect. But in her eyes, and any eyes which care to stare, I am misshapen.

I speak to her in many lying voices, in languages which she cannot know, in cadences which hurt her ears. She cannot hear, she can only understand. Her eyes are fixed within my twisted face, and I feel their scalding glare.

She sobs, and her hands flutter like moth wings to carry the tears from her painted face and drop them in the harrowed waters of the sacred river.

Helpless, I watch her melt into the substance of the river, her tears and her blood borne away on an endless silvery shroud, her flesh and her bones turned fluid in the fertile, faithful earth, which bears her up triumphantly in the infant spring, as a cluster of reeds.

I stay by her moist bedside until the snow-shrouded winter kills the reeds, and then I steal them from the frost-bound soil and make them into panpipes.

And then I play upon them, a random song of loneliness and failure. A song without tune and without beauty. A song of death and heartlessness.

She cannot hear, her eyes are fixed within my twisted face.

I mingle with the absent melody the rhythm of my absent tears.

And in a million years, it is the same again, and in a

further million years, the same again, yet as I look down
the kaleidoscope of the years, the mirrors flush the music
into new patterns and new rhythms, the music becomes
silent, and the whole play of it becomes a mime.

Titan Nine

CHAPTER 4
Horizons

"Hello, Harker," she said.

"Come on in."

"How are things?"

"Same as always. Damn awful."

She grinned faintly. Not because it was a funny line—it was a standard, incorporated into a private ritual, but it was a very old standard. She hadn't heard it in quite some time. She grinned because we weren't back then, but here and now instead. I've never been able to master this business of greeting and parting which demands such hollowness from its participants. She knew.

"Sit down," I told her. "I'll make some coffee." I seem to remember somehow that conversations always begin with coffee. Mind you, I've been out of circulation for a long time. Still, a cup in your hand and a cigarette in your mouth enable you to be doing something even when the talk threatens to lapse. And it does—all the time. I can only really talk to people when they're not there. The legacy of Block C. Sometimes it doesn't show in the dialogue, but it always shows in the fingers. Without a cup of coffee and a cigarette I have at least two hands too many for talking to friends.

They'd given me a fine apartment. It was small—everything in the fake town was three-quarter-sized, to emphasize the fact that it was lurking in a crater in a desert—but it was complete and self-contained. A nine-by-six bedroom and a closet-sized kitchen didn't bother me much. I'm no claustrophobe: I *like* walls, and low ceilings, and compactness. Empty space, particularly wasted space, is beautiful and good for the eyes, but better at a distance.

"Well," I said, handing her the cup without having to ask about white or black or how much sugar (when you haven't so many memories they're easy to keep), "what have the years done to you?"

"Disfigured me for life," she answered.

"It doesn't show."

"You don't look in the same kind of mirrors that I do."

"Mirrors, hell," I said. "You look just like you always did."

"The years haven't done a lot for you," she said.

"My troubles have aged me."

She paused, just long enough to consign the pointless exchange of gay banter to the realms of outer darkness, then she repeated the remark.

"The years haven't done you any good, have they?" Her voice was quite gentle.

"What do you expect?"

"Once now and again," she said, "I saw letters. But you only write letters when you're in a strange kind of a mood, don't you?"

"I write letters all the time," I said. "I'm in a strange

kind of a mood all the time. The letters that get through are the ones that have nothing to tell you. They stop the others."

"Your letters don't read like you," she said. "Like a weird caricature of you."

"I am a weird caricature of me," I said. No flip talk, no silly chatter. I meant that.

"Self-portrait with exaggerated color scheme and big nose," she said.

"There's nothing wrong with my nose."

"You could have put more into the letters."

"Don't talk like a shrink. You know the censorship system as well as I do. If you'd wanted, you could have got a look at damn near anything, on the grounds of being my psychiatrist. Letters I couldn't send, even private notebooks."

"I couldn't," she said. "Not until the decision was taken to bring you here."

"But you've seen them now?"

"I'm looking through them."

For a moment, I was almost afraid. Afraid of what might be in those notebooks that I wrote for me in the privacy of my cell. But nothing's sacred—they photocopy everything, and all Security has to do is ask. The mountains move, let alone pieces of paper.

"Find anything interesting?" I asked.

"I won't," she said. "I know you. If anyone finds anything it'll be someone who doesn't know you."

"Well, you don't have to bother anyway," I said. "You can read my mind."

"That's right," she said. "We can read your mind. We can read a lot of minds, but it isn't doing us any good. We can't decipher them fast enough, and they don't make sense when we do."

Business at last.

"I forgot to ask," I said. "How's TITAN?"

"There's nobody else you'd rather hear about before TITAN?" She meant Mike.

"In time," I said. "In time."

"TITAN's as well as can be expected," she said. "A technological miracle. In human terms, pretty close to being a total disaster."

"Nobody's perfect," I lamented. "So you're desperate."

"Ever since SIX they've been wheeling out the physicists in threes and hauling in psychiatrists to replace them. The whole base is a mindblower's nightmare now. Theater of the absurd."

"So you all decided that the time had come to put away your petty human talents and call upon the worn-out, pig-sick, security-smeared, maniac-murderer whose secret identity is Captain Magnificent?"

"That's about it."

"Yeah, great," I said. "But don't you think it could be a good idea to tell me exactly how I stand? Is the army so tired of wasting the flower of American youth that it decided to stock all future TITANS with totally expendable lifers from the condemned cell, or is there some incredible chain of twisted logic by which some budding genius has actually worked out that I might stand a cat in hell's chance where the nine lives of the flower of American youth seem to have simultaneously gone up in smoke?"

"We think you can go out and come back."

"The others who went out didn't?"

"All dead except one. Lindquist. The last. He's alive, but terminal schizophrenia has him."

"I see the logic," I said. "Space drives men mad. Hence send a madman. What harm can it do him?"

"Crudely put," she said, "that's about it."

"The others are all dead," I pointed out.

"Under suspicious circumstances. In locked rooms."

"I'm not the man I used to be," I told her. "I wasn't kidding when I said my troubles had aged me. I've been away a long time, kid. I might not be up to it. I really am dog tired from doing nothing but wasting. There's no use pretending. I might shit out faster than the military boys, sooner and further. You're going to have to do some very fast thinking if you're going to find me in some kind of shape to ride a TITAN."

It was fear talking through my own mouth. Some kind of thing like that is always wrecking my reunions. Within half a mile of a friendly face or a familiar ear I always retreat and some other damn thing grabs me. Self-inflicted wounds. You can lose a lot of friends that way. Also, you can talk yourself back into the jug. But some people are just downright patient. Or long-suffering.

"We can shape you up," she said. I knew I was in for hard labor.

"Okay." I shrugged, and lit a new cigarette off the butt of the old one. They wouldn't trust me with a lighter.

"Mike Sobieski's dying," she said, pulling it right out of the blue.

"We all die," I said.

"Cancer of the prostate gland," she said.

"People don't die of that. They can operate."

"Not on him," she said. "He's an old man. Prostate inflammation—even cancer—isn't uncommon at his age, but he's not as strong as most. Complications. He's always had asthma. He's got bronchitis. They couldn't operate, or they'd kill him."

"Even in this climate, he gets bronchitis?" I queried.

"Not so bad. But he's had a lifetime of it. It's weakened him badly. Every little cough is a killer now. And the cancer is spreading. It's affecting his bladder. Pretty soon it'll be his gut, his kidneys. He can't last the year."

"Did you tell him that?"

"Pretty much. They didn't want me to tell him. But he knew. I told him just the way I told you."

"I'll bet he loves you."

"He was grateful."

"It must have broken his heart."

"His heart was already broken. He isn't a fool, Harker, and if he isn't quite the orator he was when you knew him, it's only because he's old, not because he's any less of a man. He was bluffing the doctors while they were trying to bluff him. I opened the whole thing up. It's easier for everyone."

"Okay," I said. "I'm all in favor of honesty."

"He's been director ever since TITAN FOUR," she said. "The old director lost his head in the flood of bad publicity after the first disaster. Mike stepped up into his shoes. But Mike's been on the Project since it was only a gleam in a few pairs of eyes. You know what Mike used to be like when he was in college. He was probably just the same when he was a kid. He was probably on this Project from the moment he read his first science fiction magazine. He was always full up with space fuel. And he's not burned out yet. He still wants to go. Inside his head. Even though his body's giving out.

"The assistant director runs things now, in effect, but he

remains AD in name. Mike's bedridden—has been for a month—but he won't hand in his resignation and the man who'd have to take it doesn't want it. Sure, there are murmurs in high political places, but there are too many fingers in this pie for any one axman to grab the whole of the ax. TITAN is Mike's child. The dead men—and the live wreck—are on *his* conscience. If TITAN NINE comes back, it's his victory. Everybody knows that."

"Jesus," I said. "Everybody has hearts, these days. I thought hearts went out with paper roses. Even the military, hey?"

"Henneker has a heart. He'd be a general if he hadn't. Maybe president. He's a hard man and all Army with a capital *A*. But he and Mike have been hand in glove all the way. They're just about all that's supporting one another."

"If I were a taxpayer," I said, "I'd scream like hell about the way this Project is being run."

"You're not a taxpayer. You never were."

"True," I conceded. "But how do you get away with it?"

"We get away with it because people think we can do it. And just for once, in all history, we need to do it so badly that people are prepared to care more about doing it than about the way it's done. I don't say there isn't a kiloton weight up there in the sky just waiting to drop on us the moment the string burns through, but for now we hold the stage."

"And you're pinning your last hopes on little old me."

"That's right."

"You have to be crazy."

"*You* have to be crazy. That's all we need."

"Whose big idea was I? Yours?"

"That's right."

"You've come a long way since the old mind-bending days."

"That's right."

"We need TITAN NINE to bring home a live cargo," she said. "Mike needs it. Henneker needs it. I need it. The Project needs it—so far it's cost seven men and two ships, but it would still be operating if it had cost seventy men and twenty ships. The losses aren't important. What's important is politics."

"Surprise, surprise," I said, unsurprised.

"You've been away a long time," she said. "It's getting worse every year out in the good old world. The cities, the people. The conditions are getting to the point where they're intolerable. When there are too many people, people die. That can be handled. There might not be much left of America the Beautiful, but that can be handled, too. We've had contingency plans for years. But what the men at the top need desperately, need more than all the guns and the plagues, is a flag to wave. You know and I know that faster-than-light travel is no kind of solution to any kind of human problem. It's not an instant answer to the population problem or to the resource problem. But it is God's gift to the political problem, and that's the one by which the Earth moves. If we can give the president just one successful Proxima loop, we can give him a weapon to keep the people controlled for years. And that's what he needs—time to implement the contingency plans under full control. Time to kill the people discreetly. Time to save himself. The people are just beginning to realize that the world is a cage, and that they're imprisoned here. All they can see around them is darkness. They have to be shown a way out of that cage of darkness. If we can show them a road to the stars, we can make them all the promises they want. TITAN NINE is the bribe to buy off the world, Harker. We can't afford another army hot-shot cookie-chewing toothpaste-ad hero. We need a survivor. We need the ultimate survivor—a man who's spent the best years of his life practicing nothing but survival. We want a man who can live with schizophrenia, because that's what deep space is. We want, above all else, a man whose mind we can read, because if this one goes wrong we absolutely must know what went wrong, so that TITAN TEN is a sure thing."

"You paint a pretty rosy picture," I said. "We're doing all this for the president, hey? He needs the publicity."

"It's the only game we get to play," she said. "Any kick and they wheel us out and a new team in. Who d'you want to work for? The good of humanity? Freedom and justice? The American Dream? Not you, Harker. You prefer a dirty game, if there's one available. You wouldn't do it for the human race, and I wouldn't ask you. Do it for yourself, Harker. Do it because it gives you the laugh on the people. That's you, Harker."

"Quite honestly," I said, "I don't think I'm that bad. I'm tempted to tell you where you can put TITAN NINE. And one of your sweet army flyboys with it."

"But you won't."

"How can I?"

"Precisely."

"But it's a hell of a dirty game for you to be up to your neck in. And cynical about it, too. What happened to the nice, sweet, dedicated person that deciphered my mind way back when?"

"Her troubles have aged her. What am I supposed to do, become a nun?"

"Good idea."

"Well, there you go."

"There, as you so correctly state, I go. Up, up, and away. Out into the far wastes of galactic space at fifty parsecs a minute. To S Doradus and back before the kettle boils. And why? Because if I don't you'll stick me back in my cell. And why? Because you ask me to go? And why? Because you're as mad as I am and figure that only a lunatic can do it. What happens when I come back, little girl? Do you announce to the world that a homicidal maniac has opened up the road to the stars—to other homicidal maniacs?"

"You're not going to get any credit, either," she said.

"A stand-in does the press conferences and shakes hands with the prexy, hey? Yes, boys, while I was out there in the mighty deep I occupied myself with readin' holy words an' writin' home to my de-ah old ma, who has the cookies all abubblin' on the stove. Do cookies bubble?"

"There are compensations," she said.

"Name three."

"If you bring TITAN NINE back, you get to go out again on TITAN TEN."

"I could die laughing. Also pigs might fly. That's a real fine offer."

"It is," she said. "It makes you the only man in the world capable of taking wings and flying out of the cage—not just the cage you've spent your life in, but the cage we've spent *our* lives in as well. We're offering you freedom, Harker. More freedom than any of us is ever likely to share with you. We're offering you the one thing that means more to you than anything else."

"Thanks," I said.

"It's not for you."

"Who is it for? Fuck that stuff about the president and the politics and the publicity. You tell me, from your point of view. Who is it for? Mike? The greater good of humanity?"

"It's for me."

"You. Just you. Stars in your eyes, too. What did they do? Give you rocket ships instead of dolls? Give you Doc Smith to read instead of *Little Women*?"

"Just about."

"You have the wrong crew, you know," I told her. "Mike should be the brave old captain, with you his stalwart friend and second in command. You'd look well with pointed ears. And Henneker, too? Henneker the cabin boy? There's no room for me, except maybe as Fu Manchu the stowaway. What the hell game *is* this? Old maid? It sure as hell isn't poker."

"If I were you, Harker," she said, "I wouldn't worry about anybody's motives but your own. I wouldn't trouble yourself to get bitter about our little game because everyone involved in the Project is involved with it as well. Just concentrate on your end. Just go and come back. You'll only torture yourself worrying about other people."

"I'm sorry," I said.

"I know."

"I am. I've been away for a long time. I don't know how people think—not out here. I don't know how the world works out here. I wouldn't know an honest motive if you gave it to me on a silver plate."

"I know."

"You honestly think I can do it?"

"Yes."

"You honestly think I'm a logical choice?"

"Yes."

The shrinking, sinking, stinking feeling inside me wouldn't go away. I was a mess. She had to be right— where else could I get a second opinion? But it was all set wrong anyway. All going wrong. I wished that I loved her.

"Good night," she said.

"Those prison documents," I said.

"Yes?"

"I exaggerate."

"I know," she said. "Good night."

MADMAN'S DANCE

CHAPTER 5
A Question
of Characterization

The everlasting crisis of identity, of course, has no meaning except in terms of characterization. . . .

Perhaps I should say that the crisis of identity has *all* meanings—is, in fact, *total* meaning. But identity is a question of self, and here, *ipso facto,* where there is no being there is no self. Only ego.

Who am I?

Certainly not Harker Lee, who is blasted into every last cranny of this crazy nonworld. Here, there is no Harker Lee, because there is only that which is Harker Lee, and the name becomes meaningless. I cannot be Harker Lee—I am a character in Harker Lee's dream, and I must find a part to play, a character to be.

It is not the character who becomes real in the actor, but the actor who becomes unreal in the character. So to be given access to an unreal frame of reference and context of experience is a privilege, for it gives us a viewpoint from which to see ourselves, not as others see us, but as we might see ourselves if we were not cursed with subjective existence tainted with the objective selfhood. By virtue of characterization we become free to *act*, to know what it is like to be without a being-in-the-world in a world without *real* being.

I am here, dwelling with the stars, in the guts of what was once Harker Lee and is now a universe.

I am in inner space, the inner space of ego. Perhaps I might clarify my position better by asking: Who are you?

Who *are* you?

Not pure ego, nor id, and certainly not superego. What are you made of, shards of Harker Lee? You are a God, and I am your Doppelgänger, your gray brother, your son of the shadows. I am your *alter ego*.

I am a traveler upon the face of your Earth, an observer and a commentator. I am your judge and your jury, but I am your prisoner and your victim also.

I am your biographer, your prophet, your friend. I am also your guardian, who will see that you return safe and sound to your existence.

Who am I? What is my name and my part?

What can my part be but that of Lucifer, of Iblees, of Beelzebub?

Why, this is hell, nor am I out of it.

I am the devil.

I dance as Judas dances, to the madman's tarantella. We are allies, Judas and I. If you get out of line, Godman, we will straighten you out. Look out for us, Godman. Judas and I are a red-hot team.

You cannot drown us with your dreams. . . .

Her hair swirls like marsh mist about her shoulders and her neck. Its fragrance is cold and fragile—a breath of morning wind would blow it all away with a touch of its self. Her entire form is crystalline in the clouded darkness such as lingers after dawn, and she flees to her daylight slumbers within the casket of a dead tree in a stagnant swamp.

She is as old as the stones which mark her resting place. A whole far-away world that is long forgotten but which never died is hiding in the canyons of her memory. She is sister to the darkness beneath the earth, and the unlit oceans and the anaerobic fires.

You want me to follow her there, to her rendezvous with the bones of men and the stony imprints of the passage of the evolutionary procession. You would have me ride upon the frail carriage of her floating tresses, or let her ride upon my own broad back to wherever she cares to spur me. You would have me share her deathlike dreams and her dreamlike days. You want me to go with her to her distant destinies and her macabre ports of call. You want me to drink the death that is her life from the same carven cups, and open wide my embrace to encompass all her multitude of forms, and guard her from all anger and harm.

You know that I should love to plunge myself into the black depths of her nightshade existence, and swim in her sea of shadow and shame, to stay by her side whether she was allowed to fly or condemned to crawl. My mind could always tell the truth, and I could not be deluded by the mocking tyranny of your bribery. But nevertheless . . .

She dreams of an everlasting, moonless midnight, lit only by the quiet, careless stars. She dreams of a cloak of shadows which might hide her tenderness from the brightest lightning. She dreams of the ultimate end to time, when all is night and desolation, and she is equal with the whole stock of the tired human race, and the sun is an ember.

I will pass by her then, for but a moment, and perhaps I will offer her small gifts of pearls and diamonds, pouring them liberally into the ocean of her hair. She would know me even then, and we might laugh together, and make a chrysalis of our dreams in the blackened ruin that was once the universe, knowing that long after we are gone it will break and give birth to a new monadic existence.

In the meantime, we might drink strange drinks and build ruined, night-filled cities out of poisoned memories. And we would not dread the second morning of time. But while there is life in everywhere, our marriage is not even the stuff of dreams. It is a futile temptation.

Get thee behind me . . .

I am forced to pass through a town infested by a foul plague. I walk quickly along the sweat-stained, tear-stained, blood-stained, tainted road, with my collar up-turned and my eyes entrenched behind guarded lids, and my tongue pressed to the floor of my mouth. I pause only once, daring no more, as my feet grow heavy, and I watch a young man who cradles in his arms a sleeping girl-child whose body is marled with the signs in red and black.

"Awaken," murmurs the youth, into the ear of the sleeper, breathing on her pockmarked cheek. Slowly, she stirs, and her dead eyes look into his.

"I am dead," she says quietly, and without remorse.

"I have healed you," he says. "I am a healer of the dead."

"Only the dead may heal the dead, may love the dead, may dance with the dead, may pay the dead their due," quotes the child. "Are you dead?"

"No," answers the young man, "I live yet a while."

But he falls upon the road, and the child runs away to command the driver of the death-cart to bring his cargo this way, as the darkness eats his eyes and gorges upon his virility.

The child, which was only a lifeless burden, becomes so once more as the driver of the death-cart reaches down to greet her, and the driver spits on the young man, saying, "Healer of the dead, heal thyself!"

We will never have enough of masks, you and I. They are the moves in our game, the substance of our existence.

But let me test *your* pride, for just one moment. Let me tempt *you.* Let's not think that because you have all the power and all the knowledge, that I am completely without talent in this matter.

Think on this.

You have set stars in your sky as stars were set in ours. Can you conceive that it will be a *civilized* man who can reach out his hands into the sky and say, "These stars are *mine*"? Could that be a safe man, a sure man, a military man, a man of the law or . . . even this—a man of God?

It will be a man with a storm in his being, a *lust* for pride and life, blood and dominion. It could never be a man who lived within the confines of his own skull, who *knows* what he sees and hears and feels, and all that it means, who *understands* the nature of the universe and the cheating of false gods.

It will be a man who lives *without* himself, whose sensations are a part of an unknown pattern, who places his *faith,* deliberately, in false gods, idle dreams, and impossible desires.

It cannot be a man who believes in reality, but a man who believes in destiny.

If there are in the race of men those who can conquer the stars—and to conquer the stars, remember, the stars have to become a part of their lives—they will always be men of torment, outcasts, and barbarians.

Dancers in the madman's mime . . .

You and I, Harker Lee, we pieces of Harker Lee. They can't take the stars away from us. If we go home, we take the stars as part of us. They can't ever put us back in ourself, let alone in our cage. Remember that, Godman, and remember the way home. . . .

Cage of Darkness

CHAPTER 4

Me and My Shadow (Chapter 9—The Final Chapter —of "The Secondhand Life of Harker Lee")

Schizophrenia is not something you catch, like the measles, nor is it something which happens to you, like a road accident. Schizoid is something that you are.

What does being schizophrenic entail? It's like being a doctor or a hero—you can't just go out and be it, you have to have the qualifications. It's not something that everybody can be. Maybe they could if they were shown the way, but let's face it, it's not something you could recommend to your friends. In any case, they aren't shown the way. They're shown an entirely different way, and not only shown it but forced into it at every conceivable juncture. It's conditioned into them. The options are taken away from them. It's not the option of being schizoid that I worry about—it's the options that we don't even know about.

If you're a beggar who makes his/her living by being maimed so that you present a particularly pitiful sight (and this is not hypothetical—you can find beggars like this on every advertising display and TV commercial in the world), then it probably makes perfect sense to you to cripple your children in the same way. In order for it to make sense, they hand you packaged vocabularies of motives and reasons. (That's the worst—the very worst—side of the advertising strategies which are what we live by in these times. Not the capitalistic exploitation of products, but the packaging and selling of motives.) Schizophrenia is something that characterizes the ones who escape. It's a blanket label; it's not any one thing. The men who live out the terms of their natural life in Block C are the ultimate escapers. They've got away from the human condition. What a shame the human condition is a monopoly and there's nowhere for them to run.

*　　*　　*

You have no right to make cracks about TV commercials and advertising strategies when you write a spiel like that. What is it except a TV commercial in favor of the schizoid condition? You wouldn't want to wish schizophrenia on anyone, now would you?

*　　*　　*

But when you come right down to it, you see, you don't really know. You wouldn't wish it on the guy next door, but is that because you wouldn't want to wish the viewpoint on him or because you wouldn't want to bring down the wrath of the human condition upon his innocent head? You wouldn't want to see him put away in Block C.

Well, of course, that depends on who you live next door to. But you get the drift. In the final analysis, you just don't know. The whole world's out of step but Charlie, but what's the answer? Should Charlie change step? Should the world? Should the whole damn kit and caboodle stop marching and walk sensibly? Does it *really* matter so much that everybody stays in step?

But if you're rational (well, you aren't of course, *ipso facto*) you can't even claim injustice. You can only claim that it doesn't make sense. (And of course it doesn't. Not to you. You're mad. We're not.)

In the eyes of the social slot machine—our eyes—the schizo is a failure. He has *failed* to adjust to us. He has *lost* contact with his environment. He *lacks* appreciation of reality. It's all his loss. We're whole, not him. He's the square peg, but we *know* the hole is round because we're the social slot machine. (Do you have round slots?) Have you ever seen a square hole? Have you ever heard of a square hole? We *know* that nature abhors a vacuum (why did she make so much of it?) and especially a square vacuum. Absurd, no? Square holes are heresy. A sin against symmetry. We live in a radial universe, not a radical one.

You can't kick too hard, I mean, can you? You can't blame *us*. It's not *our* fault, dammit. I mean, the sun just happens to shine out of our arses, doesn't it? We didn't put it there, did we? You know it's all your fault, and you get what you deserve (we call it what you *need*). Of course you don't like it and you don't accept it, and you don't believe it. But then, you don't believe anything, do you, poor faithless creatures? (How can you *live* without faith?) We believe.

Passionately.

Rationally.

Naturally.

We *can't* believe that you can't believe. Because we're

unable to believe in the inability to believe. Naturally. It's only rational, you *must* agree. You have no passion; you've got to be wrong. That's sabotage against humanity. You're a traitor. A disgrace to the race. We feel such compassion for you.

Madness is a measure of the discrepancy between you and us.

*   *   *

Madness is a measure of the discrepancy between you and me.

Me is a believer, a mask, a label plastered on your face by the social slot machine. Belief is the important component of it. Schizophrenia is a simple unit of distance, like the inch or the parsec. And that's not a clever remark, that's a literal statement of the truth. Schizophrenia is a unit of distance along a continuum—a dimension, if you like—that exists in a real space. It's what lies between here and there, between you and me. Two schizophrenias would put me twice as far away. I'm not sure whether you'd be able to see me then. Perhaps I'd be too far away. Perhaps I'd be dead. But the important thing for all you wonderful people out *there* to remember is that you don't know *anything* about space and distance. You haven't begun to imagine.

Here I am.

There you are.

I can see you and you can see me.

But we only believe in me. We don't think that you exist.

I don't believe in you.

You don't have to believe at all. Nobody's forcing you. You don't worry about that. You don't have to.

But I have a problem.

And if I have a problem you have a problem, too.
Problems drive people out of their minds.
I want to drive you out of my mind.
How do *you* feel?

*   *   *

What's so special about Harker Lee, who isn't (I think we all agree) out of his mind? The person to ask is Jenny Segal. She's the one who's supposed to provide you with your copy of the answers. She's the one who's paid to understand. She's the heroine who ventures alone and unafraid into the Hells and the Underworlds and the Purgatories and the Limbos (yea, even unto Tartarus) to search out the Draconian psychoses and to withstand the fiery breath of their non-sense and pierce their many-colored coats of steely armor with her golden sword of understanding and her lance of explanation. She's the saint who has consecrated her life to chivalry and the quest for the grail of sanity.

And she does understand. Within limits. Always within limits. (Who ever heard of understanding without limits?) The limits of her belief. Understanding is only really possible outside the limits of belief, but we try. We don't accept that last argument, of course. Not at all.

We think you're talking through your ass.

We think you're a nut.

We DON'T understand.

And we're damn well proud of it.

How do *you* feel?

This is what Jenny says:

A schizophrenic is a pretender. He pretends to be what he is not, which is "real," in the context of society's belief. A schizophrenic suffers from a gap between his internal experience of himself and his external perception of the world only because he pretends to be what the world believes him to be (i.e., real) when he knows that he is not. The division is one of contexts. The self which exists in his own context of reality (which is unreal in the world-context) is one and the same as the self which is real in the world-context (but unreal in his own), but it appears to him to be different (and can seem so to the outside world also; hence the "split-personality" myth).

*   *   *

All of this is simply not clear. It must be patched up. It must be made simple and easy to understand.

But it's not easy to understand. That's the point. It's because it's not easy to understand that no one will even try. They have to find alternative explanations, "rational" accounts of why they don't understand. That's why they invented madness. It's a cover-up.

Then you must employ a cover-up, too. Use sleight-of-hand. Use some slick tricks and some fancy analogies. Jenny says schizophrenics pretend. So pretend. Pretend you can justify yourself. Pretend that there's a justification possible and necessary.

Can't.

Try.

I quote:

"Harker," says Jenny, "you feel that the Harker Lee which the world sees (labels) is unreal. The world feels that the Harker Lee who feels that is *ipso facto* unreal, and a hallucination. There is a basic disagreement here. All other disagreements follow from that. The world will not recognize the point of view from which you consider Harker Lee to be real as a valid one, and vice versa. It is all too easy to lose sight of the fact that we are talking about one thing only; it seems so much easier to pretend there are two. If there are two, the problem is simple: Which one is real? But there is only one, and the problem is so much more complicated: Which *context* is real?

"You deny the existence of emotions within yourself. This is not an observation, but stems from the initial dichotomy. You cannot accept the existence of emotions because you feel that they would be an attribute of the false version of yourself. If you attributed emotions to your real self, the world would deny their validity. It is simply safer to do without, to pretend they do not exist. This is the same strategy employed on both sides of the conflict to deal with the various points at issue. When in doubt, deny the existence. This is a strategy employed both by you and by the world."

Simple, really.

It begins to make sense now that certain pronouns are employed in certain unusual ways in this document. Anyone who thought that was just an affectation take three demerits. The use of the pronouns is supposed to be conveying something. It's a device for communication. Is it getting through?

Is *anything* getting through?

Now take the title of the autobiography. Secondhand? No, it's not just a tricky title. It means that the life documented therein is derived from the world outside and is not implicit and original with Harker Lee. Anyone who thinks that he lives his life at first hand is sane. Anyone who thinks his life has been traded back and forth any number of times is crazier than I am and has my congratulations and my admiration.

Some more things Jenny says about me, which may help just a little bit, give just that extra little bit of insight:

Jenny says: "You play poker very well because it

supports your conception of reality. Poker is you and not the false you that the world uses in its calculations. You win, partly because you are completely free from the error of belief in luck, partly because you are completely free from the error of belief in the absoluteness of the cards that you hold. When another man bets, he is either telling the truth about the value of his hand or lying about it. For you, there is no such distinction. For a sane man, a bluff is a lie; for you, bluff is reality, the way of life. The conditioning of society can only hinder a man when he enters the microcosm of a stud poker game. You have no such hindrance."

Jenny says: "You wear dark glasses to hide your eyes. It is a disguise you wear in argument and in all face-to-face relationships with others. The dark glasses hide the fact that the self which participates in such relationships is itself a disguise for a wholly different concept of Harker Lee. Your constant sarcasm is a similar redisguise. You disguise the intention of everything you say by making it all sound insincere. You can do this with both true and false statements because the difference is—to—you—quite irrelevant."

Jenny says: "You deliberately do what is not expected of you in order to emphasize the nonreality of the expectations which other people hold."

And Jenny says: "You can pass for sane. Especially in this day and age, when the deliberate and continual flouting of social expectations is itself a recognized and viable social strategy. You can make people accept you as a viable entity within society. You're socially adjustable, from their point of view. They can fit you in. This gives you advantages not usually available to schizophrenics. You have a very strong personality, and you're highly intelligent. In this day and age, when the world is so complicated that people actually expect *not* to understand, you awake less hostility and fear in others than you would have done at any other time in history. You can pass. And while you're passing you can relate yourself to society in a way that few schizophrenics ever got the chance to. If only you hadn't . . .''

Yes, well, I did.

There you go.

A great opportunity wasted? That's only the way Jenny sees it. One has to remember that Jenny, as a professional nutcracker, is very biased.

But you've got to admit . . .

Harker, this is you.

How do *you* feel?

Okay.

You thank Jenny for what she has achieved. You would like to love Jenny for what she is and what she means to you. But you can't. It's a hard life.

*   *   *

This is an addendum.

You think you have a self and a body. The social slot machine states that body *is* self, that self is *in* body.

You disagree.

Your self is not in your body. Your self has no body. Your self is no-body.

Your body is real in the world. It has no self; it has to be given one by the world. "I" am myself, not really a self, but an extension of body into self.

Your self exists *elsewhere,* in a space in which schizophrenia is a unit of distance. That is all of space (multidimensional). Outer space (so called) is only tridimensional and is an excerpt from all-of-space.

So?

*   *   *

This is an appendix called Appendix One. I am going to
leave it in my wastepaper basket, knowing that Major
Chalk will come in and search it at the earliest possible
opportunity, and knowing that he will not dare do
anything except route this piece of paper to its proper
place in my file—i.e., at the end of that most interesting
and confusing of documents, THE SECONDHAND LIFE OF
HARKER LEE. I am very tempted to burn it in the grate and
make Major Chalk go through the trouble of reconstitut-
ing every last word of it. I wish there was some way I could
get it to the Kremlin so that he would have to go there to
get it back, and perhaps get arrested, interrogated, and
shot as a result. Let's face it, they'd never believe him if he
said he was only looking for an appendix to a crazy man's
autobiography. Appendix Two will probably be found
flushed down the john. (That, by the way, is a lie—appendix two will be somewhere else entirely, but I know full
well that now I've written it official procedure will force
Major Chalk to check the drains.) How are you, Major
Chalk? Keep smiling.

Appendix One begins here.

My passport had a photograph on the cover, and I
thought that it might be useful to remind myself what I
looked like, because I'm going on a long trip and I'm not
sure the mirrors where I'm going will work. I reassured
myself by showing the passport to the mirror.

I'm writing this, by the way, just before I get blasted off
into nowhere in TITAN. This particular appendix is concerned principally with advice to schizophrenics.

I opened the passport to check that I was really who
they said I was, and found that my name was most
certainly Harker Lee, and that the description seemed to

fit the photograph in most respects (except for height, which is really about an inch and a quarter, color, which is monotone gray, and no distinguishing marks, because there really is a most distinct white border. Please see to it, higher authority!)

Everything is going to be all right.

A matter of the utmost simplicity.

That advice, now. The things you have to remember are these:

All truth is conditional.

That which is held to be true is that which is demonstrably true (i.e., that which can be perceived—not by you, by someone else agreeing with you—or that which can be proven by a process of unchallenged reason).

All proof and perception is based on premises. Proof arises by the logical synthesis of ideas. Perception arises by the habitual synthesis of ideas. Both perception and proof are creative processes.

If all flowers are alive, and if a rose is pink, then it follows logically that a daffodil is a plant. It is extremely important to grasp the principles which underlie this kind of argument, because they are in use constantly.

It is equally true that if a cat has nine lives and if curiosity killed the cat, then curiosity is one of the most lethal agents known, and I advise you all not to trifle with it.

The vital words in either of these logical constructions are all ifs. To say that a final conclusion is true because the premises are true is the ERROR of commitment by belief. I should watch out for this one particularly, because we all make mistakes.

It is true that the sky is blue only if I am correct in assuming that the sky is blue, after which I can prove it.

All sensory perception is as conditional as logical analysis and in the same way.

There is no absolute truth.

But even without truth at all, there is still reality, which is not conditional. The silly idea that something has to be true to be real (or vice versa) is the curse of modern society.

A lie/an illusion/a hallucination deceives. A lie is a lie because it deceives and for no other reason. A lie may be untrue, but there is no conceivable reason why it should be. A lie cannot be the opposite of a truth because a truth is conditional and a lie can only deceive if it is unconditional.

A truth might be a lie if it deceives. It deceives (virtually all truths do this) by implication.

The statement "This statement is a lie" is only a lie if it is true. It *is* a lie, because it deceives. It is therefore true. It deceives by implying a paradox which has no reality. All paradoxes stem from errors of this kind. One would think that the mere existence of paradoxes would inform people that their way of looking at things is not real, however true it may be, but not so, alas.

There is no polarity in reality.

Opposites do not exist.

Cogito ergo sum is a lie. It is a lie because it implies logic where none exists. This is an example of logic constructing its own traps. Beware of logic. *Cogito* assumes *sum*. (For those interested, one might also note that *sum* [word] assumes *cogito* [concept described by word] and therefore the whole thing is mutually self-supportive and therefore [or ergo] *ergo* is [a] redundant and [b] a false concept anyway.)

Belief is commitment. Belief in a statement, principle, or

truth inherently rejects the possibility that opposite statements, principles, or truths might exist. Yet the concept of
opposites itself arises from the infrastructure of belief.
Belief is self-contradictory. All truth is conditional and
therefore all belief is absurd. Belief denies the conditional-
ity of truth.

All beliefs deceive. All beliefs are lies.

Belief can only harm me.

I reject it.

You will find it just as easy to reject if you reject all
emotion. Emotion is the source of belief. Without emotion,
one can shed belief easily.

The sole reason I can survive the TITAN flight is because
I cannot be trapped into denial of—and thus loss of—reality.

It is all a game. The only object is to keep the piece in
play (NOT to win).

The piece is me. Identity, person, being.

I'll come back from hyperspace.

I can, and I will.

*   *   *

Appendix Two. I suppose I had better justify that last
statement. Explain it anyhow. I always have to explain
things. Well, we all have our ex-es to bear (axes?). I'll
pretend you're a moron. (Chalk, this is for you.)

Imagine a piece of paper three units by two.

Imagine the paper divided by a line into two equal
halves. The line is two units long.

Imagine that line moving sideways along the piece of
paper. It still divides the paper into two parts, but the
parts are no longer equal in size. The line, however, is still
two units long, and will remain so until it reaches the edge
of the paper, at which point the two divided parts of the

paper are six square units and zero square units in area.

The magnitude of the spaces which that line divides *cannot* be known by knowing the length of the line. (Author's message.)

Now extend the model into three dimensions. We now have a surface dividing a cube. Dispense with the squareness—we have a surface separating two volumes of whatever shape and size.

A man is a surface. He separates his inner being from the world which contains him. It is equally true to say that he separates the world outside from the inner being which contains it. We are now operating in a total of four dimensions; the human surface is itself possessed of three, just as the surface dividing the cube had two and the line dividing the piece of paper had only one.

The important point is this. By measuring the dimensions of a man, we cannot possibly hope to deduce anything about the relative dimensions of inner being and outer space, nor even of their actual sizes (the original piece of paper might have been an infinite streamer, with the dividing line still two units long).

Either inner being or outer space or both might be infinite. Either inner being or outer space or both might be negligible. We do not know. We cannot know. Our observations are founded only upon our assumptions.

In order to travel faster than light—to reach into the realms of outer space—we must side-step mass, and therefore the matter-phase. We must go, in fact, into a tachyon-phase, into a state where the relationship between mass and velocity is different and manipulable.

But in order to translate ourselves into a phase which gives us access to outer space, we must also, by that translation, give ourselves access to inner being. We know very little about either. We might be very surprised indeed to find the territories which are actually available for exploration, rather than those which we believe to be there.

Faster-than-light travel translation into tachyon-phase is an implicitly schizophrenic experience. I have some notion of what it will be like. I have some idea as to how to cope with it. The men who rode the other TITANS did not.

What happened to the other spacefarers was this: in the tachyon-phase they found themselves in a new context of reality. They found themselves, for the first time, in their own inner being. They were in no way prepared for what they found there. They were, in fact, in a context which all their socially conditioned beliefs told them was unreal and could not exist. They were each alone in a mode of reality which had been forbidden to them by the terms of their earthly existence.

They could not be expected to adapt themselves.

They were each given godhood. It is by no means easy to be a god. Their beliefs could not cope with it.

Their selves disintegrated.

Except for Lindquist's. Lindquist's self survived.

But it can't get back.

I can. You can.

*   *   *

A footnote. Probably the last words that this autobiography will ever wring from me.

They let me name the ship. I didn't think they'd do that—not for a poor crazy man who's more a victim in this game than a hero. But they did. It really is my ship.

I named the ship *Canaan*.

Of course.

MADMAN'S DANCE

CHAPTER 6

Recombinations in the Kaleidoscope

Crowds are not common in my dreams; crowds are always difficult to handle. For this reason, when the crowds do appear, pushing and jostling and pressing their empty faces into kaleidoscopic circles, I feel the pressure that much more intensely. I have always had a sort of horror of being watched, and the fact that the watchers have no faces, but only eyes, makes the horror more real.

As the mob pushes and presses, the man in the death-mask, who is always present in the crowd, but never a part of it, is withering a rose with an artful gesture of his rotting fingers. The petals, crushed in a gnarled hand, drop to the ground like stones. The man in the death-mask smiles at me, and I bow my head in acknowledgment.

The multitude is horrified.

"How can death be your friend?" asks a man in the crowd—Cain Urquhart, I think, though I cannot be sure because I cannot see him.

"Why not?" I say. "We can work together. I think we are on the same side."

This thought may be dangerous, but only if it is wrong.

Death and the devil have often been seen hand-in-glove by wiser visionaries than I. On being asked to renounce the devil and all his works, the dying man replies: this is no time to make enemies. So it should be. It could be Judas behind that mask. It might be Mastervine. Either way . . .

"I don't understand," says the voice in the crowd. Definitely not Cain Urquhart, the master of understanding. Madoc? Petrie? Chalk?

"We collaborate," I tell him (her?). "We have similar ideas and similar concerns. We are twin prisms, distributing light in different directions only because the source of light is so infinitely variable. We have the same potentials."

"Aren't you afraid?" The crowd comes closer, stifling me with its attention and curiosity. Only the man in the death-mask has space in which to move.

I do not answer.

"We writhe in agony beneath the shadow of his skeletal hand," they tell me. I cannot decide whether they are warning me or marveling at my lack of fear.

"Everyone holds that hand," I tell them. But the crowd does not understand—does not even believe me. Where is Dalquier? Or Cannon? Or Sam Mastervine? Surely the . . .

The man in the death-mask reaches his hands out into the crowd, and he begins crushing their skulls, and the bones fall like rose petals, and we laugh, sharing the joke between our divided self.

The crowd scatters.

I follow them, leaving the man in the death-mask behind me, to tidy up after himself. I cry to the crowd, because suddenly I feel that it is very important they should understand: "I am teaching you to be supermen. I teach by example. We are supermen. The cage of darkness is a barrier to be broken down, and this is the way to break it."

Now I am lonely. The crowd is still all around me, but the people are now nothing more than fugitive shadows, fading before the power of my glance, hiding from the echoes of my words.

"We *have* created something above ourself," I tell them, though they will go to almost any lengths to avoid listening. "The great tide will never ebb. We will not relegate ourselves to the situation of the beast. We will transcend man. As the ape to the man is only a thing of shame, so the man to the Titan is only a thing of shame. . . .

"We have come the way from worm to man, and we bear within us the whole legacy of the worm, as we bear the legacy of the crawling reptile and the climbing ape. We are composites of plant and phantasm, but we are nevertheless Titans. . . .

"Titan is the purpose of the human race. If we will only say: TITAN *will be* the purpose of the human race. . . .

"Remain true to the Earth, yet carry with me my extraterrestrial dreams. If these are poison, then take this poison into your bellies. When God was declared dead, blasphemies against that God ceased to be. Now the sin which preys on the human soul is blasphemy against man, against life, against knowledge.

"When your souls looked with contempt upon the body of a man, did you ever *really* doubt that you were right? That the soul should leave the body meager, ugly, and ill-provided, was that malice or reality? Thus the soul sought to escape body and Earth, and have we not done so? Could they ever cage our souls? Could their cages leach out our souls?

"Are your souls meager, hideous, and starved of wisdom? Are you a pollution upon the face of the earth? Must the afterman be an ocean of content and contempt to contain such a pollution and destroy itself with guilt?

"Not if *we* would not have it so. The hour of contempt need never come. Happiness need never be loathsome to us, or reason, or feeling, or sympathy.

"The soul *is* free. There *is* space for dreams and truth within the dreams. There is space for the heir to the crawling reptile among the stars in the sky. . . .

"We are TITANS. . . ."

They flee from my words into every corner that chance might offer them. In order to escape me, they flee even back to the arms of the man in the death-mask, who welcomes them with a smile, and a smile, and a smile. . . . I no longer laugh with him. I could cry, but there is no need. In a different time, in the cages, they will listen, and even if they refuse to believe or understand, they will take what they have to. Judas Dancer will captain a ship to the stars; Sam Mastervine will steer her; Luis Dalquier will plot her course; Nathan Petrie and Steve Cannon and Manny Madoc and Con Radley and Cain Urquhart will be her crew. Bedbug will nurse her engines, and I will wait for her in the sky.

I let the crowd run from me into the blaze of light. I remain.

I walk through the silken air, the lightness of my feet taking me upon a mountain ridge. I come upon a small man whose shoulders are badly bent beneath a gaudy bundle.

"May I help you with your load?" I ask him. My heart

is cold and stiff, as though it is locked in a granite cave, but I cannot bear to look at the hideous warping of his shoulders. It makes me feel sick.

The small man shakes his head and says, "You cannot bear this burden."

"Is it so heavy?" I ask him, with a laugh hovering upon my lips.

"It is the vault of heaven," he replies, quietly.

And he smiles.

Titan Nine

CHAPTER 5
Sobieski's Shield

They didn't want to let me in to see Mike Sobieski on my own, despite Jenny's kindly say-so. I contrived to tell the fresh-faced Major Hurst (my second-string nursemaid) to go to hell, but Sobieski's doctor (also military) wanted to stick around to make sure I didn't spit poison darts at his patient. But when I went into the sickroom, with the doctor trailing me, Mike told him to get out and leave us in peace.

"He'll only watch us through the glass, of course," said Mike, pointing at the mirror, "but I'm damned if I'll have him hovering around me like the angel of death." I pulled up a chair and situated it carefully in between Mike and the mirror.

He didn't sound any too good. It wasn't the faintness of his voice or anything like that—just a sort of sour inflection which suggested frustration and bitterness.

"How d'you feel?" I asked him.

"How d'you think I feel?" he retorted. "Numb. Only half of me in this world—the other half's chopped off and parceled up in Morphia or some such place. They kill the pain and me with it. I'm surprised they let me have my own head. Morphine's good stuff, though—lovely dreams I have during my afternoon nap. Very vivid."

"You don't take afternoon naps," I said.

"Don't tell them that," he said. "But it's not for want of trying. They ration out my real time, and there's nothing to do with the time they steal but sleep and dream. If I can. More dream than sleep, I'm afraid. But very vivid, as I say. Relax, dammit. You'll scare me to death sitting like that."

I relaxed. He was busy pausing for breath.

"Are you going to do it?" he asked, abruptly.

"Do I have a choice?" That was the wrong thing to say. I forgot that you don't say the same things to different people. You don't show the same Harker Lee to everybody. You have to change. I regretted the error.

"I hope not," he said, not offended by my remark. "If you need to choose, you're in a bad way."

"I am in a bad way," I said, muttering to take the bite out of it. "But I'm going. Of course I'm going."

"Fine."

It was his turn to relax. But he only sagged a little. He hadn't been able to muster the tension to face my reply head on.

"Blasted pillows," he said. "Ought to be possible to let me lie in a position where I can look human instead of flopping about like a worm." He tried to force himself further up the bed. I suspected that was what the doctor didn't want him to do. I couldn't decide whose side I was on, but I restrained him so that the doctor wouldn't get overexcited if he found out.

"You don't really know what you're in for yet?" he said.

"No. Hartner's going to brief me on the TITANS. With

Hurst in attendance to keep a check on classified material and so on. Jenny will take care of the psych side, of course—get me mentally fit, show me why I'm going to survive, that sort of thing. Then there'll be physical training, I suppose. But no, I don't know much about it as yet. It still seems absurd to me."

"You believe you can do it?" he asked. I knew that he only wanted to hear me say yes, but I was damned if I was going to humor him like an idiot child.

"I don't know. I'll try. You must have a good argument on paper or I wouldn't be here. But all sorts of things get committed to paper. Paper doesn't mean a thing. Jenny has a model of my mind and a computer decode. But I have a mind. There's a big difference. You know that."

"You helped build the model. The model stands up. We've tested it in the computer with everything we know about hyperspace."

"That's fine. It's my model. I believe in it. But it's analogical analysis, and you know full well that the analogue only replaces the properties of the original. It doesn't duplicate. And what you actually know about hyperspace could be written legibly on a postcard. The model stands up in the computer. That's good. But the Harker Lee you have in your files is only a paper frog that jumps when its neck is tickled. I respect the work you've done, but nothing is going to give me faith. I'll do it, if I can. But no promises. We'll have to see."

"Fair enough," he said. "That's your side of it. I want you to hear mine as well."

"That's what I came for."

"Exactly. Jenny could tell you, or Fred Jacobson, or Andy Machen. But they'd tell you in a false voice, trying to put it my way, for me. That's bad. All you want from them is their ideas, not mine. So I'm going to give you mine myself."

I nodded my understanding.

"TITAN's been going for a long time, now," he continued. "You can't even tell where or when it began. I guess it just growed. I got into the action a little late for the sweat and the searching—I came straight out of the armchair where I'd been doing the dreaming. The Project actually started when all the threads were gathered in together, but you know how much further back the thinking goes. I came straight through the corridors of power, courtesy more of reputation than imagination, when it was time to pick up the little pieces and make a big one.

"I don't suppose you know what kind of chaos ensues when fifty men who've been working on fifty aspects of fifty things all get thrown together and told that they're really all working on the same thing and they'd better get it together and build it. People's work gets all upset. The people themselves get all upset. Everybody argues. Nobody likes the Project director. Nobody likes the desert. Nobody likes the army and the Security. Nobody likes the way their shower bath is designed. *Months* of this sort of pettiness just has to be endured. It takes a long time just to get the guys back on their marks. And once there, once set, they have to go like bombs because time's wasted and money's flowing away.

"But eventually there's a spark, and you begin to get chain reactions here and there. Men who hated each other's guts only weeks before become lifelong buddies instead, and they feed each other with the data and the perspective which keeps things going. There's a sudden and terrific burst of enthusiasm, which infects everything, from the shower bath to the brass on the colonel's cap. If you're lucky, by the time that enthusiasm itself becomes routine, you have something that you're working on: a synthesized, convergent, synergistic goal at which everybody's effort is directed. Your sweat, your thinking, your life, becomes directed toward that goal.

"In those days, when I wasn't quite at the top of the pyramid, I saw TITAN as *the end.* Do you know, I never once allowed myself to believe that it would actually work? I took this problem on as a substitute for a life. It was my going out present—my immortal soul. It looked to have twenty or thirty years in it—enough so that by the time it was ready I'd be just about fit to slide quietly into my grave, so that my soul could go out with the first ship. But things went too fast for that. It didn't have twenty or thirty years in it at all. First there was urgency, then panic. Then madness. You were out when the first ones went up, weren't you?"

"I was working with Jenny. It was the big news."

"TITAN ONE flew. It went up, and it did as it was told, and it came back. I was still alive. It hadn't needed my immortal soul.

"It was great. The joke was on Einstein. No fuss, no bother. The drive worked. From a standing takeoff to a hundred times the speed of light. It worked, just as our mathematicians said it ought, just as our physicists said it could. But even they were a little bit surprised. They'd had those Einstein equations hanging over their heads like the Sword of Damocles ever since they'd ventured to make a new model of the way things work. They'd never more than half-believed, you see. Dogma was against them. They'd only dared to give half their hearts to a scientific heresy—even to their own. Even now, seven TITANS later, there are math and physics boys who believe that FTL is impossible and the FMA can't work. There are men who claim that wherever TWO went, it wasn't Proxima, and that THREE couldn't have looped Barnard's Star. They won't believe.

"But I believed, and so did every man on the base, every man on the Project. While Andy and I talked down TITAN ONE like it was our homecoming son, we were already in heaven. Whatever I was saying and doing and thinking all that day and for a week after, there was one image that was never out of my mind. Something was saying over and over, this is it. We're out. That great big cage of darkness which surrounds us is unlocked; we've beaten the universe. I felt like we'd been on trial before the Laws of Physics, and been acquitted. We were free to go. Anywhere.

"From the moment that TITAN came back, nothing else signified. I forgot my soul and my life's work and my going out gracefully. I forgot all the waste and the pollution and the destruction and the miserable people—they lost their meaning. TITAN ONE, in a single, sudden, prayed-for, but still *unexpected* moment, had translated the whole arena of human existence from the surface of one Earth already too costly to repair to the whole of a limitless cosmos.

"One day did that to me, Harker. Just one day. One day from earthbound, creeping nonentity to citizen of the galaxy. I could reach out and touch a million stars. Until that day, my dreams were only pretending. I was thinking about my life, thinking about my work, planning my existence as if it was so much window dressing. Not a genuine dream at all. Then TITAN opened the door of the human cage.

"Maybe you got a bit of it yourself when you read the papers that day. Maybe you only felt extra bitter because you were still in your cage. I don't know whether you looked out of the window into infinity, or just across the corridor into another cell, and I don't want you to tell me. With me, the burst of adrenaline that carried me high carried me high for keeps. It was the *real* moment of my birth.

"Time was quick to dive in on top of the public reaction, of course. A machine—all TITAN ONE was was a robot—isn't a man. They didn't have the same affinity with ONE that I had. How could they? The price of a bus ride was the same, the cistern leaked, and the computer cards still had them cold. They were no machine lovers. Before they thought greater things about the human race they wanted a man home from the stars, loaded down with a good corny script. Well, that was all part of it. I wanted that, too.

"We failed to deliver.

"Years have passed, and no man has come home from the stars. We have the scripts all ready—had them for years—and my God we've been tempted to use them, tempted to lie. Maybe someday we'll have to. But for now, we're still in the ring fighting.

"Can you imagine what it has come to mean for me, for all of us on the Project? Can you imagine what it meant for the man who was sacrificed because a surfeit of confident publicity exploded in his face? We had the stars given into our care, and we lost them. You can't, I know. You far less than anyone. How can I know what it's like in your world of perpetual darkness? We're at opposite ends of the spectrum of human ambitions, Harker. But we need someone from your end to gain us ours. You know, to the paper-reading, TV-devouring public, it was just news when Mason didn't come back. They felt sad for a minute, shrugged it off, watched the commercials, and life went on in the funnies and the programs. We thought there'd be difficulties in fading TITAN out of the public eye, having shouted so loud. But the public didn't notice. There were no crowds clamoring to know what happened to FIVE or SIX. The people live through their TV sets, Harker, and they take what they're given. We have to give them some real news now, Harker. For safety's sake, perhaps for all our sakes, it has to be true news. I think that's vital. If that man decides to win the next election by lying, by telling the people we have the stars when we haven't, then we never will have. The Project will be wound up—killed. The professional liars will take it over. It will become a gigantic advertising campaign. I couldn't take that. Not even that man wants that, if we can really send a man and bring him back. It'll still be a lie—we'll lie about the man. It won't be your face on the cover of *Time* magazine. But there's a world of difference between the one sort of lie and the other, d'you see? One forfeits the stars, the other lets us have them, although at their price.

"You see what I see, now, don't you. However dimly, you do see. . . .

"You know what TITAN NINE means, now. We have to break out of the cage of darkness. I don't care if it kills a hundred men—we have no choice. But we must have one live one to set alongside our hundred, our thousand dead. We must have one win to stay in the game. We need you now, Harker. You're the only man who can give us any reason to hope. It's killed strong men, good men, sane men. We need a half-man, a survivor, a man who lives with madness and doesn't give in to it. It's the only way we can continue to live."

"It's all right, Mike," I told him. "It's going to be all right."

I wasn't humoring him. I swear I wasn't fooling.

I couldn't feel his need, his emotional flames. I just couldn't.

But what could I say?

"I'll be back," I said. "I'll be seeing you."

Cage of Darkness

CHAPTER 5
An Innocent Man

I want to tell you about Nathan Petrie. I don't think he's important to your understanding of the nature of and the events connected with my life as an inmate of Block C, but I want to tell you about him anyway. You may have noticed that the things I'm telling you about the people I knew there don't really add anything to my assessment of the place. I'm telling you about them because I want to. Because, I suppose, I can't separate them from my thinking of the place. The people I knew there were the environment just as much as the locks, the landings, and the antisuicide netting. Like all the rest, Nathan Petrie was a part of my experience of Canaan.

Petrie was a sap.

I want that clear. Not a cretin, not an imbecile, not a dope.

A *sap*. A sucker. One of those of which there is one born every minute. (Sorry, that's out of date—these days it must be ten a minute if not a thousand.)

By which I mean, of course, that it is important to realize that Petrie definitely had intelligence, but was very

remiss about using it. It's one of those things that's
hilarious or tragic, depending upon what a guy looks like
and which side of him you're sitting on. Most guys were
definitely anti-Petrie (his tragedy), but I think I was on his
side (everybody's tragedy). If he'd been fat and silly,
everybody would have laughed at him, and maybe not
liked him, but they'd have let him be and even defended
him if need be. If he'd been medium-sized and handsome,
people would have liked him, ribbed him a lot, and the
girls would have flipped over him, married him, and made
a misery of his failures. But Nathan was thin and small,
everybody hated him, and it was all quite nasty.

Inside himself, Nathan Petrie was a *knot*. A knot tied a
little tighter by everybody who ever knew him. Nobody
was conscious of tormenting Nathan Petrie. Nobody hated
him with a fury sufficient to twist a knife in his wounds.
Nobody cared enough about him to hurt him with
kindness or generosity or friendship or hope or any of the
other weapons that become deadly when they're *measured*.
In Nathan's case, they would have been measured to the
last inch.

A pity, because if ever there was a man who really
needed a mile, it was Nathan.

It was all incidental and accidental where he was
concerned—and I mean *all*. In and out of him. Chance
encounters, idle words, thoughtless actions. That was
Nathan and the universe, together. Ships that pass in the
night so that one of the poor bastards gets swamped by the
other's bow wave, and the other doesn't even know.

Poor Nathan.

You couldn't even begin to understand the kind of life
he led, or the kind of life that led him. If you can see why
Nathan was Nathan, you're probably not so far off being

Nathan yourself. Sometimes I wonder just how common he is. If this is really reaching you, if you're really feeling for Nathan, then I shouldn't bother to go on reading. Go have a bath and cut your wrists.

He never bothered anybody. And try as they might, the strong arm of the law and persuasive methods even stronger couldn't quite get a grip on him for a very long time. Nathan was a simple man. He had his schemes and he had his habits. There wasn't a great deal else to him.

He swore from the moment they picked him up to the moment they locked him in Canaan with the rest of us that he never did it, that he was nowhere near the place at the time and wouldn't have done it even if he had been. (Incidentally, I'll break a rule here and tell you what he was in for—there are special circumstances which make this necessary; you'll understand in a minute.) Sure, he'd followed the girl home several times and been warned about it. Sure, he knew where she'd be at exactly that time. Sure, her boyfriend had beaten him up, and, sure, she'd called the cops on him more than once. But he was in bed asleep at the time. No, there weren't any witnesses. Who else'd live in that place? How did the knife come to be in his trash can? He hadn't the faintest idea—somebody had put it there to frame him. Would he be stupid enough to hide a murder weapon with blood on it in his own trash can?

Yes, decided the jurobot. He sure would.

As a matter of pure fact—and this is no conjecture, because the grapevine even reached Canaan—if anyone's interested, Nathan Petrie didn't do it, because he was at home that night. He *was* framed, and I know who did it. Half the prison knew. But nobody cared.

But the interesting thing is this. Nathan was not a bit

different from anyone else in Block C. A lot of killers are nice people. Nathan was neither a killer nor a nice person. But in Canaan, inside the deep cage, there's just no way to tell. No way at all.

MADMAN'S DANCE

CHAPTER 7
The Acquired Taste
of Desolation

The storm-rain floods like tears from the black eyes in the sky. The brightness of childhood is covered by the undergrowth of the dark forest of age. The branches on the frightened trees are leafless and shattered, their greenery fallen long since to the ashen ground. The burden of life hangs heavy upon their brittle frames. The valleys and the grasslands have passed into their own antiquity, forlorn, without even the company of shadows. The wailing night descends upon their hollow reaches, howling frosty winds and screaming starlight. The deathful face of time, with its features half-molten, half-given into foam, has long ago claimed the streets of existence into the cackling of vultures and the hum of flies.

The wake of man is empty of mourners.

The rivers and the marshes are fathoms deep in ancient, discarded dreams which the reaching willows may no longer pluck from the surfaces of the rippled lakes. What is done is finished and the world is wholly, truly, totally human.

And as dead as cradled bones and grave-lined rust and dust.

The silver cities are let to the cats and rats and bats, and they, too, leave only the footprints of ghosts. The world waits only for the everlasting sunset and the dreaming shadow of eternity to reawaken. . . .

. . . The smoke-veiled ground which slopes away from me, while below me half a hundred men slip and struggle in ankle-deep mud trying to shift some huge piece of machinery against the slope. Its giant wheels spin uselessly, failing to gain any purchase at all in the fluid earth. Other machines—no two are alike—light the semidarkness with streaks of blue flame, and where the streaks become arcs the ground flares and leaves a lingering glow.

The machines are impressive, but I know full well that it is only the men who are important. They work unceasingly in their thousands and tens of thousands to move and operate their masters in the most appalling of conditions. Where the machines cannot go alone, the men are ready and eager to push and carry them. They feed the juggernauts with fuel which the machines spit out in anger at some hidden enemy below them, in the bowl-valley, and above them in the mountains. The oily pall of smoke hides the array of the opposing forces from my stinging eyes.

Half a mile away, a large vehicle with thick treads and a double cupola lurches to the top of a ridge. Two rods of polished metal protruding from the twin hoods oscillate madly, but whatever effect the activity might have is hidden from me. Men suddenly erupt from its sides, sprinting madly downhill and throwing themselves flat as the tank explodes in wreaths of rose-tinted flame. I cannot tell how many men might have been left inside the leviathan, or too close to its destruction. There seem to be thousands struggling to their feet, but that cannot be. Perhaps ten or twelve.

A target is pinpointed, there is a curtain of explosions along a ragged line drawn horizontally across the far slopes, until a blossom of angry red flowers in the gloom, and there is a brief pause, taken up almost immediately by sourceless sheets of lightning, flare, and scarlet splash, and men boil out of the ground with fire and fury, dangling their burnt and broken limbs in the current of the shock waves.

Strategy is quite incalculable. Position. Fire. Run. Keep moving all the time, and finally disappear in a whimpering flood of fire. Nothing gained, everything lost; one side or other winning, but I cannot tell which.

A man races past me, shouting unintelligibly, and a small, mobile machine bounces gaily toward me. I run downhill a short distance, curiously unafraid, and drop into a trench. Seconds later, a huge bulk hurtles into the trench a little way to my right. I hear heavy breathing, a storm of racking coughs, and then it is gone again.

I am involved, but I can hardly imagine myself one of this limitless pygmy horde which labors so fruitlessly to serve its terrifying machines. I am alone and aloof. I climb out of the trench. Hot air surrounds me and clutches at my clothing, but I stand firm.

A silver thread flies from a pinnacle far to the right and unravels in a great arc all the way across the bowl. Puffs of angry red enclose it in smoke, and a stab of white gulps in the head of the streamer, but something lands at the far end of the rainbow, and there is a fragmentary rush of colored flame. The glow of an accompanying retinue of explosions illuminates a great shadowy hulk. Before the afterimage fades, it bubbles into fire, vomiting great gobs of rosy molten hail.

The black pinnacle from which the missile came becomes the focus of a thousand flickering fireworks, and the solid rock is whittled swiftly into dust and cloud.

A rain of silver rockets shoots into the far mountainsides. There is a tremble in the earth as the mountains reverberate to the impact. Several slopes slide downward with a dull roaring which drowns completely the fragile protests of a hundred thousand men whose bodies are mangled in the cascades.

Then the slopes around me erupt in their turn, sheets of flame and a vast tumult of sound which bursts and continues to expand, intolerable heat, and running men mingle all around me into a fluid mass of images whose fabric is torn by time and shattered into bloody chaos.

The survivors—seeming to be thousands, but only ten or twelve—are running uphill, their machines abandoned in their wake, still trumpeting their fury and disgust, still maintaining their own ceaseless blast.

Burning men swarm down to the plain, scattering.

Black ash fills the air, choking me and sending me writhing to my knees, gagging, and fighting desperately for air.

The bombardment ceases with a final squadron of cylindrical missiles riding white cones of flame, sweeping in shallow arcs to the roots of the mountains.

And then the charge and the pursuit: here come the machines, out of the smoke, leaping and racing on thick-tired wheels, dancing on their caterpillar feet, sounding their war cries with Klaxons and whistles and grinding gears. Shambling over the scarred, cratered surfaces come horde upon horde of the conquerors, with hard, jointed bodies like giant metal locusts, with cyclopean eyes and tentacles of rubber and steel.

I stand alone against their cavorting advance, and they pass me by.

I'm a hero.

I discover an old man on the beach which borders a pale-colored, glass-faced sea. He is pouring water from a bowl, and the slack, languorous ripples which spread from the stream are the only blemishes upon the surface of the ocean.

They are soon lost.

"Who are you?" I ask him, feeling sure that I can penetrate his facelessness if he will only give me a *clue*.

"My name is the name of the ocean," the old man replies.

"How old are you?" I ask.

"As old as the ocean," replies the ancient, his eyes rolling like gigantic waves to heave their surf-led humors from their contemplation of the sea to the time-thin sight of my shallow face.

"Will that bowl never run dry?" I ask, marveling at the steady fall of crystalline liquid from the earthenware vessel.

"I hope so," whispers the old man, with a quiet tiredness. "I hope so."

I think I am getting used to infinity.

It has three main characteristics:

Transience.

Diversity.

Alternativity.

I think I can afford to acquire a taste for desolation—or

indulge a taste that I have already acquired. There is no trap to be feared there. It is where I fear traps that the danger lies. Whatever I try to keep bottled up inside me—that is what threatens to explode me.

Titan Nine

CHAPTER 6
I'm Writing a Letter to Daddy, His Address Is Heaven Above

I was writing letters to Canaan, and they were all wrong. I didn't dare say a word. I could say I didn't like it and I felt strange, but I couldn't say a thing about TITAN, about Jenny, about Hurst. I couldn't explain to them why I felt as I did, and that devalued the whole idea of telling them *what* I felt. But I knew I had to write and keep writing, keep distributing the letters to all the people I knew that were stuck in Block C. It was the only thing I could do for them—the thing they expected of me, the thing they needed from me if I was going to live on in their minds. And they needed me, no doubt about that. Every little thing that lived on in their minds instead of dying there was precious to them, necessary to them. I wrote to Sam and to Cain and to Manny and to Luis. Short letters all, but none identical, all individual, all meaning whatever I could put into them.

Ten days into TITAN base, and I still hadn't had a reply. I thought that was odd. I know what an unconscionable time mail takes. I knew how many sticky fingers it had to pass through before it reached me. But still, I was worried. I knew they'd have written at the first opportunity they could. Judas, anyway, and Luis—the people to whom I meant most. They'd have been careful, too. Not a word out of place until contact was established. They could take risks, play games with the censor, once they were sure they were tuned in. The first letters would be absolutely by the book. They'd reach me as fast as was humanly possible, if you consider all the hands they'd go through worthy of the name human.

I had a neat stack of letters in front of me, all addressed, all stamped, and I was preparing to write one more. But the temptation overtook me, the anxiety made me pick up the phone and ring Henneker.

Just like my letters, my phone calls had to pass through any number of hands before they got where they were going. It was slow work, getting hold of men at the top. But I had the pull to get through, eventually.

"What is it?" asked the colonel.

"It's about my letters," I said.

"Come on," he replied, "you know that's not my department. I'm not the censor or the mailman."

"You're the boss," I said.

"Are you making a complaint?"

"I'm asking a favor."

"I can't let any damn thing out of this camp that hasn't gone through channels, and you know it."

"I don't want anything out," I said patiently. "It's

about letters coming in. I want to know where they're stuck in the pipeline. That's all. Just ask around for me. The prison, the boys at your end. I don't want to interfere with the precious channels. I just want to know what the holdup is all about. Just find out for me, will you?"

"It's not my job," he said. "Ask Hurst."

"Don't be a fool," I said. "You know as well as I do that anyone without rank doesn't get answers. I'm not asking for much. Just a few lousy minutes. Just *ask*, that's all."

"Okay," he said. "I'll ask. But don't get the idea you can ring me any hour of the day and ask me to call around for you. You have Hurst. He has channels."

"Great," I said. "I'll remember. But this is important. I need the answers, okay?"

"Okay," he said, and hung up.

A quarter of an hour later, I had the inestimable pleasure of meeting Major Chalk for the first time.

Chalk was a big, thickset man with wide knobby features and baby blue eyes. He looked like King Kong might have if he'd shaved. Yes sir, right down to the flat nose and the *big* mouth.

"I thought I'd better stop by," he said. Cheerfully. "Clear things up a bit."

"What things?" I asked.

"Letters," he said.

"*Those* things," I said. I opened wide the door. I invited him in. I was pleased to see him. Little did I know.

He didn't attempt to sit down. He reached into his inside pocket and he handed me a letter. I thought it was for me, from Block C. But when I opened it, without having paused to glance at its face, I found myself reading Dear Judas, I am addressing this letter to you because . . .

"You can't send it," he said.

"What do you mean, I can't send it?" I demanded, no trace of belligerence yet creeping into my voice. But even before he began to answer, I knew damn well what he meant, and I wasn't altogether surprised. Just sick.

"I mean that I can't allow it to go out of the camp." He held it up like it was a dead rattler as I surrendered it to him without thinking. I reached out to grab it back. I took it in my hand, but he didn't let go. We stood there, holding it between us like a tug rope.

"You want it rewritten," I said.

"I don't want it written at all," he corrected me. "You can write letters to anyone outside of the prison—anyone on your official list of permitted correspondents, that is. But we can't extend that list. You're still under sentence, you realize. You aren't free." He had an unpleasant gleam in his eye. He was planning to hit me with a real sickener. He'd come himself instead of sending a messenger, instead of just telling Henneker so Henneker could pass it back over the phone. I could imagine his face when Henneker phoned him. Yes, sir, I'll take care of it, sir. Yes, sir, I'll see him myself, sir. Yes, sir, I'll explain the position to him, sir. Did Henneker even know what the situation was? Did he have any power to alter it? I looked at Chalk and I knew he didn't. Chalk was radiating now-I-got-ya-ya-son-of-a-bitch. Chalk had the responsibility, and Chalk was using it.

"What about the incoming letters?" I asked flatly.

"There are no incoming letters. The army and the prison authorities both agreed that it would be best for security if we adhered to the letter of prison regulations and didn't allow you or any of the men in Block C to extend their lists of permitted correspondents. There's a provision . . ."

"I know the regulations." I interrupted him.

"Well then, you can see that our hands are tied."

"Like hell," I said. "I'm still under sentence, remember. Even under sentence I'm allowed to communicate with my fellow prisoners. You can't deny me that. You can't deny *them* that."

"I'm afraid we have to. Where matters of security are concerned . . ."

"*Security!*" I spat the word out. "Are you going to tell me that the men in Block C are a security risk? Men serving life in a lighted tomb? The men imprisoned under conditions of *perfect* security? What the hell has security got to do with it? There isn't a single secret in that letter, and you know it. Every goddam line is pure and harmless. You *know* that."

"I'm sorry," he said, being anything but. "We simply cannot let letters pass between the prison and yourself. There are regulations. There are matters of the utmost secrecy concerned. Your presence here is a secret. If one of your letters were to be intercepted, the signature would be enough."

"Hell, I'll sign them 'A friend' if you want me to. But you must let me write something. You must let them write back."

"No."

"You bastard."

"Orders," he said.

I picked up the pile from the table. "Just so much rubbish," I said.

"I'm afraid so," he replied, politely.

I wanted to ram them down his throat. He wanted me to. He was twice my size, and I could see his fingers itching. Hurst was hovering not three feet away, beyond the door which still stood ajar. He was listening, ready to interrupt if anything troublesome should happen.

I smiled. A real madman's grin.

"You don't like me, do you?" I asked Major Chalk, sweetly.

"I have no personal feelings," he assured me. "I just do my job."

"And your job is to protect me. To cover me up completely. To make sure that the world and I do not meet, even for an instant."

"You can write to your official correspondents," he said. "Provided you say nothing about . . ."

"That's not what I mean, and you know it," I said, allowing a singsong note into my voice to protect the words from the biting malice they might otherwise have contained. That malice—that *contained* malice—would have pleased Major Chalk no end.

He shrugged.

"Can I have my letter back?" I asked him.

"I brought it to show you," he said. "I'll have to take it away again. Regulations."

"Did he make up the regulation, Hurst?" I asked.

The door opened a fraction wider. "I don't know," said Hurst, still hovering without.

"Come in, you stupid bastard," I said, "and shut the door."

But Chalk stepped backward, and took it in his left hand. His right was still clinging to the letter. "I have to go now," said Chalk.

"Will I ever see you again?" I asked him, politely, not letting go.

"It's likely," he said. "I've been scanning through your files, and I find you're a card player. I play a little myself. I'd like to find out if you're as good as you think you are."

My mouth fell open. I'm not used to being startled. At first I thought he was a fool. Then I thought he was only a malicious bastard who wanted to see me beaten and beaten again.

"Oh, I'd be glad to," I said, putting real relish into my voice. "I'll be glad to. Anytime. Bring your friends."

He smiled and pulled harder at the letter. I jerked it back. It tore in two, but not into halves. He was left with the bulk of it—I only had a tiny corner. He looked at it like an eagle might look at a rat. "You can keep that bit," he said. "It doesn't appear to have anything written on it."

And he left.

Hurst came in and shut the door. He was my size, but younger. Fresh faced, like an army Whiz Kid. Keen, happy, and cookie-loving.

"Hurst," I said, "that man hates me. From really deep down. He really hates me. Now how can that be, d'you think?"

"I think we have things to do," he said.

"Do you play poker?" I asked him.

"Never," he said.

"You're a real diplomat," I told him. "A genuine American diplomat. How did we ever lose our Asian empire without you?"

We went and did the things we had to do.

MADMAN'S DANCE

CHAPTER 8
Embracing Oblivion

I walk down the slope of a vast, bubble-shaped depression.
The bowl of the valley is a somber gray, unlightened by
the leaden sky. The scene might seem drab to other eyes,
but to me it seems hostile and aggressive. The far side of
the crater appears not a simple shade of gray but an ugly
and soul-breaking chaos of dying color.

In the midst of depression, I feel fear. Part of it belongs
to me, part of it is intrinsic in the scene, but all of it is real.

The blasted landscape of the skull of TITAN ship is no less
real and no more than the blasted landscapes which my
mind perceived in the wreckage of that other world. This
is hell, nor am I out of it. Freedom is a lie. One world does
not exist within the lawless confines of another, but there
are worlds without as well as worlds within. As I walk
beneath the cold walls and the cloud-tipped peaks I am
dreaming, but the fear in my guts is just the same.

In the center of the giant wheel is an off-white patch of
what looks like dirty snow or melted candle wax. It is,
perhaps, a small blister burned on the filthy surface of the

depression, emphasizing by contrast the blackness of the soil around it.

Chopped-off peaks ring the crater, and reaching up to them all the way from the creamy hump radiate streaks of red-colored ore. The brighter-colored elements split the gray sea like red lightning. The boulders on the outskirts of the basin seem arranged almost as if in a pattern. It is as though they have been placed with infinite care and precision, but the wind and rain have displaced a few. Between the center and the first stones there is a saucer of sad gray mud, smooth and concave.

Scabs of lichenous material trail thin fingers between the red scars. I avoid them, treading instead on the softly oozing black soil.

The pit is like a sleeping beast, gray with age and diseased by decades. It is choking in the cloying phlegm of clay. Its slack, furrowed skin sags from its cheeks, and the sick white of its cyclopean eye is turned sightlessly to the gray firmament.

I can hear the wingbeat of your angels of death.

In the darkness of a starless night as I pass between the stones I hear voices, but I search in vain for their source. The sounds come from the earth, or from the monoliths, or from the dead and stagnant air.

"I am sorry," calls the first voice, sweet and deep.

"I am sorry," is the reply, flat and dead.

"Please answer me," says the first voice, after a hopeless pause. "Please answer me."

"I love you," cries the first of the voices, fearful, the words as though torn from an unwilling throat.

"I love you." The reply.

"Where are you?"

"Where are you?" The reply.

I go on my way, making no sound as my feet tread softly in the muck, and the voices die behind me in the feeble wind, and I forget them.

I feel that I am poisoning myself with the prophetic venom of the pythoness. My heart is smoldering with the acid in my veins. I am contorted into strange shapes, consumed by thirst and pricked by corkscrew thorns. I am suffering, alone but not apart from hell, whose fires do not trouble only the unjust and the impure.

I am undemanding, and unrewarded.

I am poor in spirit, and no kingdom recognizes me for its own.

I mourn, and I am not comforted.

I am meek, and I inherit sorrow and despair.

I am merciful, and no one will grant me mercy.

I am pure in heart, and I am blind.

I have endured forever, and I have shrugged off the torments which I was consigned to endure. My fear and my suffering are dissipated in the sweat which has fallen from my brow to mark my way among the stars.

The meadows of my wandering are fading in darkness, flowering with samphire and nightshade, and the only birds which nest in the stark trees are the carrion-crows.

Let it come, I pray you, the end of our escape from oblivion, and the beginning of our escape into hell.

I am ready. Call me neither coward nor hero.

I have endured, like the green grass which grows still in the crevices of the Empire of Rome.

I have neither won nor lost.

I have neither succeeded, nor have I failed.

I have traveled, and must return.

My body is ready to rejoin my soul. (Who knows the

spirit of man that goes upward and the spirit of the beast that goes downward to the earth?)

I must leave this eternity where death and time and ego have no meaning, and return to the closeted, claustro-phobic cage of darkness from which I thought to emerge. Vanity of vanities, I have discovered, vanity of vanities, all is vanity.

All is vanity and vexation of spirit.

My body must rejoin my soul.

I am leaving such friends that I might have had *long* ago in the timeless tomorrow. I feel free for one of the very few times. I am being boosted high out of the depths.

I have no weight. Free mass acceleration!

Fast, I move.

The mountain crumbles to a floor of glowing ashes. The trumpets of the sun toll like bells of flame.

Midnight!

I pity the poor, searching sea, which cannot beat its waves on shores as lonely as the sky, because there are no earthly shores unknown and unawakened.

On the day of the second wedding of the old gods, the sun glows crimson in the breast-fed sky, leaking milky clouds to the lips of the surging sea. The trumpets toll and toll and toll.

And midnight might last forever.

The clarions call forth a fourth day, and a seventh, and a tenth, their blasts of scarred sound echoing tremulously amid the pubic jungles of the hotlands.

The mountain rises again in the groping shadows of a fugitive twilight, but—love not lacking, nor even past forgotten—he sinks once more into his silent oblivion, gone with Memphis and the colored towers of Troy.

His transience is less than nothing, in this frozen dawn

of time which, being midnight, is not even one day or the next. The wishing stars of luckless days may triumph now, with their triumphs unseen by the clock hands of the factories of time. The dust of hallowed memory may stir and raise a thousand million ghosts into the stillness and the nilness.

The heralds once and for this once alone are resting on their blazoned shields, and for now and this now only my ancestors may wander through my children's tombs.

And their deaths are merely other transitory awakenings.

I have to travel a terrible road, in the darkest corners of Pandora's box, where only the last and most hateful of all the evils is left to be my companion.

All horror and pain have flown forth into the world when the sky gapes wide to contain the stars, and the doors of our cage of darkness have yawned.

And yet still we are cut by a thousand hurts, and our bodies bleed, his no worse than mine despite his foul aspect. Poison and storm and icy cold conspire to block our progress from the crannies of the box to the star-filled sky.

"I am Hope!" we cry, *together*, sweetening our plea with disastrous deception.

I try to cry out and ask the sky to take me instead of my dark companion, but I have forgotten who I am, and why.

Cage of Darkness

CHAPTER 6

"The Secondhand Life of Harker Lee," Chapter Six: How to Be a Successful Schizophrenic

I fought it.

I think I won. By a knockout in the third round.

It creeps up on you. You don't even notice it, but it's there, and one day you just turn around and take a look at yourself and it's staring you in the face. You're not sure even then how exactly you discover it or what exactly it is. It's just there, and one day you know about it.

I worried.

It's not that you get up one morning and think to yourself, Hello, I seem to be more than usually separate from the world, and my relationships seem more than usually strained, ergo I must be suffering from some kind of communicative breakdown. It would be simple if you were able to start from there, because it would give you an easier approach to the situation.

What you notice first, I guess, is the fear. There's always a fair quantity of fear hanging around, of course—loitering with intent, I believe, is the appropriate phrase—and this isn't any different kind of a fear, nor is it particularly intense. It's just unreasonable. You're scared, and there isn't any damn thing for you to be scared of. You wonder what it is you're scared of. You take a very close look at the sort of things you just might be scared of. You begin to start searching for things that you can be scared of, so that you can justify yourself to yourself.

Etc.

By which I mean, it continues. It's a process. A syndrome. Self-feeding. Once you're in it, you're there.

Etc.

You start off by chasing your own tail. It makes you edgy. You look at other people with a slightly suspicious eye. You're not so much worried about them as about your attitude toward them. Your relationships begin to get screwed up. You can't figure things the way they are. Other people get distorted. You begin to consider what they do and say in a new light. You don't know what the hell is wrong. You're bewildered. You cut one or two people to bits for no reason at all; harmless conversation tends to breed verbal violence. You hurt people with what you say.

That's when things start to go around the bend and you become really aware of a situation happening that you're in but don't know anything about. You bring yourself up short and you say, "Well, hell, what's going wrong? What am I doing and why? How does this aggravation arise?"

And then you start to be careful. You don't dare speak harshly to people. You don't dare get angry. (You're lucky if they're still talking to you, and you make sure they don't have any more cause to stop.) And once now and again, just occasionally, you'll say something you didn't mean to, which is inevitable no matter how careful you are, only things being what they are you'll begin to wonder about the self-control and whether it's slipping.

Etc.

That continues, too.

You get broody. You worry about yourself. You find that if you drink you don't get happy, you just get deeper and deeper into black darkness. Getting drunk no longer takes you into drunkenness. It takes you somewhere nobody wants to go. You give up drinking. If you're wise.

Nothing is right. The hand of the world is set against you.

You look about you for two things:

(1) You need somebody to blame.

(2) You need to be *doing* something about it.

If you've got any damn sense at all, the person you blame is yourself. If you start to blame the Commies or the fallout or the lady next door or the devil you entitle yourself to a free ticket to the funny farm. You lost. Round one and you're floored. Assuming you have the sense to be your own fall guy, you're then in a constructive frame of mind to undertake (2). You have to find that little extra from somewhere which helps you not to go too far overboard on the guilt kick. You can't avoid the self-pity. You can't avoid the depression. They're both part and parcel of the whole thing. But there's a step and a half in between a party and an orgy, and it's a step and a half you've got to do your level best not to take. If you can stand still and weather the black fits and the crying jags and not crumple up inside them, you're halfway home to the land of the living. Not to a cure, and I want to emphasize that. Not to getting rid of it, but to getting yourself to where you can live with it. That's what you're aiming at—peaceful coexistence, not war. If you opt for war, you lose. Even if you win. It's like playing poker without an opponent.

So you have your chances made (we'll assume).

You have still to take them.

(Of course it's all difficult. None of it is easy. Not any of it.)

Sitting tight is great. If in doubt, hesitate. Sit as tight as you can. Once you're in, it's easier to sink than to climb. Staying where you are is positive. It's working your way. Your first priority is staying put. After that you start looking for the effort and some way to use it to pull you up.

This is when the obsessions begin to nag at you. For every honest aspirin there are a dozen sugar pills, and they taste nicer. You have no difficulty whatsoever in finding solutions, becoming excited by solutions, falling in love with solutions. You lie in bed at night. (You *can't* sleep—not for hours and hours of trying. This is part of the positive feedback of the situation—a man without sleep is not a reasonable man.) You come up with something that looks good—superficially. A simple act. A resolution. If only you can do this it will all be all right. In the beginning, the acts are simple enough—doing them will be no problem. What is a problem is the way they go through your mind, and through again, and through and through and through . . .

Etc.

The worst and so on of them all. Over and over and over . . .

And you can't get that single blasted idea out of the very forefront of your mind. It's like a record with a jammed needle. A looped tape, Möbius looped, that plays forever. A dripping tap that you can't turn off no matter how hard you twist it. (What can drive you crazy, craziness can drive.) You can *know* that the damned idea isn't all that good. You can be 100 percent sure that it isn't going to cure you. You can know full well that you aren't being logical—or sane.

But it doesn't stop.

That thought just keeps hammering away. You repeat it to yourself, and you *just can't stop.* It keeps you awake. You can be dog tired, exhausted, and it just keeps on. You can go delirious, drugged into mental submission by the insistence of that idea, that *one* idea, and it just keeps on.

You are possessed by that idea.

Eventually, you have to go to sleep, by physiological necessity. Psychologically, there's not an instant's rest. If you dream, you dream that circuit thought. Nothing else. Your brain is stuck. There's a terrible and constant temptation to get rid of that thought one way or another. If you can't divorce it from you, you can try to divorce you from it. Pretend it's someone else. Make it into someone else. Don't. That's losing. That's shitting out. Keep that thought. Hang on to it, no matter how much you hate it.

And you wake up, thinking no time at all has passed, and it's STILL THERE.

That's a real killer.

That's when you really know you're mad.

Yet another time when you have to keep your cool. When you have to stay put.

You get up and you do things. Ordinary things. The big temptation, of course, is to do the thing you're thinking of. And you will. Not once, but a dozen times. You'll chase those ideas. They'll run you to a standstill. It's no good saying that you won't yield an inch. You will. You'll yield a mile. But every thought you kill is replaced, and you learn that. You learn to be frightened of that, and this is where you must not give way. You must not begin to sell yourself for those few minutes of blessed peace in between obsessions. You must not ever treasure those moments of peace so highly that you become an automaton—obsession, appease, obsession, appease, order, action, stimulus, reaction. That's losing. That's dying inside.

You do ordinary things. You fight against the obsession to make it give you a few moments' peace *against* its will. You work. You go shopping. You ride on buses and you walk along streets. You read a book, if it will let you, or do jigsaw puzzles, or make plastic airplanes, or paint pictures. You talk to somebody, if you can.

That last is best. It's also not so damned easy. You only think it's easy when you can take it for granted. Time comes when you need it and you can be biting your nails to the knuckles wishing somebody would talk to you, wishing there was someone you could go to and talk. For the first time in your life, you discover that people don't know how to talk. For the first time in your life you discover that *you* don't know how to talk. Because you can't just sit down and do it. You have to observe the rituals and the formulas. You can't just knock on someone's door and say "Hello, I'm mad." You have to do it by the book. You have to do it by this week's rota of permissible ways to feel and permissible ways to tell someone how you feel and permissible ways to let them answer you and permissible ways to let them pretend to understand. And for the first time in your life you find out that there's absolutely nothing at all in talk except for those rituals and permissible expressions and codes, and suddenly the language you've been using all your life becomes a useless, dead thing as far as communicating goes, and it all holds no meanings, and you can't say what it is you have to say, and if you try they can't understand you, and they just keep coming back with these silly rituals and these clichés and the multitudinous devices of speech that protect them from communicating, from thinking, from feeling, from even being in anyone's version of the world but their own except as a cardboard cutout *thing*.

And this is bad.

You have to hold still. You scream, you lose. They commit you.

Eventually, if you do enough things well enough, and if you're lucky, the obsession dies without your having to give in. It's a prideful feeling to outlast your first obsession—but watch that cockiness—here comes the next. It *is* possible to win (contrary to popular belief) by outlasting your obsessions. But to win one isn't enough, or two or three. You have to keep on winning and, as *everybody* knows, you can't win them all. Some you lose. So you not only have to win and keep winning, you have to stand the losses in between as well.

It's never easy.

And another thing you have to be careful about in yielding to these obsessions is the old saw about better the devil you know than the devil you don't. The very fact of not knowing how nasty, how silly, how futile, how utterly *mad* the next short-circuit thought is going to be is an added pressure on your mind. There's no crummy joke that fortune can play on you funnier than the obsession to do the thing you just can't do. That's a real bastard—the one you *have* to outlast because you've no damn choice. That's a real triple bind. You don't do it, you suffer it all times, all ways. You do it, or try, and they commit you, imprison you, kill you, or it kills you. Funny, hey? Or, of course, you kill yourself. But don't. You lose.

So what *do* you do?

How *do* you begin to come back again?

Yes, I mean back again, because now, believe it or not, you are well and truly and wholly *there*.

Well, again believe it or not, the first time you're there almost anything can bring you back.

The first time.

Just realizing how badly off you are, realizing it, admitting it, and analyzing it (the last two are difficult and near-miraculous, in that order) can be enough. Ought to be enough. Just knowing things are wrong and having an idea about the pattern of wrongness and the logic of wrongness can make it easy to come back. Score one for psychiatry, self-administered or paid for. But score one and only one. The one thing you mustn't do is think you've won. You have to keep winning. Not once, twice, or three times, but forever.

You have got to take the warning.

You have got to let your first time arm you—to some extent—against your second time.

A matter of days might pass. *Good* days. Happy days, even, filled with blessed relief. Don't ever waste those days! Once you're in the grip of the syndrome the quality of operations within the human sphere of existence goes down about 80 percent. Your work suffers. Your play suffers. You suffer. So when you've got those days when you can do something, DO. Set yourself up a hole to run to when the next crisis comes. You tell somebody. You ask for help. You make damn sure that the next time the obsessions get you in their claws there's somebody who can make ready with the tea and sympathy. Especially the sympathy. Paid shrinks are one answer to the need; it's better if you can find an answer without resorting to that.

While you can, you set yourself up a position in the human race that you can manage to hold. Only a fool thinks he's clear after one fall. Only a fool doesn't provide against the chance that he may fall again. If you're a fool, you lose. In the days between attack one and attack two it is *not* enough to sit still, hold tight, stand fast. You get few enough opportunities to move forward, you have *got* to take them.

When it comes back at you, you feel it coming. You know what to expect. You can move one jump ahead of it.

Which doesn't make it any easier.

In fact, it's usually worse.

And knowing it, and not being able to stop it in its tracks, that makes it worse still. You know that, too.

Etc.

And this time there really *is* a basis for the fear, and it really is something to scare the shit out of you. This is *madness* reaching out for you, and if you've come this far you *know* it. And no matter how you fight it is not diminished. It is still there, *much* larger than life.

You know the pattern by now. The long hours fretting. The *inability* to communicate on anything like a meaningful basis. But if you're wise you have one defense now, something that can't be taken away from you. It's not much—it's not communication, certainly not understanding. It's only tea and sympathy. But, by God, it's worth something. You have someone to be with, someone who will listen, or just endure your silences.

Just someone.

Without that, you're almost certainly lost. In one hell of a mess, anyhow.

It doesn't even have to be someone *important*. It helps to be able to like him, and for him to like you. But even that isn't necessary. Just a *person*. A human being. You might never ever need them again, after once or twice. He doesn't have to be a big part of your life. He just has to be there when you need someone to be there. He doesn't even have to know.

This time, the second time, the obsessions can't quite take such a hold. You've had practice. You're in training. You can take it. It hurts, every time they come, and you know by now it's *never* easy, but *they* won't get you, not the second time around, provided you've prepared for them.

But you can still wake up in the morning with the big shakes and not lose them for an hour or more. Physical things, now—especially the big shakes. Sometimes the bad vision, sometimes the nausea. Mostly the big shakes. You can take a couple of drinks and have your eyes turn fiery and be all set to break up the bar. And worst of all, you can look ahead now and you can think to yourself: this time I can take it and I can surface eventually. *What about the next time?*

And that's a killer. The hindsight protects. The foresight disarms. They can cancel, if you let them. If they do, you lose.

You *do* come up again. You last it out, wear it down, just like last time. But now you *know* it will be back. You know you're not clear. You know you have a war on, and you know you can't suffer the depletion of your forces forever. Comes the time, the big shakes will shake you to death or despair. Either way, you lose.

So you have to make use of the clear days again. You have to take yourself in hand and say: this is it. The test case. This time we go all out. This time we don't stand still. This time we hit it with everything we've got. This time we *attack*. And even then, you've got to remember that if you lose you have to come back again and do it again. That's a difficulty. You need everything you've got in order to attack; you mustn't even think about the possibility of losing, but, just in case, you've got to be able to take the failure, regroup, and come again. Not easy. That's a thin line to walk. If you fail, and commit everything to one assault, and it doesn't come off, you lose.

The third time, it's the same every step, and still you can't stop it, still you can't *reduce* it.

You can feel the strength of those quicksands, and it really terrifies you. You've never ever been afraid like this before. You can feel the implacability, the massiveness, the insidiousness, you can feel the whole thing in all its glory. (Blame the Commies, blame the lady next door, bow down to self-pity and despair, blow your hopeless brains out, mix the barbiturates, stick your head in the oven, break it, burn it, hit it, smash and slash and . . .)

(Etc.)

This is when you stand on the parapet of the bridge, weigh death in one of your hands, look down into the boiling water . . .

. . . And mock the crippled fingers of the darkness.

You get down, and you walk away, and you go home. (Or you lose.)

This is when you curl up in your favorite chair and play embryo. This is when you mime your favorite ritual in catatonic ecstasy. This is when you wake up in the cold pack and you fill yourself full of psychotropics, and this is when they haunt you with the dreaded, hideous *label*.

You show them the door and you kick them down the steps. You get up from your chair and you say no. No bending. No breaking. The precipice is only underneath your toes. Your heels are on solid rock. You need not fall, even though you *do* look down.

Maybe it helps to begin spreading the blame a little here. But you've got to spread it in the right places. Blame overwork. Blame stress. Blame traumatic experiences in your early childhood, if you're into that sort of thing. Only blame things which are intangible. Above all, blame only things which are yours to blame.

What helps most is people. What pulls you out, in the end, is people. They don't have to be doctors or samaritans or relatives. They can be bus conductors and shop clerks and secretaries and prostitutes. But not in their professional capacities. Only as people. Functioning as people. One can be enough. Two is better. A crowd can be great.

Some breaks have got to go your way. Most go against you, but any man who claims they all do is a liar and a loser. You always get some breaks. They may not be big ones, but you have to use them. You have to make breaks of your own, too. There's no such thing as luck. Chance is manipulable. By you.

You play the cards as they're dealt. But in every game of five-card stud there's a card that you play face down, and you have to play that card as a blind card, knowing what it is as well. It's not easy. It's poker. But it can be done. A good poker player wins. Not every time, but he absorbs his losses. Consistently, forever, a good poker player wins.

Never, ever blame the cards you're dealt.

If you do, you lose.

By now, you should have won. How does it feel to be a hero? Unsung, of course.

There's one thing, though, that you can't help inheriting from the whole thing, and that's a deep and constant fear. Not a shrinking, cowardly fear, but a less-than-pleasant certainty that you could always slip back, that it could always get you again, that you haven't won for good and all, you have to KEEP winning. Now and forever.

It gets harder every time.

You have to find yourself a good working order and have service checks regularly and treat yourself with a certain amount of caution and good manners. You have to remember that something, somewhere, wants you broken apart, and that wherever you are it's only just behind you. You have to expose it and know it and establish a basis for negotiation with it. You have to do it while you're sane, because while it's wrestling you down in that pit you have no opportunity.

It's sane people that need shrinks.

There is *no* cure, only coexistence.

Courage and common sense can only keep you going *in spite of it all.*

Really, it's no kind of winning at all. But it's the only kind of winning in the game.

MADMAN'S DANCE

CHAPTER 9
Crying in the Wilderness

I remember, my faceless friend, that all these torments were made by your steel-sheathed hands, even the heart of this infernal summer when the thinnest of winds burns me like vitriol, and stones by the wayside glow like salamanders in the fearful violence of the multitude of suns.

I remember, and I *will* remember.

Always.

Remember the brittle-black corpse on a bed of sand pebbles, with its limbs like fire-fraught twigs—ashen, ghostly forms which yield to the slightest question.

Remember the poisonous vapors which halo its stark form, and the unbearable heaviness of the air which walks around it.

Remember the thin dust, which the vibration of our toilsome passage made of that dead thing, rendering it instantaneously into the earth from which its ancestors dragged their original seed. And even the black dust burns, so finely divided it becomes, and the rest of the carcass is transformed into the lesser substance of the air.

Remember the sound of the hovering flies and the

marching beetles crying anguish for the wholeness of a death which robs even the carrion of their accustomed part. Even the all-conquering worm cannot play its heroic last scene in the harrowing script which you have designed to fit every act of the play that you have named "Man." Death is cruel and unrelenting in all your days and nights, and even the carrion grow hungry and cannot sleep.

Remember the grasses that conquered the empires of Rome and Babylon, sighing this day and growing dark-skinned themselves, their stems crouching low upon the ground like fugitive snakes. The wind does not sigh in the crowns of the trees, because the trees have abdicated their given kingdom, and shed their raiment out of season.

Remember the lizards in the rocks and the cockroaches and the painted frogs which are frozen by fire, their marbled eyes glaring anger and reproach from their petrified skins.

Remember. I do and I will. I survive.

You can make me forget everything except the way home. There is another shore, you know, upon the other side . . . another world.

You can't kill me. I'm you.

This totally consumed offal, without any legacy of life to give away, even to the worms, is the end that you promise to the chosen of Canaan. Not loss of life, but loss of being. Not extinction, but erasure. This end is the privilege of all that you have given to keep me company in Canaan—the faceless and the forlorn, the hopelessly insane, the images of antiman, the idols and the demons which look into my face when I am only a mask. The eyes without a face, behind the mask that is myself, remember and record these reflections of my garish, painted face, my false and hypocritical soul. I know this for what it *is*—not hell, but an attempted exorcism that would deny me even that. But no matter what qualities of mercy you renounce, however utterly, no matter how vengeful your spirit, you cannot cast away this mask that is myself. You cannot burn it, any more than you can crack it or dissolve it in acid.

Remember, my faceless friend, that if the mask is all that I am, it is all that *you* are, too. You remember that, Godman. When I pay court to darkness, embracing oblivion, it is you that trembles on the brink of nonexistence.

Kill me, and there is nothing left.

Think, my faceless friend, which things of this kind need to be wrought by your steel-sheathed hands, and which are better left unmade. It will do no good for you or me to say: forgive them, for they know not what they are. In this architecture of this reality they have no existence and leave no legacy.

Not even as ghosts may we taste the verminous kiss and the bliss of decay.

They are nothing, and nothing is what you would make of us, if you would make us a part of them.

I *will* remember. . . .

This cratered world called Yrilene, a shattered satin skull, where the heart which beat within the loculus beats still, an everlasting pulse of force and promise.

In a dream called Yrilene, chapel bells are summoned to sound from cities buried in the sea, and the richest of splendors decorate the myth. The bells ring and ring again, to celebrate the marriage of Harker Lee and his sister of the shadows.

The gilded stars look down, and the sacred images of father and grandfather and forefather's sons are given life by the lambent life of Yrilene, and smile their sullen blessing.

Beyond the hills, I can hear breaths of sweet nocturne, the scent of lavender, and the dreams of amaranth. The caprine company and the ophidian walkers in the night have laid themselves to their eternal rest, and the gibbous admirals of evil have paused in the passages of the storm-black night. The alchemy of Yrilene holds us cradled, safe for an instant, and we suck from her blood-filled mammillae to toast the deaths of murderers and martyrs.

I am dressed in my coat of many colors, and I hold the hand of Harker's shadow-bride. There is no escape. There is no relenting in the pressure of existence.

The puppet master bids me dance.

Dance we all. It is a feast—a carnival. Harker is dancing, and every man in the multitude has a shadow-bride to be his own, until midnight, when the chapel bells will cease and the great bell tolls, and all the brides will turn to dust, and the toastmaster will bid us all unmask.

We *all* wear masks.

But we have no faces underneath.

Titan Nine

CHAPTER 7
The Titans

Fred Jacobson, the assistant director, gave me the definitive history of TITAN. I don't think anyone else dared to be so free with highly classified information.

FMA stands for Free Mass Acceleration. Apart from the official, sanctified jargon, it is also known as "the female principle."

It seems that Einstein, for all his heroic attempts to make life into equations, wasn't quite right. Not, you understand, that he was actually *wrong*, but he just tended to oversimplify a little. It happens to the best of us. (And the worst—more often the worst.) The Einstein theory really had very little to say about traveling faster than light except that it was patently absurd. The idea of the tachyonic phase—wherein things could only travel faster than light and whereby traveling slower than light became an absurdity—cropped up first in somebody's fertile imagination. But it did get people to thinking, even without any observations to back them up.

Einstein, it seems, was a bit of a fundamentalist. He never quite appreciated the hideous complexity of reality.

156

He thought that mass was mass, and only one form of energy. According to Jacobson, there is mass and mass. Bound mass, free mass, and energetic mass. So what's the difference? Don't ask me, I only work here. The man was knocking himself out trying to tell me in the simplest way he could, but it's just not my field. I didn't have an adequate command of the jargon. I couldn't quite follow him into the further regions of abstrusity.

The sum total of the theory was this: that effective mass can be reduced to zero by the adroit manipulation of a countermass. Once mass is zero, one doesn't have to bother one's pretty head about minor concerns such as gravity or elegant equations which tend to involve one in the mysteries of infinity.

Hence, TITAN ONE. A tin can loaded with hardware. They sent it out and brought it back. It went out a little further than the orbit of Pluto, and spent a good sixty hours, in three bursts, at faster-than-light velocities relative to Earth. The purpose of the flight was purely and simply to prove that it could be done. No measurements were taken, no useful data were gleaned. It was simply a yes/no question, and the universe gave the right answer.

Perhaps the nicest thing about the Project at this stage was its cheapness. No rockets. No waste. No fuel. TITAN ONE was flown on the same sort of power that you use to heat your house. All the hardware came back intact, and it soft-landed, too.

It was the technological accountant's dream. A ticket to the stars for the price of a hamburger and a cup of coffee. It was Mike Sobieski's dream, too, or it became that dream—the escape from what he called a cage of darkness.

A second ship was built—much bigger—intended eventually to accommodate personnel and all kinds of equipment—lab fittings and operative hardware. This ship became TITAN TWO and was dispatched on a programmed flight which would take it once around Proxima Centauri and back again.

In the meantime, the first ship was touched up again—no point in putting it in a museum just yet—and modified so that she could go out again and accomplish just a little bit more. She was still designed purely as a probe, though. She was sent out to loop Barnard's Star. Both probes came back, and the human race had touched the stars, although with mechanical fingers. What we learned from these probes came as no surprise.

There was already quite a lot known about both the stars involved, including the fact that they had no planets. But TITAN base was obliged to know that both stars possessed a retinue of dust and debris of various density and composition. Many people took this as an indication that with only minor changes in the way things were/ might have been, the stars *could* have had planets, and other stars almost certainly would.

And so the second ship was refitted as TITAN FOUR and was sent out once again. This time it had a name—the *Ambassador*—and a pilot. The pilot's name was Doug Mason, and he and his ship were the subject of one of the biggest PR campaigns in history. Mason was an experienced air force flyboy who'd rocket-jockeyed a good deal in his time.

The press coverage was extensive. Millions and millions of words were printed about what the whole thing meant to the human race. The public didn't actually get to know much about TITAN—only that FOUR was lifting at such and such a date, and was due back in approximately so long.

But they got to know an awful lot about Mason and about the great big wonderful galaxy.

Doug Mason and TITAN FOUR simply disappeared from human ken. They went into tachyonic phase right on schedule, and that was the last the world ever heard of its ambassador to the stars.

You can imagine what happened. At TITAN, panic, fear, and execution. In the world, not a lot. Doug Mason was just another celluloid hero, just another figment of media imagination. Who cared? Who'd ever cared? The public had become virtually immune to the reality behind the headlines. Nobody told them about TITAN FOUR's failure, and they didn't make a fuss. But the cage door, which had been officially declared open, was now shut firmly once again. There was just no point in throwing more parties in advance, to wish the heroes on their way. TITAN died in the media, and continued on its own. The pressmen and the cameras came to watch launches, came to be ready for return deadlines, but nothing went out. Nothing was going to go out until someone came home. The next time the opening of the cage door was advertised, it would have to be for real.

There was absolutely nothing that anyone could know about what had—or might have—happened to TITAN FOUR. Once Mason took her into tachyonic phase she was beyond human ken. The signals she might have sent just couldn't get back. Once a TITAN was lost, it was lost forever. And TITAN FOUR was lost.

Mike Sobieski had already conveyed to me the emotional meaning of the loss, and that was far more important, really, than the loss to the economy.

The new ship was bigger, better, and safer than *Ambassador*. Not that the first ship hadn't had its complement of backup devices, fail-safes, and duplicate controls. Nothing should have gone wrong with *Ambassador*. But one can always make extra certain. One can always find a little more safety margin to allow. Jacobson, like Mike and many others on the project, was always of the opinion that it was not the *Ambassador* but its pilot who had failed, and so they duplicated him, too.

TITAN FIVE—the *Destiny*—carried Patrick Bowen and Michael Janusson (Pat and Mike. Neither was Irish. Janusson was USAF; Bowen was army). Janusson was set to look after the ship. Bowen was set to look after Janusson. Anything which took out one of them would have to take out both.

Everyone knew, however, that there was just one thing Janusson and Bowen might need that they couldn't have, and that was time. The tachyonic tin can couldn't be brought back sub-c just like that. There was no ejector seat. The brakes just couldn't make an emergency stop. They were sent out with instructions to keep as close to the magic c as was reasonable, but even then, time wasn't really on their side. The phase shift was a delicate operation—it wasn't like flicking a switch. If something did go badly wrong aboard the *Destiny*, neither Janusson nor Bowen would be coming back.

And they didn't.

Ideas now had to be found and they had to be good, despite the almost total lack of data. There was a split in the Project, about what was going wrong, about what could be done to stop it going wrong again. The military blamed the technical staff, the technical staff blamed the pilots, and the PR brigade hated everybody because the public and political image of the Project had been shot to hell. PR didn't know whose fault it was, but it sure as hell wasn't theirs.

This was a bad time. But Mike Sobieski weathered it. The sacking of the first figurehead had been ritualistic. There was no point in being recriminative. TITAN had to be given every chance to sort itself out. Mike thought there was only one way to look at the problem. The ships came back on their own. If they didn't come back with men aboard, then something was going wrong with the men.

The scientific method provided one logical step. The next ship had to be sent out with no provision whatsoever for manual interference. A robot tin can carrying a coffin. In the coffin—a passenger.

They built a newer, glorified version of the first robot probe. They used the same FeMAle that had brought TITANS ONE and THREE safely home. They trusted her. They dressed her in steel and put her robot controls in a sealed cavity. The living quarters were simply one tin can inside another—a cage within a cage, exactly like Block C. TITAN SIX was scheduled to loop Proxima at high speed and then come home. The drive had already done a longer trip just as fast.

Even so, perhaps the Proxima loop was just a trifle ambitious. In all, the ship would be trans-c for several days. Why not a couple of hours? Why not a couple of minutes, just to try? But there was no such thing as a couple of minutes, or a couple of hours. Phase shift took twelve hours at least. That was the minimum time the ship could spend pretending to be a creature born and bred to tachyonic existence.

The "pilot" of SIX was Kel Furin. He was in no way connected with the military, though he had passed all the tests which the military could devise in order to test his fitness (in their eyes) to undertake the mission. Furin was a physicist—a personal friend of Sobieski.

The new ship was called *Hope*. I don't know who named the ships, but the sequence of names was close to black comedy. The people who built and sent out those ships meant every word of it, though. From their point of view there was no kind of comedy at all in the name *Hope*. That ship really did carry their hope. There was nobody on the base, by the time that TITAN SIX went into tachyonic phase, who hadn't encountered the suspicion that the human race might never be able to claim the stars, whether they could be reached or not.

There were no press releases at all concerning TITAN SIX. The fact that a fourth man was being sent into deep space was simply not talked about, as if it were rank bad taste to even think about it.

And, thanks to the discretion of all the Project people involved, there were no headlines when SIX made her reappearance right on schedule. They failed to make radio contact with Furin.

He was dead. He had killed himself by electrocution.

Every man on the Project knew that he hadn't done it for terrestrial reasons. Something out there had made him do it. Something out there was hostile to human life. The conquest of space was to be no kind of cakewalk. Space was fighting back.

In came the psychologists then, in their legions. Jenny was already on the Project, but not until SIX came back was she a major figure. She'd known Kel Furin, too.

TITAN SEVEN was built from the ground up. They knew they didn't have to worry about cogs and circuits now. But they didn't leave out a single thing. If anything, they made even more certain than they ever had.

This time, the capsule wasn't so much a prison cell as a minihospital ward. There were two men again: Cartland and Napier. Cartland was a careful, clever young man with a reputation for absolute stability. And not just a reputation. The brainwashers had virtually dismantled his mind to make sure it was put together exactly as they would have wished if they'd been designing him. I can imagine how hard they must have searched for Cartland. He was on the technical staff of the Project—a clock watcher and a button pusher, pretty low in the hierarchy. But he was what the situation—at that time—seemed to demand. Napier was Cartland's watchdog. He was a psychiatrist (and perhaps a bad risk simply because of that). The logic of including him in the team was that if something did go wrong he was at least capable of describing what it was. He was there to collect data, to make sure that when SEVEN came back there would be something to go on.

There were cameras to watch Cartland and Napier, record every second of their time on SEVEN. There was a vast battery of instruments, some scheduled to give constant readings, others that they were obliged to use periodically.

With the number of instruments that were there to gather data, it was quite impossible to deny Cartland and Napier the wherewithal to commit suicide if they so desired. They knew that, and they accepted the risk. It wasn't made easy for them—they weren't issued knives—but it was known by all concerned that suicide was in the cards.

The cards turned up just that way. SEVEN (which was called *Lady Luck*) brought them back. Dead.

TITAN base knew how, and when. But they didn't know why. Cartland and Napier hadn't bothered to put their reasons, or their thoughts, on record. In fact, they hadn't *done* anything at all, except die. They hadn't moved from their beds—it was electrocution, as with Furin. They had survived only two hours and a few minutes of hyperspace. (Their deaths were not simultaneous, but Cartland—the man picked for his stability—survived Napier by only seven minutes.)

All the tapes, all the film, all the monitors told TITAN exactly nothing that they could use.

And so: Lindquist.

They were determined that Lindquist wasn't going to kill himself. They built him into a machine. He was totally immobilized. The machine breathed for him, fed him, extracted his wastes, and would beat his heart for him if he somehow forgot to do it himself. They rigged Johnny Lindquist so they could run him by remote control. They weren't even satisfied with that. They put him into a perpetual sleep. He wasn't to be conscious for a single moment while TITAN EIGHT was in tachyonic phase. He'd be able to talk to them all the way out to the testing ground, and they intended to bring him around as soon as he was safely sub-c. But apart from that, they asked nothing of him but that he should live, and they gave him as much help as was mechanically possible with that.

These were desperate measures. TITAN was a desperate Project.

They profiled him—took a comprehensive tape of his mind as revealed by resonance phenomena. They made a start on an analysis, exactly along the lines of the Lee-Segal handbook for brain-pickers. They put a monitor tape on him so they could track his mind activity while he was in hyperspace.

Mike Sobieski still insisted on Proxima. It was no good sending him out to do a lightning tour around Pluto. It had to be Proxima. The stars were the purpose of the Project, and Mike insisted on dealing with the stars.

Lindquist was a volunteer. He was army, but I don't think his military status came into it. He was one of a couple of hundred volunteers from TITAN base. TITAN EIGHT was a one-way ticket to hell, and everybody knew it, but there were still two hundred volunteers. I don't know how they chose Lindquist. Probably by ballot. Everybody loved Johnny. Outside the base, he was nothing and had never seemed likely to be anything. He'd flown a rocket just once, but not an important rocket. But he was a great guy.

The machines saved him, of course. You can rely on machines. Machines aren't human. They don't give in. Johnny Lindquist came back. Alive and in one piece. But not quite the same piece they sent out. It looked the same, but it wasn't. The piece they sent out was intent and serious, full of memories of smiling and friends and youth. He'd smoked and he'd drunk and he'd screwed his share of women. He had a lot of life and every reason to want it back. Every bit of it. . . .

But he came back completely catatonic. His body was all there, heart beating, breathing, blood flowing, nourished, and clean. But his mind had gone away. It just wasn't there anymore—either that or it had changed beyond recognition. It took hours of studying tapes and monitors to find a trace of Johnny Lindquist inside his skull. They found traces. Only traces. Lindquist's mind had been exploded, and there was only wreckage left.

You could still find traces of him inside his body. You could see them there, on the tape. I saw them there myself. The monitors clicked on and on, and the flickering needles gave out fugitive evidence that somewhere Johnny Lindquist still existed. But *so* far away.

He was ultimately schizophrenic. Hopelessly insane. They said. But their words weren't in any way adequate to describe. Their words were worthless in the face of what the universe had sent back in exchange for Johnny Lindquist.

TITAN EIGHT, by the way, was called simply *Traveler.*

They found a whole host of new theories to account for Johnny not holding out. They knew from the monitor he'd stayed together for a day or more, then got steadily worse. They knew it was only a matter of time extending that day into days, and then to weeks. If they could lay their hands on the right kind of mind . . .

There were still one hundred and ninety-nine volunteers. But they chose me instead.

Cage of Darkness

CHAPTER 7
Survival

We know very little about human nature. We know almost nothing about human capabilities. There is vast scope for discovery about man and what he can do. The fact that there is vast scope for discovery does not mean that such discovery is to be sought, or that it will be of any significance if and when it is found.

Such discoveries are made in terms of endurance. They have no universal meaning at all. Such meaning as they have is entirely personal.

A man who walks from the Atlantic to the Pacific across the United States will be applauded and mocked. A man who sails around the world in a small boat or swims the English Channel will be applauded, but not mocked. A man who spends years squatting atop a pole or drinks fifty pints of beer faster than any man has ever done it before will be mocked, and applauded in a mocking fashion. The discrepancies in the way these feats are regarded in the eyes of the world are not rational. To embark upon any of these projects is not particularly courageous. They are all possible. In every case the challenge is internal—to force oneself to accept the rigors and the particular hardships involved. Success, too, is measured only internally, by the degree to which hardship has been accepted, endured, conquered. In all cases, the feat itself is meaningless except in an internal context.

The men who live in Block C are neither applauded nor mocked. They are forgotten. They embark upon their Canaanite existence without courage, without even enthusiasm. For them, the rigors and the hardships are not a challenge accepted but a situation given. The time of hardships is not finite—once condemned to Block C a prisoner is there for life. The feat of survival is a greater one than any of those I quoted earlier, but it is quite as meaningless in any context save the internal one. There is not even any achievement involved—merely survival. Yet this survival offers each man a vast scope for discovery about what he is.

What was Con Radley?

When you are hungry, you want to eat. That is what being hungry means. That, says the crowd (this is the faceless crowd which applauds, mocks, or forgets), is natural.

When the crowd says natural they want to imply that it is right and proper and the way God planned it. What they actually do mean, however, is that they either like it that way or they welcome the opportunity to put on a brave face and play their own version of the endurance game. (This is why there is such a vast difference between eating being natural, shitting being natural, and fucking being natural.)

Apologies for the interlude, but it really is necessary if we are to discuss with any depth of meaning the question of what is/was Con Radley.

Con Radley was a hungry man. It was exactly the same as the hunger you know so well. In terms of the way things actually *are* it was a perfectly natural hunger. He felt it. It was there. It existed.

And people didn't like it. It wasn't, you see, a hunger for food.

What is more, people certainly did not welcome this particular opportunity to don a brave face and accept it.

So the crowd naturally called it unnatural.

Needless to say, nobody gave a tinker's dam about Con. Nobody cared what he felt or thought or who he was. They only cared about what they felt and liked and liked to think and feel. After all, when you come right down to it (they say), in the final analysis (they say), ultimately (they say), God had put Con on Earth so that he could be part of their environment, and it was damn well up to them to say what he should be and feel and think and do. He hadn't anything to do with himself.

I'm not going to tell you exactly what kind of a pervert Con Radley was. I mean, you don't approve of me writing about things like that, do you? You'd prefer that Radley didn't even exist, especially in this document, to which you think he isn't at all relevant. If he's here at all, you want him kept well back out of sight. You want him to be unmentionable.

All well and good. From this moment until he goes the way of all bit-part players, you won't even notice that Con Radley is in any way different from your own sweet self. He'll be mentioned only by name, if at all.

You can make up your own mind about who and what he was that made you hand him a free, one-way ticket to Canaan. After all, if you don't want me to talk about such things, it's only natural that I should comply.

But I want to say this. In Canaan, Con Radley had no option but to discover things about human nature—his own human nature, that you tried to steal from him by sending him there—that you haven't even dreamed of. It may mean nothing, except to him (it doesn't matter whether you applaud, mock, forget, or kill), but to him, it means everything.

It means: up yours.

MADMAN'S DANCE

CHAPTER 10

While the Gods Sleep Restfully, the World Is Free from Nightmares

I descend into a long basin of land, tapered like a spearhead, which ends in a narrow neck between two cliffs. The surface is scattered with boulders, as though the faces of rock on either side have been blasted apart. I can see long figures moving about on the clifftops above me, but the valley itself seems desolate and silent. Once, I pause to watch a landslide tumble down the sheer wall to the right of me, leaving yet another diagonal scar in the face of the rock.

I find, when I get there, that the pass is blocked. I cannot hope to get through that way. The barricade is made of loose boulders, and the crevices are filled with lubricant ash. I try, at first, to pick my way carefully up the rocky slope, but I sink and slip and slide, and I make no progress at all.

"There's no way."

I turn to find an old man standing behind me. It is he who speaks.

"Where did you come from?" I ask him. I was alone, I am sure of that.

"From the hills," he replies.

I contemplate his answer briefly, and then I repeat the question. I have found that it pays to repeat questions. The answers are almost never the same.

"From beyond the slopes," he replies this time.

"Then there is a path," I conclude.

"No," he says, "there is only the other way."

"And which is that?" I ask.

The old man walks away, treading lightly upon the fluid surface. I watch him closely. But he is right. There is no way but the other. His feet do not touch the surface. He dissolves himself into the rock. His shape blurs in the clear air, and he passes into shadow beneath the bright sun. He fades into the barricade. He becomes invisible.

Lifting my eyes to the jagged ridge of the cliff which towers high above me, I discern a tiny silhouette.

It is waving.

Nevertheless, I think that I have come through the worst. It is not easy. It is never easy.. But there is yet another way. I can go back. I can go around. I have all the time that I need. If I were Sisyphus, I would abandon the rock and go to the mountaintop without it. If I were Tantalus, I would go hungry. If I were Ixion, I would be patient, because I would know that someday the wheel would return, and that existence is only a matter of waiting for it to do so.

I think that you and I are at rest. Not that our troubles are over—merely that we have come to accept them.

Neither you nor I can work miracles. I think you have accepted that at last. You are content to be a conjurer—you have abandoned your futile quest to be a *real* magician. We are most certainly on the way home. We have looped the star. We have come close to it, and we have passed it by. We are aimed for the sun.

I am not complacent. I look at the sunrise, and I do not call it dawn. There are more false dawns than real. But I remember, and I endure. The dreams flow by, taunting me with their petty frustrations and their giggling specters and their veiled meanings. I am not afraid of them. They try to make everything fearful with their coy hints and their baseless insistences of danger and significance. But dreams are froth. I know it, and so—I think—do you.

If this is the calm before the storm, all well and good. Let me taste your lightning. I will find it as bitter as I ever did, but I will drink it down. I remain unbroken. We are whole.

We are going home.

At the crossroads where the dead-ended highways meet, I find a featureless milestone, a weatherworn signpost, and a scarecrow in a tattered military uniform holding aloft a cross and speaking to a multitude which passes him silently by.

"It is coming in clouds of night," he pronounces, in accusing, prophetic tones. "Shadowless in the black sky. The good crops will wither, and from the derelict land and the dust of city streets there will spring new wheat, in the cause of compensation.

"And those whose crops are blighted will cry out aloud for help, but there will be no one to turn to, save for those to whom they sold their bread in years past. And these, who now have plenty, will set the price at the very highest, and will spit on the erstwhile rich, in the name of compensation."

I remember that in the long-gone days when I was given my first pair of wings, my father warned me:

"Do not fly as high as your dreams might take you."

But I trusted my dreams. How was I to know that dreams can be faithless? How was I to know that I was set apart, by the mark of Tom O'Bedlam, that dreams were meant for other men, and that to me they could be only a curse?

How?

I, child of the winds, flexed and furled my giant wings with a feeling of great power, and I soared away into the black, brooding skies. I flew above the clouds, bathed in airborne fountains, and danced in the ballroom of the stars.

I flew to the distant moon and cooled my feet in her oceans of tidal dust.

I flew to the sun and glided in and out of her flowing tresses of fire, crying aloud to hear the echoes fleeing through her honeycombed caverns of light.

I tasted the sweet blood which oozed from the many spear wounds of heroic, immortal Mars.

I blinded my eyes in the poisonous vapors of Venus's samite shroud, and washed them clean in cold starlight that fell from the clouds of the Milky Way.

I painted a portrait in the liquid, glowing face of inmost Mercury, and failed to recognize the man behind the face, although I knew him well and remembered his name.

I cast my clothes to the wilderness of wild rock, to giant death-worlds in the arctic solar sea. My fingers touched the rings of Saturn and were not bitten by the cold. I was naked, and I did not bleed.

And the gluttony of my gaze reached further yet, and out and out, expanding ever faster at the speed of light and beyond, shedding glare of its own into the paths of the treading stars.

And I returned to my father, full of the triumph which I could hurl against his ancient wisdom.

But he only replied, "Do not fly as high as your dreams might take you."

My father advises me still. He is in the asylum. He remembers Icarus. I remember Titan. I am Titan.

Titan Nine

CHAPTER 8
Five-Card Stud

Ever since I first passed through the gate of TITAN base, I'd been looking for a game of cards. I'd been away from the table a long time. The games in Canaan were tough, but they just weren't poker. The whole essence of gambling is money. You can't play poker without cash. I needed something to take the edge off my nerves, and poker was the only thing I knew capable of taking off as much edge as I had accumulated in my weeks at TITAN. The pressure of what passed for reality in that place was too much for a little guy like me to take twenty-four hours a day without some way I could press back. I needed a smaller place to work for a while—the microcosm of a card game. I needed to spend a few hours in a world where I could lead a whole and effective existence.

Chalk was a purist. A five-card stud man. Five-card stud is the most skillful game in existence, bar none. Far more skillful than chess or go or war. Those games are *pure* skill, surely, but a game that is *only* skill merely demands that you beat your opponent. You only have to be better

than the next man—and that means that the skill
potential of those games has never been explored, except
by computers, which aren't very good at them anyway.
Stud is different. In stud, you not only have to beat the
man, you have to beat the cards. It's not enough to be a
better player. The best player in the world gets losing
hands in direct proportion to the number of opponents.
You have to win the game, rather than simply beat your
opponent. Opponents are easy—behind the workings of
chance there's the structure of the universe. You need
patience, memory, control, perfect understanding not only
of the men you want to beat but of the cards you have to
beat them with. Nobody faces that sort of a problem across
a chessboard. And even if you play perfectly, even if you
are the best in the world, you still can't win them all.
Nobody has a God-given right to win at stud. That's the
essence of real skill. You can have it and use it and still
lose.

I don't find it too difficult. I'm not Luis Dalquier, but
I'm good. I have style. I've played games which have
made me sweat, games which have made me grit my teeth.
And I've played many a losing game. But I always have
the style.

I confess to being addicted to the game. I need the
game, because it's the only thing that can involve me
totally, can transplant me from the hostile outer world and
offer me a haven where I can really *be.*

I don't enjoy poker. It doesn't give me any pleasure, not
even to take big money out of a game. In point of fact, I
never really play for big money. I never ever had big
money to play with. It didn't make the game any less
meaningful. It just has to be real money, and money you

need. I play for the rules and regulations, for the laws of the poker universe. It's a life of its own. But I'm not happier there than here.

I got Goodman to play—he was fairly keen and he knew what had passed between Chalk and me through Hurst. Chalk brought along just one friend—a Lieutenant Hartley. Both were secret agents from the depths of Security rather than toy soldiers like Goodman.

From the moment we picked up the first hand, I guessed that Chalk was a believer. The day he gave up believing in Santa Claus he began believing in the Cincinnati Kid. He was out to get me, and he *believed* he could do it. It meant a lot to Chalk to see me beaten; I don't know why, but there are a dozen reasons I could understand. Chalk was the kind of guy who is always out to get somebody. I was victim-of-the-month, that was all. He'd probably faced any number of people he was out to get across a card table, and simple logic said that some of them must have got away. But he was cocksure now, he was keen, and he was confident. That testified to the fact that he was good, but it also testified to the fact that he had a crazy kind of faith in fate and fortune. I was glad to see it, because that made him—ultimately—a loser. I didn't get cocksure myself, because I knew that every loser in the world wins his share of evenings.

I started to play knowing that I could lose, and knowing that if I did Chalk would treasure the memory till the day he died. It didn't bother me. Most poker games find more than one schizo sitting at a table, and even if it doesn't take one to know one, you usually find out.

We began quietly, playing for mediocre stakes. I had a few weeks' pay to play with. I hadn't spent a penny in all the weeks I'd been at TITAN—there wasn't much opportu-

nity—and I'd been surprised to find out that they were
paying me at all. But they were, and quite handsomely,
too. Danger money on top. I didn't know that I was ever
going to get a chance to spend it, but it was very useful
nevertheless.

I spent the first hour being quiet, finding out what sort
of a game it was. I bet the value of my hand, or a little
over, and I dropped a couple at the showdown just to let it
be known around and about that I told outrageous
untruths at times. I didn't drop much, but I lost fairly
steadily. It didn't bother me in the least—giving money
away to begin with is never bad strategy at poker, as long
as you give it away in small quantities. The other guys in
the game knew what they were doing. We were playing a
pot limit and they used it—they didn't give away much
with varying bets. They played moderately, but forcefully.
They made their money work. It took some time for me to
get an idea of exactly how hard they *did* work their money.
They all lacked imagination. Players who play together a
lot often do; their game tends to become stereotyped.
Chalk and Hartley were obviously Mutt and Jeff, and
Goodman was no stranger to them.

Chalk raised often and he raised high. In order to hold
my hands I was forced to raise back, with more or less the
same frequency. We were both fairly modest about it in
the beginning, but looking four hours into the future I
could see that some real money might fly when we got
hard down to it. Hartley raised hardly at all, and it didn't
take me long to realize that Chalk and Hartley had what
might delicately be called an "understanding." Chalk
raised most often when Hartley had high cards showing,
and Hartley was a good, steady caller against Chalk's
raises. It was obvious that when Chalk risked his money,

he would far rather it ended up with Hartley than with anyone else, if he were to lose it at all. Goodman played a sound, steady game, but over a period of time Chalk and Hartley's sandwich tactics pulled his money away in dribs and drabs. He was patient enough, waiting for one he could take them both for a ride with, but it was like shooting craps. Over an evening's play, he was going to end up slightly down rather than slightly up.

Having Hartley on his side wasn't really a tremendous advantage to Chalk, because Hartley wasn't very good. That soon became moderately clear. He was too mechanical, had too much faith in the system—he couldn't really measure the game to good effect. He kept himself in cash, around the even money bracket, but that was largely thanks to Chalk.

We began playing about ten, and after my poor start I began to make tracks, and until two I won fairly steadily. I backed off from a lot of Chalk's raises, and with help from the cards I managed to draw him out a little and whittle down his cash as well. He wasn't keen to back down against my raises, and as time wore on he became the game's prime loser. Hartley dropped a big one to Goodman, which redressed the balance between those two, and at two I was ahead more or less what Chalk and Goodman were down, with Hartley holding par.

The screws really came on in the next half-hour as the betting was driven up by some hands. I lost one big pot to Goodman, and two hands later Chalk cinched me on one I'd thought I'd win. I could see the light of battle in Chalk's eyes as the pile in front of me dwindled rapidly and I went into the red. He began to push harder, and I folded time and time again while my money walked steadily across the table to him. Then I played three of a kind against a double pair, and magically it was all back with me again. But we still hadn't whittled into anybody's stake to any real depth. Chalk made up his mind to take me, and his belief suddenly began to show.

Once, twice, and then again, in ten minutes between 3:15 and 3:25, Chalk and I pushed the pot to its limit, and he lost all three. I practically cornered the market in cash. Goodman was a bit down, Hartley a lot, and Chalk was practically destitute. The stakes were still trifling, of course, so all in all I'd picked up a thousand or eleven hundred. But measured against the game I was the clear conquerer. The major was very upset. We doubled the initial stakes, by mutual agreement; everybody knew it was about due, and we settled back to a quiet routine. Doubling the initial stakes does a lot more than double final pots, because pots tend to increase exponentially, so that small and simple move had made a big difference to the potential of the game. It was time for a rethink. Goodman won some back from me, and Hartley depleted Chalk's stock even further. Chalk introduced some new cash into the game. He was obviously having a hard time. He dropped his cigarettes while passing on the cards to deal. He picked them up and gave one to Hartley while Goodman and I lit up from our own supply. His eyes were getting hot and red, and I knew the strain was getting to him.

Hartley dealt Goodman a five, gave me a king, and dealt Chalk a jack. He turned himself up a nine. I found that I had another king in the hole. I bet, Chalk called, and Hartley raised. Goodman met it with a careless resignation which suggested that the raise was quite irrelevant to him. I was surprised to see Hartley raise, but I knew that his raises were rarely worth worrying about,

and did not seem to figure in his understanding with
Chalk. I played possum and called. Chalk reraised by the
maximum permissible—the whole contents of the pot. The
sequence was unusual, but not unheard of. It was entirely
possible that Chalk was raising on the strength of Hartley's
raise. Hartley called the reraise, and so did I. For a
first-round pot, it was now quite large. And as it increased,
so did the permissible bet.

Nobody improved openly on the next round. My two
kings were still beating everyone else. I bet the limit.
Hartley ventured another small raise. I figured it was time
to stop pretending to be dead, and I reraised. Chalk had to
put in a lot to call—a lot more than he'd already risked.
He needed a pair—jacks, by preference, because his other
card was lower than Hartley's nine—to even contemplate
calling.

He called.

So did Hartley.

And I began to wonder. I'd seen the understanding in
operation for several hours, but this seemed to be needless
extravagance. After all, I had the high card showing.
Hartley had been stamped on twice for his low raises, and
showing nine, seven he could hardly be confident. Yet he
called.

He dealt the cards. I showed king, queen, eight. Chalk
had jack, eight, three. Hartley had nine, seven, six—an
outside straight if he had an eight in the hole, but one
could hardly imagine him still in the game if that were so.

I bet five hundred.

Chalk only had about five hundred in front of him,
despite having brought out his secret reserve. Nevertheless,
he said, "Your five hundred with a thousand." He took out
a pen and a checkbook, and he began to write.

Hartley put in his chips.

I sat back to think.

I knew Chalk wasn't a lunatic. I knew that even a lunatic would be disgracing himself if he raised on that sequence. Did he think that I was a straight and simple liar? How could he afford to raise even if he did? Could any man on Earth really have that much faith in the destiny of a pair of jacks? What the hell could he do if I raised three thousand, as I was manifestly being invited to do?

I flicked the corners of my cards, fingering them nervously. I looked very worried, and Chalk smiled. Hell, I *was* very worried. Especially when I got an odd sensation about the feel of the cards. They were worn enough, sure, and those we'd been playing with hadn't accumulated memorable marks. But these just didn't have the feel of having been played with. They hadn't soaked up sweat. The wear was old wear. During the light-up between deals, while Chalk had passed on the deck and dropped his cigarettes, they had worked a gypsy switch. It was clear now—Chalk had done the shuffling before he passed on the deck. The deck Hartley was dealing from wasn't the same one. It was stacked.

"Chalk," I said, "how much am I worth?"

"Huh?" he said. Polite surprise was written all over his face, but I knew that inside himself he was sensing a real kill.

"Hell," he said, "you can cover the bet. You got it there."

"How much am I worth, Chalk?" I persisted. My voice was flat and cold. I was threatening him. I could see the doubts begin to rise.

"How do I know?" he fenced.

"Because you know me better than I do. I don't keep a close check on all my assets, because most of them are no use to me. But you know what I own. You know my file backward. You know to the dollar exactly how much I'm worth."

He swallowed, looking puzzled. He knew I wanted to raise, but he couldn't see what the fuss was for. He knew I had more than three thousand, given what I had in front of me.

"I guess about eight and a half thou," he said.

I was surprised. But I had every confidence that he was right. There was the money I'd been paid for the mind-reading job, and there was what I owned before I first got put away. All no use, but you can't take it with you, and they can't take it off you. It was all on tap. I could bet with it. There was my insurance policy as well (courtesy of TITAN), but I wasn't going to die tonight. I thought I could wheedle another ten thousand out of various sources if need be, but I didn't see that kind of need.

"Okay," I said. "I'll call your thousand. That squares the pot. But I'd like to lay a little side bet. I'd like to bet my eight thousand, five hundred that you don't win this hand."

Chalk didn't move a muscle. He was frozen.

Hartley went as white as a sheet.

I could imagine the conflict inside Chalk's mind, hidden behind that sweaty, tight-held countenance. Greed, pure and simple. Not just the big hand to take the guts out of Harker Lee, but the added bonus of total annihilation. And doubt. Hideous doubt. Could anything go wrong? Was I only betting on my kings? Did I have something else to go on? Remember, Chalk had an ace in his hole, and he was aiming to pair it last card. He hadn't anything yet. He was betting on the sure knowledge of what was yet to come.

"Provided, of course," I purred, "that we have a gentleman's agreement about anything we might bet after the last card. You know, I could raise more." I stressed the word "raise," deliberately goading him.

He was afraid, but he was determined as well. He knew something was funny, but he knew the cards were stacked his way. He couldn't go wrong. He couldn't turn down the opportunity. No way.

"It's a bet," he said.

Hartley had put down the cards, waiting for us to settle it. He reached for them again now, to continue to deal. I brought my hand down on top of his.

"Just a minute," I said. "I want to cut the deck."

I'm sure the lieutenant looked absolutely ghastly, but my eyes were firmly fixed on Chalk. I wanted to see him shatter.

And shatter he did.

His jaw relaxed. Sweat seemed to ooze out of every pore on his fat, greasy face. His eyes seemed to have difficulty in focusing.

"You can't do that," he breathed.

"Why not?" I demanded.

I smiled. I was superficially relaxed. My heart was going like a hammer, but there was no outward sign. I was in the catbird seat, and I was tightening the straps. I felt Hartley's hand beneath my own slip back, flaccid and nerveless.

I turned to Goodman.

"Can you think of any reason why I shouldn't cut the cards?" I asked.

Goodman looked at Chalk, and he looked at me. It was obvious what was happening, and he was remembering that over the years he'd suffered Chalk and Hartley, and their understanding. And he was a good guy. Army loyalty just wasn't in the race.

"No reason at all," he said.

"Quite so," I said. "Now look at it this way, Major Chalk. You have an ace in your hole, right? Don't ask me how I know, I'm telepathic. That means that there are three aces left in the pack. One of those is scheduled to come to you next card. You put it there, so you deserve to forfeit that one. There are still two more. You can still win, can't you? You just can't be sure of winning. Well, that's poker for you. Can I cut the deck now?"

The major looked at us both, and he knew he was beaten.

"Go ahead," he said, in a voice that grated because his mouth was stone dry. I'll swear he still thought he might get one of the other aces. Well, he might have. But he didn't.

Hartley's shaking hands took the pack once I'd cut it, and dealt me a third king. Then he paired Chalk's three for him.

It all served to add insult to injury.

"One dollar," I said, throwing an odd bill into the middle.

Chalk silently folded his hand.

"That's right," I said, wonderingly. "I do appear to have cinch, don't I? Still, I'll let you out of your misery. I've got three of these. What have you got?"

Chalk put his hand back into the deck and began to shuffle.

"It's my deal," said Goodman.

"You owe me eight and a half thousand dollars," I told Chalk.

Goodman took the cards. I pulled the cash out of the middle and inspected the check.

"Suppose he had gotten one of the other two aces," said Goodman, "and you hadn't improved?"

"I'd have lost," I said.

MADMAN'S DANCE

CHAPTER 11
Lost in the
Metaplastic Maze

There is a fountain which rises within the roots of a great ash tree where I rest one day in my traveling.

A giant of a man, with a great beard and breastplate of carven gold, approaches the tree and asks—apparently of the tree—whether he might drink the water of the fountain and thus take into himself the sap of the tree, so that he could thereby know all that the tree knows and all that it yet might know.

And the tree allows him to do so, but plucks out one of his eyes as a tribute, and sets it in its branches as a gorgeous fruit.

Now the great warrior drinks, and he knows all that he has asked to know. Sadness descends upon him like a cloak when he perceives the hollowness of his self, and in particular his empty heroism. Both in his backward path and in his forward path, it seems that he is nothing. He will not weep, because he thinks to do so will dishonor his sword, but his face is drawn across with grayness, and lines are graven therein, as though he has become suddenly most ancient.

Slowly, he continues on his way.

I have drunk from the spring myself, and I know that it is only water, but my eye is not hanging from the branches of the tree like a succulent apple, and I have not asked the tree to permit me a share in its store of knowledge.

A multitude of small, colored birds fly about the tree now, and each of them in turn hovers by the strange new fruit, and each in turn takes a tiny bite therefrom. Then they fly away, in all directions, into all the corners of the world, and as they fly they weep the tears of the warrior's surrendered eye, which falls like rain upon the ground.

And their colors slowly fade, because they, like the warrior himself, inherit all the burden of a lifetime in a single moment. But they do not die.

They do not die.

I take advantage of the rarest of all chances when I have walked a little further along the road. I find a statue of Justice which has been temporarily imbued with life by a fragment of chance. She is on her bended knee before a group of small children, sorting through their petty disputes. One by one, I watch the children turn away from her blindfolded face, and each begins to cry as each limps away.

Then she stands, and faces me, though I know she cannot see me because of the stone bandage which imprisons her eyes.

"How can you read the inclination of your scales?" I ask her, pointing at the scales which she carries in her left hand, though it is useless to point, because she cannot see.

"I cannot read," she tells me. "I am blind."

"Then how can you judge?" I ask her.

She laughs and laughs and laughs, her mouth gaping wide with the rushing mirth, her stone bandage stirring not a fraction of an inch, though her loose dress flaps like a storm-pressed sail.

She makes no answer, but she waves aloft the sword which she holds in her other hand.

One by one, she beheads the children.

I know my enemies.

They bear marks upon their foreheads, and the signs label them with stupidity, blindness, intolerance, and avarice. Their bodies are fueled by the hungry engines of their vanity. They are not remorseful, they make no apologies.

Their errors are obstinate in their insistence on a counterfeit reality. It is cowardice which makes them oblivious to the humiliating truth. They make certain that their meager concessions and their pitiful overtures to honesty do them no harm, rob them of no illusions, and help to prop up their tattered self-confidence. With armor of happiness and weapons of faith they tread their downward path to a meaningless fate. They cry and they crow and they make false images to mirror their imaginary affections, as if the effluent of their tiny minds could alter the course of aeonic destiny.

I, in my pretty disguise as cloven-hoofed Satan, choose to offer solace to their prisoned minds by selling them vice in the absurd commerce of evil, but my sense of humor will not permit them to have any real joy of it. They are seeking the cheap fabric of a synthetic existence, and willingly pay the price, which is their own humanity.

There are puppet strings tied to my fingers, and I can make the world dance to an idiot's tune. I pour filth upon their heads, and they pay no more heed to it than if it were the gentle rain which falls from heaven. Each day they are further dissipated upon the great rack of my ever-present hell, but they are forbidden to feel horror or disgust, by virtue of the fact that the gloom of the pit is the covenant which they themselves have sought and signed and sealed—and thought themselves the winners of a bargain.

They cannot even suspect the poverty which they crave and the pain which they court, for they will not gamble what they have, and they use it all to buy the anesthetic of furtive pleasure and the meager squeezing of bloodless stones.

The opaque eyes in their powdered clown masks will not see the emptiness of their minds, but prefer to adhere with wormlike tenacity to the thin curtain of matter which is set in the floor of the cage where I keep them for amusement. They live in a Lilliput of the soul, yet imagine themselves gods and Titans.

Among the jackals and the rats and the scorpions and the spiders and the bloodsucking bats they make their home. They are my guests. And yet they imagine themselves the Lords of Creation. And with what fervor do they point to one or another among them whom they imagine to be uglier or filthier or more riddled with the plague than the rest. Their minds permit an infinite quantity of self-pity and the denigration of one another.

I love them all, my wonderful enemies, in the way that they love one another. I laugh at their miseries and their hypocrisies, and most of all at their feeble, futile castles in the stagnant air.

And the path of my journey lies clear before me across the sky. I can see it now, where it was hazy before.

I will pass through the earthly depths where devil-drums will sing my praises and set out a rhythm for my feet to follow, and I will need no rest, not even in the heights where the mountains meet the sky above the clouds.

I will search the caverns where every shape is gray, and return to the gentle light of a kindly sun, and roam the pitfalled pages of my youth.

I will fight with every army that ever went to war, and learn to savor in the utmost the agonies of death and wounding.

I will leap to catch the starlight and the comet's tresses. I will tramp the mighty skies, along the avenue of the zodiac, and saturate my tiny self with every pain and pleasure known to the frivolities of flesh.

I will aim for heaven, and leave my heart in hell. And descend via misspent time and ill-spilled blood, by the lost, forgotten years, tasting the wounds and the tears, looking for lust and ecstasy, and experimenting with eternity.

I will grope in passing fancy for the empty womb, but pass on and through to the luxuries of unknown, unsought dooms. The sands of time will run through my shriveling fingers. Ape and bird I will be, and fly and cry while I grow scales and mollusk shell. I will search the ultimate oblivion of fleeing life in the primeval sea.

And on and on, through lifeless paradise and limitless death.

And I will return, because the journey is cyclic.

I will stand, as I do now, on the threshold of eternity, again and again.

I have discovered that you are dead. The universe is mine.

Titan Nine

CHAPTER 9

The Waiting Game

It was about ten when I knocked on Jenny's door. I was almost surprised when she answered.

"Hi," she said. Sounded unenthusiastic, like: Oh, it's *you.*

I wandered in and sat down.

"Long time no see," I said.

"All of thirty hours," she said. "You want some coffee?"

"That's right. What'd you do today?"

Her answer floated back from the kitchenette. "Work."

"The new tape the same as the old one?"

"Just about."

"I had a look at your torture chamber. Jacobson showed me around with a ghoulish grin on his face. I asked for a demonstration, but poor Hurst looked quite pale and I didn't have the heart."

"It is a bit cramped," she admitted, leaning in the doorway while she waited for the water to boil. "But it's only for a few weeks. And you'll be so full of happy thoughts you won't even notice the time pass."

"Happy thoughts," I echoed. "Houdini couldn't have

got out of that thing with all the picklocks in his armory. D'you really think it's necessary?"

"No."

"But it's safe?"

"No chances. We do it all the easy way. I don't think the equipment matters. All we want to know is whether your mind can stand up. I think it can. But the others didn't. So we take no chances."

"It's a hell of a way to travel."

"For the time being, it's the only way. It brought Lindquist back in one piece. We'd be fools not to use it to bring you back in one piece."

"Does it occur to you that if deep space doesn't drive me mad, the Iron Maiden treatment might?"

"Not you, Harker. Not you. You're a practiced survivor. Anyhow, come back catatonic if you feel like it. Feel free. We'll fish you out of it."

She came in with the coffee, and I sipped gingerly. I couldn't understand why everybody was so perpetually ghoulishly cheerful these days. Nobody was sparing my feelings.

"All the king's horses and all the king's men couldn't put Humpty-Dumpty together again," I observed.

"So they should have hired a psychiatrist."

"You aren't a psychiatrist. You're only a theorist."

"I'm the world's foremost expert on you. And I've practiced. Psychiatry, that is."

"In the midst of all this happy jollity," I said, "I feel about as merry as an undertaker at a christening. Sometimes I get the feeling nobody thinks I can do it except me and thee, so nobody cares much. I feel like the butt of a big joke."

"So laugh."

"It's not funny. I have my doubts, you know. Real doubts. Sometimes I mull over your fascinating logic—you know, Harker Lee is the one man we can send to spend six weeks in hell, because he's done it all before.

"Well, that's right. I have done it before, and it wasn't nice. So maybe it wasn't spectacular; I just stared at spots on the ceiling till they crawled, and gave up talking for Lent. Big deal. But it wasn't that easy. There were an awful lot of things involved in my recovery after that breakdown, and one of them was a knowledge that it could be beaten and if it could be beaten it wouldn't happen again. You know, that's a whole lot of different circumstances to the ones I'm likely to find out by Proxima Centauri."

"The trip won't take six weeks," she said. "And most of the weeks it does take you'll be normal space at sub-c and you can talk, and there's no reason why you shouldn't be absolutely okay."

"Has it ever occurred to you that when a guy standing on top of a high building manages to talk himself out of jumping off it doesn't necessarily mean he could survive the fall if he did?"

She sighed.

People who understand you are often very difficult to talk to. They understand you too well. They know when you're talking beyond your real feelings, and they know why. If they play the game, you know they're fooling. If they don't play the game, you can't either. Sometimes it does me good to talk, to say things I don't mean. But I need an audience. It's easier by mail.

"So what do you want?" she said. "You want to go home?"

"Can I?"

"No."

"Then that's not what I want, is it?"

"No," she said, tiredly, "you want to sound off. You want to feel sorry for yourself and make me feel sorry for you, too."

"So humor me."

"Has it occurred to you that it isn't so easy for the rest of us?"

"I'm the guy qualifies for the coffin if it doesn't work."

"Exactly," she said. She sounded bitter—something I'd not known her sound before. She didn't usually show ragged edges. She was normally determined and dedicated. No frayed nerves at all. But not now. Pressure was beginning to work on her. Why? Surely not because it was little old Harker that had his head on the chopping block? Maybe it was a build-up over a long period, I thought. The strain of work, the strain of seeing Lindquist every day, his tape clicking away, the strain of seeing Mike, too, with *his* time running out.

But she was carrying on: "All you have to do, sweet child, is lie on your cushioned couch in your steel vest, all your needs supplied directly and automatically. And live or die. Just that, no more. It's no trouble at all. The worst place you can end up is nowhere. I know damn well you're scared, but how the hell can it hurt you when you've been crying good and loud for the last ten years that you're dead anyway and only walking around because they won't put you in the ground? All the time I've known you you've complained what a damn hard life it is and how little difference it would make if you were dead. So this job comes natural to you. Tailor-made. You have nothing to lose. Well, we have. We have to live with the problems and keep living with them and keep on fighting them. You don't."

Hoist with mine own petard.

"Great," I said. "You send me out because it doesn't matter a damn whether I come back or not."

"To you, Harker, to *you*. It matters to us whether you come back or not. It's we who have to face the consequences if you don't."

"That's a pretty heartless attitude, if you don't mind my saying so," I said.

"That's right," she said. "But it's you who's doing all the whining."

"I'm only the fall guy," I said. "I don't get to whine."

"I just wish you wouldn't."

"I'm sorry."

"You're just the victim," she said. "We're the murderers, and we have to keep right on murdering until we need to murder no more. Do you think we like that? Do you think that we like being dragged into your morbid speculations and your fears, day after day? Don't you think we're scared for you? Don't you think we might have morbid speculations of our own? Don't you think we might feel guilty?"

"I'm a murderer, too," I said.

"Then you know how I feel."

I did know how she felt. It was good to know that she really did feel. There had been times when I was in doubt. I'd finally made her mad at me. I needle people deliberately. I always have. But I felt sorry because I'd needled Jenny. I'd come for a little self-help, as a predator on her good nature. I hadn't intended to trespass on her finer feelings.

There was a silence. Not a pregnant silence, but an empty, vacuous silence. A silence that needed to contain something, but didn't.

An aborted silence.

"I'm sorry," I said, to intrude something into the pause.

"I know," she said. "I know you didn't mean that." She was still bitter, softly bitter. I lit two cigarettes and passed one to her.

"It's tough," I said, meaning tough for her.

"It's never easy," she said, calming quickly.

"It won't be your fault," I said, "if it doesn't work out."

"It will," she said, and she wasn't going to hear any arguments.

"You're scared," I said.

"That's right."

I put my hand on her shoulder. "You never said anything before," I said. "I didn't know. Miles of computer printout and a few years, and a few letters. That's all I am. You know that. You don't love me. Hell, you don't even like me very much."

"Don't be an idiot," she said.

"Meaning?"

"What I said."

"You like me."

"That's right."

"Thanks a lot."

"I suppose," she said, "that if it were you that had to send me out there, on the heels of seven dead men, it wouldn't matter a damn."

"It'd break my heart," I said, "if you didn't come back."

"Your heart's already broken," she said.

"It'd break again."

"Well, it'll break mine if you don't come back."

"You don't love me."

"You don't love me. You don't have to be in love with someone to be on the same side."

"That's nice," I said. "That's very nice. I'd rather be carrying your good wishes than the hopes of the human race. I can keep your good wishes when I come back."

"That's right," she said.

"By the way," I said, "talking about the hope of the human race, who does take the accolades if I do come back? Who do you gypsy switch for me?"

"I thought you knew," she said. "Young Hurst is going through training with you. Not for nothing, you know."

"Yeah," I said. "He's the hero type."

Cage of Darkness

CHAPTER 8
The Man Inside

If Bedbug ever had a name, we took it away from him. We called him Bedbug instead, and that became the only name he had—*all* he had, in fact, in the whole world. The only thing that was truly his. If we ever offered him anything else, he refused it. Maybe that's why everyone outside Canaan hated him so.

Bedbug is approximately six foot six, and very wide. He weighs about two hundred and sixty pounds. He has hands which can pulverize stones. He has a colossal skull, and nobody knows whether the brain inside it is proportionately colossal, or whether the bone is three inches thick. Nobody ever cared enough to find out. Big brain or no big brain, Bedbug was categorized as the lowest level of idiot, and that was that.

You know what an idiot is, don't you? An idiot is someone stupider than you. He's someone measurably more stupid than you. (You insist on his being measurable, because we live in a world of advertising fidelity, where all labels have to be legally provable, all soaps wash whiter, and all idiots can be treated like dirt. Sometimes hallowed dirt, but dirt nevertheless. There is no soap that can take the labels off people.) An idiot, you say, is someone who can be tried, convicted, condemned, and numbered by something you call I.Q. I.Q. is measured by trying to make somebody do something and penalizing him if he doesn't. It's something we invented in order to better castigate the stupid for being stupider than we, lest others should castigate us as well.

We made a mistake when we labeled Bedbug an idiot. Bedbug hasn't got an I.Q. and never did have. He can't be numbered, except maybe by the algebraic x. And you wouldn't want to number anyone like that, would you? Except, maybe, the soap which somehow never seems to wash whiter than anything. You do realize, I hope, that I'm not saying Bedbug hasn't got any intelligence. What I'm saying is that nobody was ever able to get into contact with it. Nobody has ever been able to shake it out so that they could count it and keep the change, so they could weigh it and find it wanting. Equally, they couldn't hammer it and find it malleable (Bedbug, classification ineducable); they couldn't bend it and find it plastic (Bedbug, condition incurable).

Bedbug is a nice guy. He is probably the only man in Canaan capable of real gentleness and kindness and love. Possibly the only man on Earth. Because Bedbug alone hasn't had his identity kicked into a jelly and sieved through a computer card. People tended to think of Bedbug at one time as a big, shaggy animal, some kind of lovable dog. That was a mistake. Bedbug isn't like a dog. Bedbug isn't like anything we know about. (Is that why we hated him?) Bedbug is a man, but not a man like us. The way he thinks and feels is his own, purely his own, and none of us will ever get near him. No one can come within a million miles of understanding him, not now, not in the days when he was a gross, grotesque freak of a baby, not ever. By the time he'd emerged from the womb, nobody who'd looked forward to knowing him wanted to continue to know him, or ever to try to know him. That was okay—they'd have been on to an automatic bummer. They wouldn't have stood a chance.

Maybe he sensed that, when he poked his head out into the daylight, and that's why he never bothered to exert himself in the least to try and know them. I can't say. I'm no closer to Bedbug than you are. I'm one of you, not one of him.

You can call it unfortunate if you like that no one could ever give him anything—not even pity. You can call it tragic that no one could ever offer him their crude and savage version of help. You can call it unfortunate that the world simply dropped him and left him to rot in a crazy house.

I don't call it anything, and neither did Bedbug. It's the way things were. That's the nineteen-seventies for you.

Let me give you a sketch of baby Bedbug's life. It's largely fabricated, as you will undoubtedly know, and you also know that I have one hell of an imagination, but I don't think you can call me a liar here, because I think this account reeks of reality.

It was a vast hospital. Such things grow by force of necessity. As society progresses, social maladjustment increases exponentially. (You can check the graphs.) There used to be a time, in the Golden Age (joke) when there were so few people we had to label loony that all you needed to accommodate a whole stateful was one cellar, a couple of cages, and a thriving clergy. By the time Bedbug was born in the seventies three people in four needed institutional head-shrinking at least once in their trivial lives. Psycho shops were busy places. Funny factories throughout the land were having conveyor belts put in.

No one had time for hopeless cases except amateurs and experimenters. You can call it a crying shame if you like, that no real pro could spare the sweat to tinker with Bedbug for a couple of hours a week, but let's face it, it was more a merciful escape. Whether you agree with me or not will depend on how shrunken your own head is.

But they fed him, clothed him, and treated his diseases. (Society isn't all bad—did I ever say it was?) They gave him opportunities to talk, which he didn't take. They gave him music to listen to, but they never found out if he even heard it. They tried to house-train him, and they gleefully chalked that up as their sole success. It wasn't the training, though. Bedbug couldn't be trained. It was simply his way. What he did, he did for his own reasons.

He walked, too, and used his hands cleverly. But no one ever managed to get through to him that what he ought to do with his hands was what they wanted him to, not what he wanted to do himself. This hurt their feelings greatly. Because he walked and used the toilet they were convinced he could understand them if only he'd *want* to. But he didn't. That's partly why we hated him.

One day, however, the great wheel of unhappy chance found him out. (Yes, I'm going to talk about the events leading up to the incarceration. I know I said I wouldn't because it doesn't matter, and that still goes. The events I am about to detail are quite fictitious, coming out of my own handsome head. I don't know why Bedbug is in Block C, and it *doesn't* matter. In all probability, the truth is stranger than fiction. But the fiction is more real, and that's what I'm going to set down now.) As I was saying, one day . . .

After twenty years and maybe a week or two more, of only occasional, cursory, and incidental attention, Bedbug was *discovered*. Obscure geographical regions do not mind this happening to them (though they might if they thought seriously about the consequences). Girl starlets positively dream of its happening to them. Bedbug, characteristically, did not even know that it had happened to him. In the beginning.

His case and his cause were enthusiastically adopted by a group of young doctors. Youth, as you know, has its own built-in drive and determination, and nutcracking as a profession is fitted with a compulsion to interfere. A bastard branch of medicine, shrinkery had adopted for itself the surgeon's holy motto, IF IN DOUBT, CUT IT OUT, and the primary directive of the needle-wielding experimental physiologists, SHOOT ANYTHING THAT MOVES.

These youngsters were therefore experimentally minded and unawed by the most mountainous of Mahometan challenges. They started, of course, with a handful of behaviorist tenets; cause and effect, these particular youngsters believed, was the God-given core of all things scientific. Stimulus and effect. Study stimulus and effect and you could crack any nut.

Unfortunately, Bedbug reacted to no stimuli.

Did they pack it up and call it a day? Like hell they did. These boys had no experience to chalk it up to. The discards of the last generation were already marked down in their black books as the first of their triumphs.

Bedbug MUST react!

He didn't mind the electric shocks.

He did not react to all the things they showed him—pornography, mirrors, signs.

He didn't mind the ultrasonics.

It didn't do anything to him when they stuck the needles in, masturbated him, dropped spiders down the back of his neck, filled him brimful of psychotropics, emetics, or laxatives. He didn't respond when they said please. The witch doctor failed to raise a laugh. The rite of exorcism was a dismal flop. Total darkness and blinding light came alike to him, as did stroboscopic alternation of same. Complete immobilization, ice baths, and sensory deprivation bothered him not in the least.

Apart from the processes of natural life, there was only one thing that Bedbug was known to do, and that was dream. They could spot the rapid eye movements while he was asleep. (Not while he was awake.) So they tried keeping him awake, keeping him away from his dreams. Had it failed, they would probably have resorted to starving him, asphyxiating him, or vivisecting him. All in a good cause.

As it turned out, though, there was no need to go to extremes. Torturing him with lack of sleep, denying him access to the only world that *he* knew to exist, eventually elicited a reaction.

He killed them all.

Every last one. He smashed up a lot of the hospital in the process, but he killed *only* his tormentors, and *all* his tormentors. He did not run amok, he simply knocked down a few doors, bent a few steel bars, and mashed the people he wanted to mash.

Nobody ever tried again.

Breaking out of Block C is impossible. Bedbug can do it. It remains impossible. Bedbug is Bedbug now. Incorruptible.

We all hate him.

Well, not quite. Everyone in Canaan likes him.

MADMAN'S DANCE

CHAPTER 12

In the Prison of My Dreams

She is naked, and because she knows my mind and its subtle convolutions she dons glittering jewels, which become stars decking the firmament of her body and soul. She is, herself, as dark as the night sky, and she is beckoning, and laughing with a hint of mockery. She is one, and she is a thousand, and she is a million. She is not temptation (*I* am temptation) but promise, promise fulfilled a thousand times, and times without number.

While she dances, the stars that she wears circle and wheel and sparkle and shine, and sing the hollow lament of the rhythm of the spheres. The pallor of the stones in their setting, and their life and their vibration fill me with an amber liquid sensation which drags at my throat and warms me within my breast like a glowing coal. The chaos of the cold stone lights and their sensuous welcome make me mad with misunderstanding.

And when she lays her body on the ground and allows herself to flow and fuse, she smiles with transport, the blackness of her eyes is limitless, and the lissome curling of her body as gentle as slow water in a level stream. She taunts me with her eyes and bewilders me with her gemstones, and she moves herself into strange imaginary constellations as she rolls. She is free and honest and she does not pretend, but the music of her movements has only lies to tell me. Her arms and her legs, her thighs and her breasts shine with constant sweat like distant stardust, drawing my vision beyond the limits of resolution, where I can see nothing real except with the treacherous eye of my mind. Her breasts, when she is clothed, bear shells of ruby-red sarcophrase and stars of white sapphire. Even then, she disturbs my silence as deeply as my own fears, and the very scent of her body casts my thoughts into a wild abyss of hope and dream and foreboding from which I hurl myself with desperation and dread. Hidden menace dances perilously close to haloed triumph in the sonorous melancholy of the pavane, and I am forever looking over my shoulder lest some faceless presence be lurking there to threaten my exclusive reward.

I think I see before me the echoes of another existence, peopled with madmen and—worse still—mad gods. I look at her, and out of the corner of my eye I see a looking-glass Alice, a strange fragment of a long-destroyed incarnation. In the lamplight stars of her decorated skin, I can almost see diamonds on a pack of playing cards, and jacks and queens and bullet-riddled aces. And a hundred thousand children and young men who claim to be the faded hours of Harker Lee, consigned and consigning to the oblivion of dead memory and replowed engrammic earth.

Who sends these ghosts to haunt me?

And the candle whose light is reflected in the facets of the stones of enchantment flickers and dies, and there is no light to fire my fancies and my fantasies, and I lay myself to sleep in the cradle of her thighs.

But in sleep, there comes no rest, for I pass only from dream to dream to dream, and there is no possible remission in the fateful continuity of life. I feel that the constancy of the flow of images is breaking me apart; I cannot stand the everlasting flow of it all, and I can no longer split the current of images into separate scenes. I am caught in a long transition, dreaming that I am dreaming that I am dreaming, and I flee down endless corridors of sleep, rebound through an infinity of mirror images, with not the least prospect of escape. There is no court of appeal. And yet, why should I need one? You are dead, Harker Lee, whoever you were. You cannot haunt me—why am I forced to live with these—the residue of your futile life—why? Who pursues me? I am alone. In all the universe, there is only myself. I am all that there is: I, mock-Satan, hiding my face behind a million masks and discarding a million more. There is no one here but my victims.

No one.

Leave me alone. I *will not* be a prisoner in my own skull. I *will not* yield to my foolish fears. If the hound of hell himself is after me . . . why, then, I will wait for him and he will lick my hand.

Yet the ghost whispers in my ear that you have me prisoner, that you have me locked in the condemned cell. Who is this ghost? There is *no* man-in-a-death-mask. There never was.

Who dares to put me to the question? Who dares to pretend to be my judge? This is hell, nor am I out of it, and I am Lord in hell as in all the universe. There is no one. . . .

I did *not* see Attila born.

I did *not* see the sun rise on Agincourt.

I did *not* see the collapse of the Aztec Empire.

I was *not* present at the death of Tamburlaine.

This hound of hell is chasing me, through all the fading years he seeks me still to seize me in his savage teeth and stain the waters of the world with my heartfelt tears.

My jailers threw away the key a thousand years ago. They have left me here to rot away. But the bones they left in hiding are growing flesh again, and bloodbeat is returning to my veins. They think one day I'll break in two, so they hate me all the more, and while they wait for me to break they'll add it to the score.

Their fear is eating their hearts like acid, they really want to run. But they need someone to blame it on, and it's going to be me.

It wasn't me who stole your wives, it wasn't me who killed your king, it wasn't me that burned those effigies of Jesus, it wasn't me who scorned your gifts of love.

It won't be me who dies tonight, whatever you might do. There's nothing I can do for you; it isn't me you fear. Tonight the falling stars are faster in their fall, like pointing fingers in the sky. And the words they spell in starlight might tell you that I'll die. But your words and signs can't hurt me, if that's the thing you want. If you want to see the streets run red, if you want to see me bleed, the hound of hell can't catch me, you can't hold me till he does, you'd better use a goat.

However much you hate me, I'm not going to die tonight. Not for you, not for anyone. This time, you can do your own dying. Not me. Not me.

I don't care what your name is. I don't know any Judas. I never did.

Titan Nine

CHAPTER 10
The Man Who Came Back

The doctor to whose care Lindquist had been consigned
was named Martinez. He was a little guy who looked as if
he ought to be smiling all the time. He wasn't smiling
now.

"How is he?" Jenny asked. Pure ritual.

"The same," Martinez told her, inevitably.

No better, no worse. How much worse could the poor
bastard get? He just lay there, looking every inch a
cadaver. No engagement whatsoever with his body. Blank
features, blank eyes, absolute stillness. There was a silver
helmet on his head which was connected to a computer
input. Across the room was a console with a plotter and
lineprinter. The chatter of the printer had been gagged so
that it did no more than murmur, but the plotter had been
able to keep its occasional click. And click it did, about
three times a minute, to testify that Johnny Lindquist was
still in there somewhere and could still flick a pointer with
the best of them.

"Look at the plot," said Jenny.

The paper was hanging down to the floor and rolling up. I tore off a strip and inspected it. I saw more or less what I'd expected to see. Big, slow deltas.

"So?" I said.

"Never mind the waves," she said. "Look at the subplots."

The subplots were the resonance currents—the traces which correlated best with the cytoanalogues in the brain—the life of the mind. It was impossible to track each neurone block, of course—even the helmet hadn't that much ambition—and a lot of incomplete patterns and ephemeral patterns didn't register, but the resonance finder went down deep—well below the crude frequency-sort into alpha, beta, and so on.

The real analysis would be coming out of the line-printer, but you can usually gather a good idea of what's going on and what's not from a brisk scan of the trained eye through the subplots. My eye, of course, wasn't trained.

"What can you see?" asked Hurst, who was suitably impressed by the clinical complexity of the operation.

I felt obliged to pretend so as not to disillusion the poor boy. I was surprised to find that I could make some sort of sense of it. I hadn't forgotten everything.

"Normal paleocortical activity," I said. "But with no knowledge of the mind-code it's difficult to see . . . is he right-handed?"

"Yes." It was Martinez who answered.

"Well, the impulses from the left neocortex are considerably different from those in the right. The fields are unbalanced—the right half is depleted. So if the left neocortex correlates with right-handedness he's not making a lot of use of his learning. If his cytoarchitecture is stacked normally he's a very active little lad inside his skull. The pons is cutting out all the bodily responses, though—not even a twitch."

"You're missing the point," said Jenny. I wasn't surprised.

"So okay," I said. "Did we come here to play guessing games? You're the one with the mind-reading license. It's only a hobby with me."

"Will," she said.

"How's that?"

"He no longer has free will."

I looked back at the trace. "Am I supposed to be able to read that?"

She shook her head, with slight impatience. "You can't read it," she said. "But it can be deduced."

"Yeah, well," I murmured, still ardently searching the trace for clues, "I guess I failed the exam."

Will is a modifier capable of altering the spatiotemporal activity of the neuronal network by exerting fields of analogue-predilection that become effective via the reactive properties of the vital cortex. There are two ways it can fail: if the modifying principle breaks down, or if the reactivity of the cortex is depressed. Either way you get an instant zombie.

I couldn't find a thing. I dropped the trace.

"Let's stop messing around," I said. "Is the printout intelligible?"

Martinez carefully tore off the pages of the lineprinter output, which were stacking themselves politely on the shelf provided for just that purpose. He passed them over to me without comment.

I looked at the garbage, trying to make sense out of computer jargon for the first time in several years, finding it harder than looking at graphs. I couldn't see a thing.

"It's all Greek to me," I said. "Just gibberish."

"Perfect score," said Jenny. "Not many people spot that. Most of them ask me what it means."

"What does it mean?" I asked.

"Now you've spoiled it. You were right the first time. It *is* gibberish."

"What's the point of having the computer turn out gibberish?" I asked, reasonably enough.

"The computer is programmed to make sense," she told me. "It has the decode process that we worked out before we sent him up operating quite normally."

I thought for a minute. "You're saying that his personality has been completely disintegrated?"

"No."

I gave vent to a quick snort of exasperation. "Then he's got himself a whole new private language. He's acting out fantasies that bear no relation to his old reality. A sort of metamorphosis of the mind."

"That's right. We think his mind has suffered a kind of perspective-inversion. His viewpoint was turned inside out, if you like. If *before* we consider him to have been *inside* himself, looking *out*, using an *inner* ego to act as arbiter and interpreter, then *now* he's *outside* himself, looking *in*, using an external—or at any rate totally *different*—ego to act as arbiter."

"How can he be outside himself?" asked Hurst, who was lost several minutes back, but was still trying valiantly to take an interest.

"You think he formed a new ego because his old one wasn't up to it?" I asked.

"What else can we think?" asked Jenny, rhetorically. "Johnny was a sane man. A very sane man. He was what one might call a counter-solipsist. A solipsist thinks that everything else is a figment of his imagination. Johnny, though, thought everything else was solidly, dramatically real. The solipsist can account for everything—he need never lack an explanation. But Johnny could exist only in the one reality-context. He had a *strong* mind—a very strong mind. But it was like a diamond—brittle. Uncrushable, but quite easily shattered.

"Johnny thought he was a unit of a universe. He hardly had any concept of self that was independent of that universe framework. In a different framework, which is obviously what he found in tachyonic phase—how could he adapt? What chance had he? But you, now—your concept of self is very different from Johnny's. It doesn't matter whether either of you was right or wrong, sane or insane—those things are relative to context. We're now beyond context, and it's your mind that is definitely the more *useful*. Understand, I'm not saying that Johnny was sane here and insane there, while you'll be sane there but insane here. Certainly not. You'll be as insane relative to the tachyonic context as you are to the Earthly context. But you have the flexibility. You have the adaptability. You see what I mean?"

"In a word," I said, "maybe."

"In hyperspace," she said, quite patient, because she was sure of her ground and could restate her case any number of ways, "the sane structures of Johnny's mind became useless. They shattered, were thrown out. The same thing would have happened if a mind which was 'sane' relative to the tachyonic phase was suddenly precipitated into the slower-than-light phase. Sane minds are narrow minds. But a mind which allows for other reality-contexts as a matter of course is a different matter.

It's 'insane' relative to any particular context, because it's badly adapted—a bad fit—but it can make some sort of adjustment to almost any context—if, that is, it can make adjustments at all. Your mind has adjusted to *here*; there's no reason it can't also adjust to *there*. You won't be sane—I'm certainly not saying that your schizoid view of reality is any more true than Johnny's normal one was. But it's the view we need. If we're right—and you can prove us right or wrong very soon now—space travel is for schizoids. Socially adjusted schizoids only, because it's just as bad to be a dogmatic schizophrenic as to be a dogmatic realist, but for schizoids, nevertheless."

"And ain't that a laugh?" I said, still looking at the printout. "But I don't see why it prints out anything at all. Why gibberish? Why not question marks?"

"It's not the same sort of program that was built from your model," said Martinez. "Your program is to assign keywords to patterns and thus gives us a picture of what you're thinking about and the patterns of change that occur. This program assigns letters and not words, so that something comes out even when no keyword in the vocabulary is applicable. We search for patterns in the letters—new, synthesized 'words' and frequencies of juxtaposition."

"You're trying to decipher his mind from pure theory?" I said. "I've heard of ambition, but . . ."

"We have his old model as well," said Martinez. "It may help. And we've come a long way since your initial breakthrough. There are theories about universal patterns and tendencies to make assignations in particular ways. Also, of course, we have some theories about reality-structures now that we didn't have earlier in the Project."

"Yeah," I said, "but theory is theory is . . ."

"We have a pure mind there," said Jenny. "The only one we've ever seen. A virgin mind, untroubled by heredity and conditioning. That's human nature, coming out of that computer. Johnny is a valuable commodity."

"Sure as hell," I said, with aggressive sarcasm. "Very valuable. To whom? To him? Very valuable indeed. And I suppose your machines will keep him alive till he's five hundred, considering he's not about to do anything ill-advised that might jeopardize his health, like living? We've got men in Block C like that—you try hitching Bedbug to your machines. He's pure human nature, too. Dead from the neck up and the waist down."

"You could put it that way," said Jenny flatly, forestalling Martinez. She knew me.

"I've heard of taking arms against a sea of troubles," I said, "and by opposing . . . well, you know the rest. But do you honestly believe that you can send me into chaos—a mariner drowning in a sea of troubles—in order that I can make some sort of sense out of it? Order out of chaos? Who am I, God?"

"No." The denial came from Martinez.

"Just an impure case of human nature," I said, dryly.

"Anything God could do . . ." commented Hurst. I guess ten minutes without an inane remark must have been pushing his record fairly close.

"Thank you," I said. "Faith is a wonderful thing."

I looked again at the trace that was telling the story of Lindquist's mind. If you set a monkey to producing random letters in a sequence, rumor has it that he will one day present you with a copy of the complete works of Somerset Maugham. You can see why no one's bothered to try the experiment. What was Lindquist going to produce? THE SKYLARK OF SPACE? A LA RECHERCHE DU

TEMPS PERDU? CATCH A FALLING STAR AND PUT IT IN YOUR POCKET?

None of them. If he tried really hard, the net production of his thirty score and ten years might be THE QUICK BROWN FOX JUMPED OVER THE LAZY DOG. Complete with typographical errors.

"Do me a favor," I said. "If I come back like that, put me in a glass box and put me in the foyer of a strip club. Don't let me fall as low as this."

"You won't come back like that," said Jenny.

"Well if I don't, put Hurst in the glass box instead. He's the guy who gets to be me if I don't, isn't he?"

I don't think Hurst liked the idea.

I left Lindquist to his private agony. Jenny stayed behind. Hurst followed me, dogging my footsteps like the avenging angel.

"You remind me of an old joke," I told him.

"Which one?" he wanted to know.

"You're never alone with schizophrenia."

Cage of Darkness

CHAPTER 9
Contacts

Some of the men in Canaan have wives and children. When he is condemned to Block C, effectively he has already lost them. It is not always as simple as that. They often continue to haunt him, just as—I imagine—he haunts them in their own version of existence, for years. The fact that the haunting is a haunting of love and futile need and the carcass of hope rather than a specter of vengeance does not make it any the less terrible—nor, indeed, any the less fearful, though the fear is of a different kind. It is the appearance of the vengeful phantasm that is feared, while it is the departure of the phantasm of human contact which is dreaded as the ultimate extinction of being in the world.

The incoming letter is always and absolutely devoid of hope and life no matter what its contents. The Dear John letter, when it comes, is virtually a euthanasia. It is the outgoing letter which is the focus of uncertainty. That is the contact with something to offer, apparently. That is the contact which will always retain some kind of mean-

ing. The incoming letter cannot prevail against the
environment; it can bring in nothing of the outside world
for more than a fleeting instant, because nothing of the
outside world can survive in this kind of a cage. The outgoing letter, on the other hand, carries part of the inmate back, away from the prison, out into the daylight. It
is a kind of escape; it tells the inmate that he still has some
kind of existence in the world which human consensus says
is real. It may be only an existence scribbled on paper, like
the works of an author long dead, but it is an existence of a
kind and an existence which can continue to grow and
ramify as long as the inmate can put pen to paper.

The outgoing letter, I *must* make you realize, is a thing
of the utmost importance. This is vital to your understanding. Will you please accept, if only as a working hypothe-
sis, the extreme importance of the outgoing letter? I
promise you that this will be the only favor this document
will ever ask of you.

Now think.

Censorship operates with respect to every piece of paper
that passes in and out of Block C. They censor the books
that come in, and if you underline words in the books they
rub out the lines on the way out. All lines can be erased.
There are only pencils—soft pencils—available to inmates
in Block C. When a prisoner writes a letter, he presses
down hard, to make sure that even if the words are rubbed
out the impression remains. He runs the risk of having his
letter destroyed in consequence, if he strays too far over the
borderline of what is "tolerable," but it gives him a little
extra latitude. I have known men who would quite
literally write certain passages in their letters in their own
blood to prevent erasure. This is futile, because such letters
are virtually certain to be destroyed.

These are some of the rules of censorship:

A prisoner must not write about prison conditions.

A prisoner must not write about prison guards.

A prisoner must not write about prison events.

A prisoner must not write about escaping.

A prisoner must not write about desperation, about the possibility of his committing suicide, nor about anything which implies that his condition, mental or physical, is intolerable.

I offer these without comment, save to say that each and every one of these rules may be transgressed to a degree which the censor may consider "harmless." One never knows where the line is drawn. More important, one never knows whether one's letters get out unviolated or not, or to what extent they have been violated if so. Incoming letters which might tell a prisoner about such censorship are themselves censored.

There are other rules:

Letters may be sent only to, and received from, people on a list of authorized correspondents which the prison authorities must approve.

Only two letters may be sent per week. (There is no limit on the number of letters received in a week.)

One may write only to individuals that are personally known to the prisoner, never to individuals who are not known to the prisoner and never in any circumstances to an organization of any kind.

Again, no comment. But an observation: people outside try many devices for making their letters less easy to censor—pressing down hard to make an impression, using all kinds of code and invisible ink. Most fail. Many letters are simply intercepted. There is no way for the prisoner to tell his correspondents on the outside about the things which may or may not have been censored from letters. Any such reference is automatically censored.

* * *

Perhaps there is one thing more to be said about contacts, and that is about the guards. They are always present. There are always a lot of them. They are human, too.

But there are always the cameras as well. At every junction there is a camera set high in the wall. Total surveillance at all times. We can never know who it is that enforces the rules and regulations of the prison. Perhaps the guards would let us live, just a little, if they could. But they have one endless chorus which puts an end to all our efforts to make human contacts out of them. The regulations rule absolutely supreme.

"It's not me, mate," the guard will say. *"It's the camera."*

MADMAN'S DANCE

CHAPTER 13
Eternity in the Balance

I enter chaos.

I see the fury of irrationality. I am that fury. The four elements—fire, water, earth, and air—have beaten their plowshares into swords and are bearing arms against the people. The universe is being torn apart by the massive forces of their bickering.

Beneath me, all around me, within me, the surfaces split. They show me sheer faces of bloodstained rock, and then they slam together again, mocking me. Fountains of molten rock and flame leap into the skies, dying like roman candles. People climb the fountains like beanstalks, ride them like broomsticks, and shatter into sparks.

A pulpy liquid mass that is the grass that conquered empires is still half-visible here and there, but in most places it is reduced to black ash indistinguishable from the ash of the petty emperors. The birds are flying high in the fiery sky—I wish I am a bird—but when the flames rend them, they are not born again. I am the phoenix, too. Only I. Only one.

There is no place of safety in the turmoil. The paint on

my mask is melting, and I can feel the electric sparks within my brain surging and swelling, preparing themselves to be a cyclone. The suns are neither aloof nor uncaring. They spin like wheels and flare and cough. They are vomiting fissioning hydrogen.

In time, the atoms will be torn apart, and the electrons and the mesons themselves. The worlds wave like flags in the random wind, flapping and clattering and complaining. Each time their colors are visible they shudder and change. Vast clouds of dust are rising everywhere, blotting out all semblance of eternity, carrying with them the roasted spores that might have been some kind of hope for the rebirth of time, in another place, if there is another place, and not just nothing wrapped around the far horizons.

Slivers of flesh and fragments of souls slide from the edges of ever widening cracks in the fabric of space, to fill the yawning crevasses and overflow into nowhen.

A blister of substance bursts somewhere close at hand, and I am bathed in flame and flux. For an instant, the stream of serum is whirling around me in a hot-air cocoon, and the harsh light of it plucks at the skin on my eyes. Then I am clear again, watching my infinities give up their sick ghosts into the painted skies.

Traveling from the far end of a new-formed furrow in the universe, a vast wave of living tissue is swept by black flood water toward my station, as the barrier between space and unspace which supports the tide bucks and heaves in the grip of a fever. A second wave, approaching the first from the nearer end, picks up colossal speed, and both waves rear up on their hind parts, growing a million eyes apiece to watch the coming crash. The edges race ahead as the wave fronts become concave. The vast bowls of amoebic plasm become steeper and steeper as they reach for one another.

They meet.

A kaleidoscopic image of scattered eyes is all that comes of the furious copulation. There is no chance for anything else to happen. Just eyes, fluttering and rattling like marbles in a whirling box.

I watch a chain of mountains explode, gunning their hearts at the multiple suns. But their substance is only flotsam and jetsam in the wreckage of the sky. A fissure splits beneath my feet and gradually spreads—I am straddling the gulf, with one foot on either lip, and the debris of the universe flows around my feet as it surges to fall into the sightless depths. The gaping abyss grows and grows.

I watch the vivid lightning dissect the darkening blurs that is all that remains of the horizons. I see pinnacles and spires tumbling into dust. I see in the sky that was above me, but is falling slowly like autumn leaves, the wrathful reflection of a vast holocaust which is consuming me. I see the flames themselves—all that is left now that matter is destroyed—cavorting in my wounds, I see the plumes and vortices of my crumbling being, red in the castellate flames.

At last, I cry for help, and the sound of my voice, being the only thing in the whole chain of universes to be found within sleep within sleep within sleep . . . is an infinite scream.

But the *answer* . . .

Now I stand on top of the largest mountain in the world, and it is firm beneath my feet. The western horizon is a hundred and three miles away, but the road which leads to the eastern horizon is only sixty-four miles long, because the mountains of the east are quite large.

On top of the mountain grows a single flower. A lotus. Which opens its petals every morning to give birth to a tiny (not altogether human) child which grows until the sun is at its zenith, and which spends the afternoon placidly decaying into old age and senility.

I watch the child during the whole of a morning, while he plays, and learns not to play.

In the afternoon, I talk to him, about the possible existence of life after birth. Our conversation is pleasant, and we have a mutual understanding, despite the fact that we disagree.

But in the evening, he grows maudlin; he curses and abuses me, his envy and his anger spilling out from his lips and blackening his image. He complains of the coming agony of darkness and the eternal oblivion which will only pass when he is born again into the same day, over and over.

I speak to him softly, but I cannot console him.

In the end, he has only one thought in his wizened head, and that is a somewhat bitter one.

"If only," he says, "the sun might rise tomorrow in the west and set in the east."

I ask him, very quietly, for help, though I know he is already dead.

But the *answer* . . .

Then there is a cold wind and a cold night wrapping my face with wax and needles of pain. There are faceless people huddled all around me. They do not know one another, but they press closer and closer in fear and misery, hoping to avoid death by freezing. They do not try to know one another; they dare not even speak. They do not *want* to know one another, but they all need to share the little warmth which they have between them.

One of them might live through the night.

They do not touch me.

Someone approaches, hidden by the darkness.

In sudden fear, the people find their voices, and they cry out, "Who are you? What do you want?"

No voice answers them.

"We can give you nothing," they say, "We do not know you. Show yourself so that we can know whether you are a man or a creature of the darkness."

Suddenly, there is light, as the stranger lights the hair upon his head. It burns with a fierce, unquenching flame.

"I am a man," he says.

But with his face haloed by fire, his eyes gleaming like sapphires, his voice hot and sweet, his hands catching and holding great sparks which he holds forth as gifts for the people, he seems so like a god.

I cry to him for help. My voice is sharpened by the icy air, and my words fly like a dagger to his face.

I see his face now, and it is no face at all, but a death-mask.

The face behind the death-mask, I have every reason to believe, is my own face.

And the answer . . .

Titan Nine

CHAPTER 11

Just Lie Down and Relax— This Isn't Going to Hurt a Bit

The physical side of TITAN was, so far as I was concerned, a good deal less troublesome than the psychological. The hardware—such of it as I was allowed to feast my unsecurity-cleared eyes upon—was fearsome in aspect, but dedicated to reducing life to the utmost simplicity.

High gee and low gee were not particularly demanding to one of my asthenic physique. It took a little practice, certainly, but I soon adjusted myself to the sensations involved. I had no predilection toward skysickness.

However, high and low gee in a centrifuge rig-out is one thing; an iron maiden is quite another. You all know about iron maidens—boxes full of spikes beloved (it is said) by Torquemada and his merry bunch of religious enthusiasts. The TITAN iron maiden was less picturesque, and they were more careful inserting the spikes, but the principle was exactly the same. You know the hole at the bottom where the blood runs out? That was there, too.

Liquid food was delivered into the femoral vein. Urine was taken out of the bladder at about the same location (but through a different tube). Gut, testicles, and sundry other bits of apparatus were placed under metabolic suppression, so they didn't miss out on their habits too much. Wrists, legs, and waist strongly manacled.

I pointed out that I couldn't scratch my nose. They assured me it wouldn't itch. I didn't believe them.

They gave me courses in isometrics and transcendental meditation, and they were just as serious about both. I had no illusions about the potential usefulness of either.

"If I was determined," I said, while they were locking me in for the first long practice run, "I could pick a hole in myself with my growing fingernail and short-circuit all the apparatus with the leaking blood."

"Your fingernails won't grow," they assured me.

"Exactly how much of me is going to function in the way that nature intended?" I asked.

"All of you," they told me. "We're just giving nature a helping hand."

"What about my brain?"

"If your brain operated as nature intended," they pointed out, with commendable wit, "you wouldn't be here. We'll put you in a state of light tranquilization for the duration of the flight. Not enough to make you high or knock you out. Just enough to keep your adrenal cortex in line and give the rest of your bodily emergency mechanisms a sense of responsibility. You'll probably notice a slight psychotropic effect; you won't be allowed to get as scared as you otherwise might."

"You try and stop me," I threatened. "I shall be scared

shitless every light year of the way. I'm a coward through and through."

"You'll die laughing," they promised me, undiplomatically.

"Are you sure this Heath Robinson affair will stand up to the gees on takeoff?" I asked.

"Easy," they assured me. "How d'you feel?"

"Just terrible," I said, with winning honesty. "How long am I scheduled to be locked up for the dummy run?"

"Twelve hours the first time."

"You're joking."

"Two days the second time," he said. "The third time it'll be the real thing. Full dress and remember your cues, or else."

"When's takeoff?" I asked, innocently.

"Zero hour," they informed me, helpfully. "Classified."

"You've been in a flat rush lately," I said. "Must be close."

"No rush," they said. "We always work this way. We never hurry. Just work fast. No corners cut. You'll be fine."

Promises, promises.

"Right," said the medic, before he left me alone to my torture, "we're on our way. There'll be someone to talk to at all times"—he indicated the mike over my head—"so scream all you like."

"Does Hurst have to do this, too?" I asked.

"Oh, yes," he assured me. "Anything else?"

There was no way of passing the time. It had to pass all by itself. I didn't talk much to begin with, but soon I realized that the mike was a good friend. I'd thought it would be easy; after all, I spent years in the deprived environment of Canaan. But at least, even in Block C, I had room to move, and I could scratch my nose any hour of the day or night whether it itched or not.

There's freedom and freedom.

Twelve hours felt like twelve days. I wondered what the weeks of the real thing would seem like. . . .

Cage of Darkness

CHAPTER 10

We All Need Somebody to Look Down On

Manny Madoc was, by profession, a purveyor of pornography. By implication, this made him a corrupter of the innocent and a destroyer of society—a menace second only to that of Cain Urquhart and his happy band of bombers.

In actual fact, he was a rational, even-tempered guy with a kind face and a helpful disposition.

The world was not kind to Manny. Which shows what lousy taste the world has, because Manny belonged to a class of person whose presence on Earth is absolutely vital to the well-being and peace of mind of the common man. (Need I emphasize that I am not referring to his stock-in-trade?)

Manny Madoc was a much-arrested man in his early days (his days in Block C are most definitely his later days), owing to the fact that he was generally too poor to raise the protection money adequate to safeguard his calling. The substance of the charges irregularly laid against him used to vary over quite a range, but usually consisted of (or were at least inspired by) public-spirited attacks upon the morality and the propriety of the material which he marketed somewhat inefficiently. (He also printed it himself, in a small way. He was devoted to his vocation.) Occasionally there was a drunk-and-disorderly or a petty larceny thrown in to add insult to injury. Once they nailed him for slander, and another time they came within an inch of crucifying him with a blackmail allegation. If he'd been black, foreign, or Jewish it might well have stuck, but despite his name he was lily-white and a good Protestant.

He spent, in all, fifteen or sixteen of his best years being hustled by the nasties and busted by the gendarmes. Five of those years he spent in the jug—two of them because one time he figured he couldn't possibly do worse on his own than his last lawyer had done for him (a four-hundred-dollar fine) and discovered how wrong he could be. Being neither an efficient legal diplomat nor an orator of genius, he neatly avoided the statutory fine and ran straight into the jail term.

As a further guide to the guilelessness (nay, even stupidity) of Manny's character, it may be productive to proceed further with the tale of that particular sentence. He was sent first of all to a pleasant open prison where, except for digging the occasional field or resurfacing a road here and there, life was moderately bearable. However, having been assigned the rather comfortable and enviable job of painting the prison outhouses, he conceived a daring and pathetically simple plan of escape. Needless to say, he was picked up within a matter of days while in bed with his wife. He was not returned to the pleasant establishment but sent instead to a more secure place of confinement, where he found himself for the first time among murderers rather than among thieves. (Murderers of somewhat lesser talent than the Canaanites, the Law would have us believe.) Although minor murderers tend to be of considerable moral standing (and therefore out of sympathy with Manny's outside career), he found them more congenial company than he was used to.

Of the crime(s) which resulted in Manny's becoming a member of our own select group in Block C, I have nothing to say save that they occurred at a much later date than the part of his life which I am studying here. If you remember, I am painting this word-picture of Manny the jaded pornographer in order to preface an argument to the effect that Manny is one of the people we need.

Argument follows immediately:

Manny is a failure. Manny is a sucker. He was custom built to be a modern-day scapegoat. He is a perfectly proportioned fall guy.

Manny is a walking joke. The world could ill afford to lose such a man. There may be a hundred more like him, but the world of today cannot afford to lose a single one. We need a thousand.

The desperation of our need for this kind of social victim can be seen in the millions of people who pay close attention to the grotesqueries inhabiting the scandal pages of many a top-selling newspaper; in the millions who wallow thrice weekly in television soap operas chronicling the shame and humiliation of common people who may easily be identified as the Joneses next door; in the millions who can gloat over the horrific intimacies of agony columns and courtroom dramas and brutal cartoons and deodorant commercials.

Manny is the guy you score off. Manny is the guy who finishes behind you in the human race. Manny is the guy who cops *your* share of the world's deluge of bad luck.

Manny is the guy who slips on the banana skin, who is comically impotent, who is firmly trodden into the dirt by the weight of authority which *you* can carry with ease. Every time Manny gets a bit part in a newspaper carve-up, he does his bit for your edification and gratification and self-glorification. You only have to pass him on the street to feel good and clean and human inside your sweaty skin.

You *need* Manny—Manny and a million others. You, the self-satisfied people, the comfortable people, the I-know-what's-right-and-what's-wrong people. The bitchers and the binders and the vicious mockers who delight in the failure of the victims trapped and tortured in the communal net authored by your wishes and knotted by your silent voices.

You.

Manny's shoulders are the platform for the tenuous pride of the common man. Manny's misfortunes are the vicarious delight of the respectable man. Manny's failures are the safe foundation for the contentment of the common man.

And the punch line of the joke?

Block C, where else?

You need these people to live so you can kill them. Block C, for crimes too hideous to contemplate and quite irrelevant.

Go ahead and laugh. It's your joke.

There's Cain, too. I mentioned Cain, if you remember, when I began to describe Manny. Cain Urquhart was a man who used to place the blame squarely where it belongs—on everybody. His own share of the blame, needless to say, was ameliorated by all kinds of extenuat-

ing circumstances—primarily that he, at least, had tried
(is trying still, and intends to go on trying) to *do* something
about it.

Cain always knew the world was all wrong, as does
everyone else, but perhaps he used to feel it more than
most, because he was definitely not prepared to tolerate it.

In fact, like most people whose lives are deeply steeped
in dogma and belief, Cain was extremely intolerant of
anything and everything which met with his disapproval,
no matter whether that disapproval arose from an emotional reaction, a conditioned fear, a whim, or simply
because his beliefs insisted that he hate. All the other
sources of disapproval, of course, became interpreted in
the dogmatic terms of those beliefs (you can't just hate
things; you've got to have a belief which lets you). Dogma,
as you well know (unless you are dogmatic yourself), can
accommodate any amount of perversion by fear, greed,
hatred, lust, and sheer meanness, and still remain absolutely inflexible.

To sum up Cain, he was a man who believed in right
and wrong.

It was probably a mere accident of fate that he didn't
happen to be a devout Catholic or an Orthodox Jew or a
Nazi, a spiritualist, a conservationist, a sex maniac, or a
psychiatrist. He was stamped by a stamp of a different
color, that's all. Cain was an anarchist.

There was a time when ANARCHY was a proud word
standing for the absence of anything in the form of
organization or government. In those days it was a sensible
philosophy and by no means dogmatic. It spoke for itself
(so to speak). These days, however, the word has assumed
a dogmatic meaning by virtue of the fact that it has been
taken over by the believers and made to stand for the

absence of anything in the form of *wrong* organization or *wrong* government. (Or *right,* if you happen to be a different kind of believer.) Cain, of course, was an anarchist in the recent sense of the word.

His behavior was 90 percent similar to that of the other brands of believer (Nazi, sex maniac, etc.) in that he went around nursing a strong dislike for disagreement and worrying about things. His dogma leaned toward the activist philosophy, which meant that instead of reacting to disagreement by dignified ignorance (like, say, Flat-Earthers) he believed in killing them (like, say, in the Spanish Inquisition).

Cain Urquhart was not a leader of men who could sway vast crowds with hysterical shouting. He was an underfed, undersized, undersexed, underdeveloped, underrated underdog. He had a few friends, though, and they used to meet occasionally for a communal hate-in and to make a few bombs.

He was grossly misunderstood, mainly because most people didn't seem to share his deep love of social explosions.

He was never credited with any really spectacular bangs. The Golden Gate Bridge, the Washington Monument, the Taj Mahal, the Church of Christ the Saviour in Addis Ababa (full) and the East Chicago nuke were all the explosions of other, more charismatic bombers.

All in all, at a rough guess, I don't suppose Cain killed more than twenty or thirty people, whose cash value was only a matter of a few thousand (they were all capitalists), and probably no more than three were cops. If you add this up, it credits Cain with destruction of about .0000000000000001 of the gross national product and about the same (perhaps a little larger) fraction of the human race. The population explosion undid Cain's explosions people-wise in about seven seconds, give or take a Chinese or two. Still, as Karl Marx and Jesus are both reputed to have remarked, every little bit helps.

But what would you do without Cain's intrepid band of outlaws? Where would you find your society demons? Your political crusades? Where else could you buy such absolute sincerity and purity and rationality in which to clothe your hatred? Cain is just one more of the vast legion of off-the-peg victims who enables you to destroy without a qualm. You need him. You really do.

If you're lucky, you might live next door to a Cain Urquhart, in which case you have an ever available laugh at the bastard's expense. You don't have to wait for the aphids to wreck his roses. He only has to step out of the door.

Go ahead and laugh.

Everybody needs a good laugh once in a while.

MADMAN'S DANCE

CHAPTER 14

Vanished from My Hand, Left Me Blindly Here to Stand

There was a time, in my earliest childhood, when my life was like any other, unless my memory, or my sense of timing, plays me false.

I remember holding toys in my open hands, and finding that water tastes bitter, and cursing the world for it.

I remember shouldering arms against a sea of troubles.

I remember erasing in my mind all attempts to find love, to pretend hope, to regret the death of happiness. I strangled every strangling frustration. With barbed wire.

I remember the weaponless executioners, passing by, knowing and uncaring, as I suffocate beneath the plague of indifference.

I never blamed luck. I never could believe in luck.

I never blamed myself. I never could believe in myself.

239

I cursed, but I could never find the delicacy of hand to make the soap doll anything but faceless.

I laughed, like an idiot, when anything died.

I cannot go back to such strange and heartbreaking beginnings, not armed with the knowledge that could make those days of innocence into an everlasting tragedy. What I did not know, I will not tell myself. I cannot return, in any case, because the child that grew up to become half a man is beside me now. I cannot enter his spirit, nor he mine. We coexist. We understand each other exactly insofar as the crocodile brain which shelters behind the pig brain which shelters behind the human brain can understand its playmates. We each have our journeys, we are each in the middle of them.

They are not the same. We have different goals and different values.

Because I am only half of a man, and that half mostly words, I am often called upon to settle disputes when I pause momentarily in my journey. The three goddesses, who have decided to set aside the infamous judgment of Paris on the grounds of corruption and dubious constitutional validity, come to me with a rotted apple from which one bite—and all the gold—is missing.

They ask me to award it to the most beautiful. They have one-track minds.

The first of the three, and the tallest, who has eyes flashing with star-glare, approaches me and says, "I can give you the knowledge of the world, and a lot of power."

I am a man without ambition, and I certainly have not the vanity of kings.

"No," I say.

When the second comes to me, I ask her, "What is the nature of your bribe?"

She replies, "The future. The gift of success. What you can do, that you will do."

No one knows better than I my intrinsic limitations. I prefer her serenity and quietness to the bold, offensive beauty of the first, but I am not in the habit of working for nothing.

I go looking for the third, who is slender and shadowy and—insofar as my own poor judgment can possibly tell—the most beautiful of the three in actual fact. She is glowing with golden light and life.

"What have you to offer me in return for the apple?" I ask her.

"Only dreams," she says. Either she has confidence in my honesty and in herself, or she has lost interest since Paris. It is not, when all is said and done, a very nice apple. Not any more.

I pause to contemplate my decision, in the meantime taking another bite out of the unsavory fruit. I discover a large maggot within it. At the sight of the maggot, all three goddesses shudder and turn into old hags.

I throw the apple away, and it falls into a fast stream, to be borne away by the current. When I look back, all three of them are still chasing it. The maggot is chasing them.

I console myself with the thought that I have the dreams anyway, though the promises they make me are forgotten as soon as I awake. No one, after all, can hold fine sand or cool water in his clenched fist.

Helen of Troy stands on the terrace which tops the wall where it curves away from the sea. She is accompanied by a guard.

Her eyes are roaming the distant horizon of the sea, and she stands with such intense stillness that it seems she has been there for some hours. She might be waiting for a sail to appear in the distance, or for the rising of a special star.

Her mouth forms words, but she does not speak aloud. The name of Harker Lee forms on her lips several times, and it seems that she might be praying. But her eyes are steady and staring, not closed, and her head is high, not bowed.

She wears a long garment of silky white material, folded but not pinned at the shoulder or tied about the waist. Her long black hair is decorated by clasps formed into golden wreaths, and spiraled by a ribbon of creamy lace. She wears scarlet moccasins upon her feet. Around her waist is a bracelet of wrought glass, carrying tiny patterns of metal filaments, which send silver hyphae into the flesh of her arm, reaching for the autonomic nerves.

She begins to hum a slow, sad tune, while her gaze still lingers on the face of Alio Shan and the pearly path of moonlight which crosses the sea toward the giant wall.

Her face is very thin. The cheekbones stand out. Her complexion is distinctly yellow. Her eyes, instead of irises, have tiny skulls, each with two black pupils.

I am a thousand ships too late.

Still, I can become addicted to the sight and taste and touch of her body, which she still wears well. Especially in such times as she extends herself upon a couch, or dances by starlight. The shimmering wraiths of her jet black hair fall like waves of a restless ocean, or sway as though at the ministrations of a warm wind. My eyes are transported into distant dimensions, where I can see only a universe of cut glass and dark skin, with the parts of her body and the elements of my soul dissipated into the slashed lines and the many-shaped translucent faces.

Her skulled eyes continually search through this many-colored mosaic chaos, like two identical liquid globes of gold and chrome and anguish. They move to a secret cadence, following an invisible scent that trails like the wake of a fleeing snake over and between the light-filled surfaces of this crystalline space.

She is lost in the magic of my own liquidness, trapped by the shapelessness of her form, the easy disconnection of her attributes, but she retains a gentle rhythm, an integrity, a unity, which defied the cutting edges of the diamond leaves and the angry sapphire thorns of the mallarmite roses. She does not bleed; she cannot weep. She flows like purple wine or heavy oil. Her omnipresence is overpowering, a folded, cloaking sky woven with a multitude of silver sperm.

THIS IS TITAN BASE CALLING CANAAN. TITAN BASE TO CANAAN. ACKNOWLEDGE PLEASE. . . .

And the answer. . . .

Titan Nine

CHAPTER 12

Standing on the Brink
of Infinity,
Looking at My Watch

When they took me out of the iron womb, I couldn't walk. Nobody was even sympathetic. After all, I'd had nothing to do but sit around, had I? Everybody else had been *working.* There were a lot of people worse off than me, weren't there?

Name two.

Only I still couldn't stand up. Hurst had to carry me out of the mock-up into the jeep, and then out of the jeep into the apartment. He was a big, strong lad, and I didn't promise to return the favor. Jenny was waiting for me at home, and Hurst disappeared discreetly.

"It's nice to have friends," I commented, as he disappeared.

"Him or me?" asked Jenny.

"It's nice to have more than one friend," I said, too tired to make meaningless discriminations.

"How d'you feel?" she asked. She really was a one for asking silly questions.

"How the hell d'you think I feel?" I sat down on the couch and massaged myself lovingly.

"You want some food?"

"Damn right. And a cigarette. And a drink. Not necessarily in that order, but all now. Then I'll feel human enough to take a shower."

"You don't have to be human to wash."

"No, but it helps. Come on, woman, move. Weeds, booze, and food, and don't waste time."

She gave me a cigarette and lit it for me. "No drink on premises," she said. "Blame yourself. I told them to send some around with the food."

"I thought you'd be only too happy to cook it with your own sweet hands," I said.

"Housework ruins sweet hands," she told me. "Don't you ever watch TV?"

"Not where I was," I told her. "Beyond even the reach of TV."

"Next time," she said, "it'll be for real."

"Glad to hear it," I said. "But not tomorrow morning, please."

"When do you want to go?"

"I have a choice?"

"All the choice we can give you. As soon as humanly possible, but it's up to you to decide what's humanly possible. You're cleared now. It's your party from here on."

I was suspicious. "I don't really have a choice, do I?" I

said. "This is a line. You're trying to get me to voluntarily take away some of your precious responsibility. You were right a while back when you said it's easier to be the fall guy than the guy who has to push him over the edge. I'm falling. Like a sack of potatoes. I'm ready when you are, only not tomorrow morning. Please."

She didn't say anything for a moment or two. I guess I'd sounded a little sharp. But I'd just been in the maiden for two days, and I was sore.

Finally, she caught my eye and looked hard at me, to prepare me for the fact that what she was about to say was serious. Not that I ever thought any of it wasn't.

"Monday," she said.

"It's not my birthday," I said. "It'll do. It's been Monday all along, hasn't it? I didn't really have a choice?"

"We'd have postponed it if you'd said so."

"No point in hanging around."

"I don't think waiting would do any of us any good."

"No."

There was a discreet knock at the door. Jenny answered it, and came back with a tray. There was steak and potatoes, but only in very small quantities. The rest was all mush. The booze was beer. I don't like beer.

"Got to take it easy," she said.

"So it seems," I said. "Don't get the choice, do I?"

She shoved the tray into my lap. I'd recovered enough by now to sit up and make use of the coffee table. It was at an awkward height, but you can't have everything.

"Tell me," I said, "one way and another I've accumulated quite a cache while I've been here. After the flight, I'll be modestly well off. What can I actually *do* with my money?"

"Whatever you want."

"They'll let me off base, then."

"Under escort, yes. I'm afraid you'll have to put up with the company of a Major Hurst or similar for pretty much the rest of your life."

"They won't get bored. I suppose the idea is to drive me back into space in order to get away from them."

"You'll go back."

"Do I get a choice about that?"

"Some. But you won't have much competition in the field of starship piloting. And we will put pressure on you. But I think you'll ride TITAN TEN without having your arm twisted. And ELEVEN. And . . ."

"I can count."

"Quite so," she said.

"I see," I said. "When I come back, I count. I'm one of the family. I matter. My opinions have weight. I'm not just a pawn. I get promoted to queen. Or thereabouts."

"Thereabouts," she said.

"I always wanted to run a Project," I said.

"All you have to do is come back," she assured me. Promises, promises.

"I'll tell you what I do want," I told her. "I want a crew. I want some choice about the boys I take out with me. I want Judas Dancer and Luis Dalquier. I want Sam and I want Con."

"You want them all out of the prison."

"That's right," I said. "All of them. Bedbug, too. Will I have the weight to pull that?"

"I think so."

"The army and the prison won't stop me?"

"I don't think *they'll* have the weight."

"The army gets the publicity—Hurst poses for the pretty pictures."

"That may figure outside the perimeter fence, but inside the base—inside the Project—you're the man that counts. Mike will back you. If Mike retires, Fred Jacobson will back you. I think it can be done."

"I'm not fooling," I said. "I want those men out. All of them. Including Bedbug. No matter how old they are, or in what physical shape. Even if we can't use them as pilots and/or passengers."

"We'll use them," she promised. "We'll find a use for them."

I hoped she wasn't stringing me along. I really hoped that she meant what she said. I wasn't making any threats, but I knew in my own mind that I wasn't going anywhere near the stars if those men were still locked in their filthy dungeon. Once was to try. If it got serious, well then, I could turn my attention to the serious side of life.

"It could be worse being right than being wrong," I said, absently intruding into the conversation another thread of thought I'd been working on.

"No," she said. She knew what I meant. She'd thought, too. She'd been thinking for years.

"Mike Sobieski's dream died with Lindquist," I said. "The human race can't have the stars. Not the way he wanted it."

"You're a member of the human race," she told me.

"I wonder."

"We'll adopt you."

"Because you need me. Big deal. All these years an outcast, and then, Come back, Harker—all is forgiven. I don't even have to forgive. I don't get the choice. It's you that hands out the labels. Human, schizo."

"When you pilot that ship," said Jenny, "you're human. You're carrying Mike Sobieski, and you're carrying me."

"Are you sure?" I said. "Are you sure that come next year, or the year after, both you and Mike might not sit down and think: the road to the stars isn't open. It's as firmly shut as it was before FMA was ever thought of. Only madmen can go to the stars. Only our filth and our vermin. Do we really want that? Can the human race really permit the stars to be polluted as the Earth was polluted before we invented places like Block C? Do we really want the stars on those terms? Isn't that the way it'll be when the truth does eventually leak out? What happens when they begin to line up for their tickets to the stars and they find a notice on the ticket office saying SCHIZOIDS ONLY? Are you sure that when I come back from Proxima Centauri and I say Hello, how are you, I've just conquered the stars, you won't hate me for it? Are you?"

"I'm sure," she said.

"And how many others?"

"I don't know."

"Quite."

"It doesn't matter."

"Listen to you. Like hell it doesn't matter. You could turn around in ten years' time to the assembled ranks of your starmen, culled from the finest asylums in the country, and you could say: Sorry, boys, the taxpayer has decided that if his little boy can't be a spaceman he's damned if he'll let some punk out of a funny farm be one either. We can probably channel you into sewing mailbags and making road signs, provided that you put up with the environment provided. Otherwise, we could shoot you. How d'you feel?"

"That's childish," she said.

"Precisely," I said. "That's why it's such a real possibility. Have you seen your local taxpayer recently?"

"Have you?"

"No. But I have seen that scientists never consider the consequences of their actions. Not the real consequences. Think of the silly bastard who invented the wheel."

"Now you're simply retreating into foolishness."

I finished eating, and I put the knife and fork down very carefully.

"That's right," I said. "Put to flight by contemplation of the enormity of it all."

She poured me a drink and offered it to me. I shook my head, and she sipped it herself instead.

"If I come back," I said, "will you marry me?"

"What would that prove?" she said. "Either way?"

I didn't know. I didn't press for an answer, either. At that particular moment in time, it was a pretty silly question anyway.

"You might wish you were wrong," I said. "You might."

"Harker," she said, "you're a fool. I hope with all my heart that you come back. And if you come back, we win as well as you. Some of them might hate you, but since when has that been new? No matter how much they hate you, we can't afford not to make use of you. We need the stars."

"Don't we all?" I said. "Don't we all?"

Cage of Darkness

CHAPTER 11
Time Isn't on *My* Side

The men who live in Block C didn't voluntarily shoot themselves full of cocaine or chew peyote in order to give themselves a special kind of experience. They weren't momentarily dropped from the routine of life like the victims of diseases or car crashes. They were put into their present circumstances as a punishment (a *debt* to society).

They have been given *time*. Somebody else's time. Their own time has been taken away from them, in order to pay that debt. (What does society do with the debts they collect? When is the big payoff?) Mind you, it could be that fair exchange is not robbery (courts don't commit crimes), and the time the Canaanites are given is equal in value to the time that is taken away from them. How can you measure it? (No one in Canaan has a watch.)

The men in the deep cage aren't the only ones who make big deals in time, of course. Look around you, at the civilized world. Are most of those people selling their labor, selling their skills, their talents, their abilities? Hardly. Three men (and women) in four deal almost exclusively in time. They trade in their own time and get, in part exchange, derelict factory time or tattered office time. Plus, of course, a wage. Time is money. (Would you buy a secondhand car from Father Time?)

But the worker's time is measured by the hands of the clock. Only a segment of the day has to be traded in. And there are weekends and holidays. In Block C, the men have made the total trade. They retain not a single instant of their own time. They have, instead, an eternity of prison time. If factory time is derelict, what can one say of prison time? An icy waste of time? A time-vacuum? A quicksand of time?

We do not have words.

We have philosophies: do your time; don't let your time do you.

We make comparisons: there is hard time (slow, troubled, agonizing) and sad time (when you're dying). When one man tries to unburden his troubled conscience onto another, he may be accused of stealing that man's time. But usually, in Canaan, we acknowledge theft as a legitimate activity. We are usually ready to listen.

This is what I know of one man's troubles:

Poor Judas never had a chance. This is a sob story. It is calculated to pluck at your heartstrings and make cinematic violin music. If you don't enjoy it, that's your privilege. Could your heartstrings be out of tune? Almost certainly. It's too much to expect that *you* could play Dancer's music. You don't belong to Dancer's world.

And that's the real killer.

Nobody lives in Dancer's world. Most certainly not the people who *are* in it. Because Dancer's world is beyond the limit of endurance. It is an inhuman world, and he didn't make it with human beings in mind. Why not? Where would Judas Dancer ever see a *human* being? There are too many of them. You can't see humanity for the sheer weight of the flesh. World population, five billion. Everybody knows. Human? How?

Forget the myriad deaths that the strange face of tomorrow might threaten you with. They aren't important. They don't matter. *Everybody* dies. It doesn't matter how or of what. Forget all the poison and the disease. Forget the starvation and the thirst. Forget what the TV screen tells you. That kind of peril is always around the corner. It's what they're saving you from, and what they'll *always* be saving you from. And they'll continue to save you, just so long as tomorrow wears a face that is worse than today's. They have a vested interest in that Dracula mask that tomorrow always wears. Forget it. It doesn't matter a damn. Death, for all its lopsided smile and its drooling blood, is not what scares Judas Dancer. It's not what moves him. It couldn't ever be. Judas Madman's dance is not a dance of death. Judas Dancer's chessman motives weren't forced on him by the way he was going to die. What's *important,* in Judas Dancer's world, is what you *live* with.

And what did Judas have to live with?

Four billion people on the day he was born. Five billion on his tenth birthday. How many now? Don't ask me. I lost count.

So what?

Is five billion people too many? Is four? Is three? Too many for Judas Dancer. I don't know about you. Hell, I don't even know about me. It all depends where you are and where you can go. I know where I am. Where are you?

Crowding causes stress. Stress causes shock. Shock causes Judas Dancer. Madman's Dance is a shock-strained world. It behaves kinda dazed. It doesn't know quite where it's at. It can't walk a chalk line. It needs lots of hot, sweet tea and sympathy. It has wild eyes, and it swears itself blind it'll never be the same again. When it can swear at all, that is. Mostly it just mutters.

Madman's Dance is the world, of course. Not Judas. Judas isn't dazed. He's sharp and pointed. He can walk a straight line over broken glass. It cuts his feet to ribbons, but he can keep straight. And narrow. He has tame, quiet eyes and he swears all the time.

Sometimes, though, he mutters. Just a bit.

Judas isn't the product of evolution. He isn't a machine shaped by a few million years of environment and ancestry. Shock isn't part of his innate psychology, his basic anatomy, the purposeful state of his being. What comes out of Judas isn't just the nature of the *beast*. What comes out of Judas is what went in. Interpreted. Processed. Analyzed. Analogized. Reacted to.

GIGO.

Judas is a bone broken because he was bent too far. He's an innocent little blood cell lysed by unfair osmotic conditions. He's a heart stopping because his blood is bubbling nitrogen.

He has rhapsody of the depths. He's really deep down.

Where else could they put him when he surfaced but in a decompression chamber? Along with the rest of us. We all got the bends. We're as bent as that cracking bone.

There's no way on Earth of stopping Judas Madman's Dance. It's Newton's third law. Action: crowding. Reaction: shock. Or maybe it's Newton's second law. Then again, remember the first. Judas can always keep a straight line. There's no force big enough to turn him aside. How could there be? Mass infinite, acceleration absolute zero. How does *that* compute?

When Judas Dancer was living in his mother's womb, he was driven mad by his mother's blood. Mummy had no bandages. She had blood instead of embalming fluid. Mummy even had guts. The world got to Mummy, all right. She had no defenses. Perpetual stress causes perpetual shock. First the adrenaline goes. It takes such a pounding that in the end it just leaks. You live your life on a permanent Hill House high. Your brain races—high gear and no way to shift. The gears can't take it. The pituitary just can't cope. Your blood goes sour. Okay for Mummy. Just keep taking the pills. But what about the bastard in the cage of flesh? He's sharing your time, your blood, and you're in shock.

So who's Judas?

Judas Dancer, unborn, was soaked in stress long before the day he was born. An insane fetus.

It didn't show. He wasn't born microcephalic, phocomelial, or mongoloid. He was born baby shaped. With just a shade more luck, he could have won competitions. But there was always just that little bit too *much* competition. Baby contests take so much more winning these days. Like wars.

Baby Judas was colored shocking pink. What else? His whole system was chemically unbalanced. His blood was mad, and his brain never had a chance. His tissues were mad long before they began sucking up the world. He never had a chance. Neoteny cuts both ways. You can absorb the world into your pattern of growth. Great stuff. Judas Dancer absorbed the world into *his* pattern of growth. That's Judas. That's the world.

Okay, what about the world? Here we are. Day zero. Judas has just emerged.

That's nothing remarkable. You don't even notice. It

happens six times every second. Or is it ten? Do you know? Do you care?

Six times a second, all over the world, lunatics are coming out of their madhouses. You don't give a tinker's dam. Quite right. You have your pride. Mirror, mirror on the wall is the portrait of Dorian Gray. Too bad.

You measure madmen by what they do to you, not by what they are in themselves.

(Did it ever occur to you that *you* . . . ? No, of course not. Sorry I asked.)

You wouldn't recognize a madman unless he scratched your eyes out.

You educate Judas Dancer in exactly the same way you've been educating your children for centuries. Sorry. Did I say "you"? I meant *we. Us.* You *and* me. The old pals act. The old school tie. Brothers of the revolution. Champions of the circular argument.

As I was saying, we schooled Judas just like anyone else. His madness made no difference to his educability. We pavloved him regardless. What Mummy and Daddy didn't like they belted out of him. What Mummy and Daddy did like they bribed into him. In the age-old tradition of the beggars of Calcutta, we carved and crippled Judas into his appropriate slot. We knocked the rough edges off him and stuffed him into his hole. With a hammer. Lubricants milk and blood, with just a soupçon of kindness. We betrayed his thinking capacities with arbitrary assumptions. We betrayed his behavioral development with rituals. We carefully obliterated the links between his thoughts and his feelings, between his experience of himself and his experience of the world, between his emotions and his actions, between his wants and his needs. Christ Almighty, we did a job and a half. We killed him dead, and hell, with just a shade more cooperation and gratitude we'd have turned him out as sane as you or I. Sorry, as sane as you. With me is where he ended *up*. Back in the womb, again. Alas.

All in all, Judas's life was nothing unusual.

Judas was only a *little bit* unusual. It wasn't really his fault, though perhaps I shouldn't make excuses for him. He just wasn't very good at being a puppet. He got confused. The strings just weren't attached. Maybe if we'd hammered a little bit harder and hadn't allowed ourselves to weaken so that we intruded that seasoning of kindness, it would all have been just fine. He could have been a worker. Bluff, hearty, salt of the Earth. He could have been a brain. Sober, serious, pillar of society. He could have been a snob. A sham whipping boy for the sneers of superior men. Or maybe a clown. One of those quaint and charming cynics, or perhaps an intellectual. Maybe even a media man. He could have done *so much*. His whole life was ahead of him.

Too far ahead. It would have beat him on the flat. He had no chance uphill.

We mustn't blame ourselves. Judas Dancer *was* mad. Quite insane. A disgrace to the human race. His shock-strained system persisted in rubbing his feelings up against his thoughts, his thoughts got mingled in with his speech, his feelings interfered with his actions. And for the final humiliation (of us, that is, he didn't even *real*ize) who he was got all snarled up with what he tried to be. No chance. He was a positive danger to society, and he went right ahead and proved it.

We all knew it was going to happen.

We're all shocked. We're all sorry. We're all hypocrites. When I come to think about it, I'm not quite sure why

Judas came to Canaan instead of one of the other 4,999,999,999. I suppose it must be a matter of degree, or something. Judas is a graduate of society, class of '93. Highest honors. On the other hand, it might be that there was something special about him after all. Who would know? Is there any such thing as a single, individual human being? A unique? A singleton? A one-and-only? Is any man an island? Was there anything genuinely, honestly, authentically original about what took place between Dancer and his mother, his father, and his neighbor? Surely not that most of the dramatis personae ended up dead. *Everybody* dies.

Judas Dancer might just be a random factor plucked from a pool of five billion. You and he together might even constitute a statistically significant sample. (You don't believe it? So what kind of a sample do you usually use when you decide what to believe?)

Do *not* identify with Judas Dancer. Do *not* attempt to relate to what he does and says and thinks. Do *not* try to learn from your experience of him. Don't listen to a word he whispers in your ear. It's only a dirty word when all is said and done. Shut your eyes. Forget it. If you can, with all that adrenaline in your system.

I could tell you whom Judas Dancer killed, but I won't. It doesn't matter either. It doesn't even matter that Judas is on good old Block C (Block Canaan) with the rest of us chosen people.

After all, he's among friends.

MADMAN'S DANCE

CHAPTER 15

Specific Spatiotemporal Patterns of Neuronal Activity

The ground beneath my feet is a mobile brown mud, streaked with yellow and black. Caught in the steaming broth are algae and diatoms, their flotsam staining the mud green in places. Scaly insects and tiny frogs dart across the surface, sometimes floundering, sometimes snatching up smaller skimming insects or swimming, spinning rotifers. Occasionally, the gurgling of an animal throat, the splutter of a writhing body in deeper water will indicate that there are larger predators waiting in their hiding places.

The swamp winds around and between the twisted roots of immense trees, whose foliage forms a dappled canopy way over my head. Many of the trees resemble maidenhairs or twisted replicas of weeds grown many times too tall. Some have stalks like monstrous sticks of rhubarb,

with adventitious hairs as thick as my arm all the way up
the grooved stems. The forest floor is covered with clumps
of mangrove and rhododendron bushes, their tangled
branches hanging Medusalike over the stagnant water into
which their black roots vanish.

Many interwoven, mottled creepers festoon the larger
trees and provide, in their turn, an anchorage for ferns and
fungi and algal webs.

I see, between the threads of the green curtain, the
wings of dragonflies and the scales of fishmen, all hiding,
all their forms twinkling briefly in the filtered sunlight.
Thousands of gnats and midges and other minute jewel-
winged flies with slender bodies and multilenticular eyes
form an ever-present cloud that engulfs me.

The world feeds on my blood.

Tiny mites and other forms too tiny to see individually
swarm over the cork bark of the trees, turning the wood
into a living shell.

There is a stretch of muddy sand beneath my feet.
Across the brown surface scurry a horde of sandhoppers
and spiders. Dead and rotting shellfish are washed up by
turgid ripples into a thin wash of scum around the edges of
the sandbank. Small lizards perch above shade-green
pools, remaining perfectly still, save for their tongues,
which flash back and forth with orgiastic fervor.

The sounds are all individually slight, but cumulatively
they are well-nigh deafening. There are scratches and
clickings, the sawing of insect legs and the clucking of
amphibian throats, the screaming of a million deaths per
minute. There is a steady sucking and hissing in the body
of the water, a groaning and creaking in the forest itself,
the chatter of rain in the sky. The raindrops never reach

the swamp—they are swallowed up by the crowns of the trees. Every single one.

I am frightened, dissolving into the alkaline water, eaten by the carrion flies, petrified into the boles of the trees, sliced and hung out to dry in the sunless, sickly air with the lianas and the bindweed.

I am drowning.

TITAN BASE TO CANAAN. TITAN BASE TO CANAAN. COME IN CANAAN. TITAN BASE TO CANAAN.

The man in the death-mask is stretched out before me—a corpse. The forest is feeding on his flesh-smeared bones. I watch them eating slowly through his mask, holding my breath until I can hold it no longer. The mask dissolves into a thousand beetles and worms.

But they have already consumed the face inside. They have been working from within as well as without. I do not know who he is—which of us, if one of us at all. I do not know whether you are dead or not.

At least I know that. I do not know. I have been forced to cry for help and recognize that. But I am still screaming, somewhere in chaos. I have merely fled through a continuum of awakening. I am running through the pages of sleep, but I can find only more dreams and more. I can find neither the beginning of the book nor its close. I cannot find doors, I cannot find windows. I can only wake and wake and wake, while that scream goes on forever in a universe that is empty of everything save the scream, and I cry and cry for help.

But the answer: the *answer* . . .

CALLING

You made the Law within which the Earth existed, and by which mankind had to learn to live. And I had to learn to live. And you, if you could. If you did. If you have . . .

The Law provided that there should be going forward as well as going backward. It provided that we should exist in aeonic time, between the crevices of the ticking clock and above the clicking register of creations. You provided for standstill and rewinding of the clock, rewiring and the setting of alarms. You gave us the procession of night and day, but also said that night would be, and day would be in the random flux of chaos, where we should find them. That was madness, and we welcome it.

You decided that there should be no death save destruction, and that which could abide could be

CANAAN

immortal, and that the gate of heaven could not be opened by those who suffer under the Law.

You cast us down to dwell in the deepness of your Earth, while you went away to find out whether there are bars around our cosmic cage.

Into this wild abyss I was escorted, and my path amid confusion and tumult and discord I charted with my companions, a dancer whose name is Judas and another whose name is very probably

TITAN

nothing more than another mask to conceal him. I took the advice of chance in order to choose my way.

The way was hard and fierce, because this is a world filled with anger and primal fire. The countenance divine is

CALLING

thundered and scarred, and I know that if settlement and peace are to be found then it is only at great expense.

It is as though you said to me:

I have lived in your world which has treated me in its

fashion. Now you shall live in mine and see your world treated in my fashion, and you shall share it. You are
CALLING
challenging me still, and you are laughing as you point to the forbidden stars.

I see that I am unwelcome in your world, though you do not hate me, and my threats—and eventually my claim upon your throne (which was madness and welcome)— mean nothing at all to you, if you mean anything to yourself, which now I concede that I do not, and have never, and will possibly never, know.

C . . .

Is there an

. . . ALLING

answer?

Titan Nine

CHAPTER 13

Tomorrow Morning
Is the Beginning of
the Rest of Your Life

On the eve of the journey, I wanted to sit right down and write a letter to all the folks back home, to say hello, and maybe a speculative good-bye, and to wish them all the best, even to tell them that my God I'd do my best to get them out. I wouldn't have raised any false hopes—they wouldn't have believed me. But Major Chalk had killed my letter-writing stone dead. I had no private agony columns any more.

I was too jumpy to play patience, let alone poker.

I'd have appreciated more than anything else a chance to get away from the base, but of course that wasn't on the prescription either. I was beginning to suffer from a kind of misanthropic claustrophobia. I couldn't bear to be touched, and as zero hour approached with the hands of the clock, people seemed to converge upon me, to become imminent. It wasn't that there were so many of them, just that they seemed to be getting as close to me as circumstances would allow. I felt like a millionaire about to make my will asking for the loan of a five-dollar bill to light my cigarette. Everybody was anxious to get a slice of me for their souvenir collections. Never before had people been so ready to laugh at my jokes.

There was no escape. I was a cog trapped inside a machine. Locked, engaged. I couldn't move without shearing the pins of my purpose.

I got rid of Hurst. He was finally allowed to fade into the background, where I'd tried to put him all along.

I know that nobody was getting any sleep that night, including me, and I just wanted somewhere that I could be, for just a little while.

Jenny's part was almost over, and I would have been very grateful for something to say to her. But what could I say? Let's go to bed and have something to remember each other by? Not with the microphones and the hidden cameras. Not with the mute eyes of the world and posterity, like Pinkerton's, never sleeping, devoting their precious time and attention to me. I'd been in Jenny's pocket for far too long. The only conceivable thing I had left to say to her was good-bye.

So I went to see Mike Sobieski.

He was nine parts of the way to happyland. Drugged to the eyeballs. He couldn't even see me.

"What's the time?" he said. His voice was firm, but none too healthy. He was living by hanging on to the hand of the clock. Doing his time the hard way, minute by minute.

"It's twelve-thirty."

"You should be in bed," he said. "It's way past my bedtime, too. But I guess it's a special occasion. We can stay up late if we want to. It is you, isn't it, Harker?"

"It's me."

"Can't trust myself these days," he complained. "I dream too much. All this firedamp they shoot into me. Don't keep needles anymore. Have to use a gas pump."

"Bad?"

"Bad! How the hell do I know? I'm as high as a kite, and I haven't been down for a week. I wouldn't feel a red-hot poker if it smacked me in the gut. I could be dead and I wouldn't know."

The whole string of patter was distressingly false. Those drugs might be killing all the pain, but tomorrow's lift was flooding him with thoughts, and thoughts were painful—not in themselves, but because of the way they were running around his mind like bulls in a china chain store. I wondered if it might not be better to leave him to the ministrations of the doctors, but I didn't suppose that the ministrations of the doctors were the most important thing in the world to him. My TITAN might be. He was only living the Project. There was nothing else left in him. He and Lindquist—a pair of one-eyed jacks.

"Anybody else with you?" he asked.

I shook my head, but he was still struggling to look expectant, waiting for an answer.

"No," I said.

"My wife's gone home?"

"I don't know your wife, Mike. I didn't see anybody."

"What's the doctor doing?"

"Sleeping. The nurse is outside."

"Good," he said. "That's good."

"Take it easy," I said. "There's a fair while yet. It's all a formality tomorrow. Nothing can happen. Just take it easy till I get back. You can get excited then. I'll have a drink for you, to celebrate for both of us. You get excited then—and to hell with the heart attacks. But not now, Mike, okay? I can't take it. Just quiet."

"I hope you can get in here," he said. "With all the people. There's bound to be people. No way of avoiding them."

"I'll tell them all to go to hell," I assured him.

"Of course you will. Don't spare the president. Tell them to go to hell. Shout into the microphones. They'll cut it off the tapes, though."

"Cynic."

"I can afford it now. Project directors aren't allowed to be cynics, but it's after midnight now."

"You're still Project director," I told him.

"Because I haven't the strength to sign my resignation or the grace to want to? I'm an embarrassing accessory. The skeleton in the closet. Beyond that door—maybe just beyond the end of my own nose—Fred Jacobson is director. He can keep his face straight. I can pretend to be human now. I'm off the job."

"That's not what they say," I told him. "It's all your baby."

"Yeah, well we all know what they say."

"They mean it."

"I hear what they say. Please do not disturb. You can look but you mustn't touch. Patients should be seen and not heard. Everybody has to die by the book—discreetly. That's what the doctors say. They're my voice now."

"You don't have to listen to them," I told him. "You're the boss."

"Don't you believe it, son. Once they get you down they

make damn sure you die by the book. Don't die in bed, Harker. Die on Sirius Five or some planet of a sun we can't even see. Do it your own way. If you don't want to die their way they won't let you die at all. Just keep you on as a machine."

"I know," I said.

"I only really sent for you to say one thing," he said.

"What's that?" I asked.

"I wanted to promise you I'd be here when you come back. They think I'm a good bet to fade out before then, but I want you to know I'll wait. I'll see you right, Harker. I'll be *here.* You remember that."

"I'll remember it, Mike," I said. "You'll be here waiting for me. I'll come straight here."

I stood up and began to back away.

"Harker?" he said, his voice suddenly harsh.

"I'm still here," I told him. "You want me to stay?"

"Hell no," he said. "I'll be asleep any minute. Just wanted to ask you something."

"Okay, Mike."

But he didn't have a question. I knew he wasn't out of his mind on the morphine high. Everything he said he knew he was saying. It was all important.

I went away, and I closed the door. Without a question, he wouldn't be waiting for an answer. He knew I was coming back. There'd be time.

I rang Jenny from the nurse's desk.

"What do I have to come back to?" I asked her.

"Figure it out," she said.

"I count my blessings every time I have a second to spare," I said. "It comes to zero every time."

"Pessimism," she said.

"Truth," I said.

"Where are you speaking from?"

"Hospital."

"You want a sleeping pill?"

"You have to be joking."

"You won't sleep."

"Neither will you."

"I'll take a pill."

"I've got to go now."

"Good night."

"And thanks."

I put the phone down, scowled at the nurse, and went back to my apartment to sleep. I tried not to notice the eyes that followed my every move.

Cage of Darkness

CHAPTER 12
Strategies

There are various strategies for doing time, but virtually all of them are applicable only to the ordinary prison term. The experience of Canaan time is intrinsically different, and the available strategies are considerably restricted.

Struggle—the refusal to capitulate—is obviously quite out of the question. One can be a rebel for two years or five, but the idea of maintaining a posture of rebellion indefinitely is quite meaningless.

The strategies available to the Block C prisoner are therefore the strategies of retreatism, a conscious exception from the deathly environment. In the beginning, this is always adaptation. It is always conscious. But, as time goes by, there is always the doubt that conscious adaptation is only a cloak concealing a complete participation in the deathliness of the Block.

Every man in Canaan dies there. Twice. There is death absolute, and death strategic. There may be years between. The men in Block C may well be the only men in the world who have experienced death, studied it, discussed it, and reached conclusions about it. On the other hand, there may be six or ten more Canaans in this country alone. There may be thousands of dead men in the world—whole communities of them discussing their deaths in terms of pieces removed from a chessboard, folded hands in a card game.

How can we know?

There are other deaths than strategic and absolute, but I have not seen them in Canaan during my stay. Luis, who has been here longer than any of us, tells us about death by resignation, death by fear, death by the literal coming apart of the personality. Not merely premature burial, which we all discovered, death-before-death. Luis has provided us with accounts of those who have discovered destruction-before-death. They do not last as long, in the between-time, so I am told.

Perhaps if it were not for Luis, many more of us would find destruction rather than the soft death. But Luis is a master strategist—a strategist for all of us, not merely for himself. He is an environmental engineer, perhaps the greatest of them all, because the environment which provides him with his clay is surely the poorest of them all.

Luis Dalquier has taught me more than any other man I know.

He was a gambler of genius. He was not the greatest hustler in the world, by any means, but he must have been one of the greatest players. Talent he had in truckloads, but it was talent he didn't know how to exploit.

The first thing which makes any man a great poker player is an absolutely firm disbelief in luck. Luis knew there was no such thing, and thereby gained an advantage over virtually every other man that ever saw a hole card.

A sucker, like everybody else, can read a stud hand as it

lies. He knows the probabilities of his improving to the various potentials which reside in his incomplete hand. He knows the possibilities inherent in his opponents' hands, and he knows the probability distributions relevant to their improvement. (Anyone too stupid to calculate this much doesn't even rate as a card player.) What separates the greats from the goods is the control and the judgment and the respect which is added to that basic knowledge. No matter how sharp a guy's probability theory might be, no matter how perceptive his psychology, if he believes even a tiny bit in luck then he is a loser at heart. Because a man who knows that luck exists knows that it is luck which decides his eventual fate in the game. Once a man starts believing that his next card, or his opponent's card, or the card his opponent already has in his hole is determined and/or determinable by fortune, fate, kismet, destiny, the cosmic pattern, the outlay of the universe, the will of Allah, or the great unknown, he is a *loser.* Dalquier was not a loser.

The second thing which makes any man a great card player is *feel.* The great card player, like Luis, is never a thinker, a calculator, a concentrator. Poker is the toughest game in the world on a man who tries to rivet himself into the game. No one has perfect concentration. You can have everything in the world going for you and still shit out through simple tiredness. But not Luis—Luis didn't ever need to figure the odds in his head. He didn't need to debate the chances inside his head once a showdown was reached. He didn't need to make his consciousness monitor his betting. It flowed through him like an electric current. He knew it all by feel. It didn't come naturally to him, by any means. It was *programmed* into him by hard math and hard practice and hard psychology. It came to him slowly, that feel, but it came. He won it.

Nobody ever told Luis that the cardinal principle of card-playing is that bluff is to conceal, not to deceive. He discovered that himself, built into his growing understanding of the game. He was an automatic concealer. He never lied because he had a wholly natural in-built total disregard for the truth. He never knew the meaning of truth, never even thought that it might have a meaning. To him, truth had just as little referent as luck (or God, or kindness, or altruism, or heroism, or humanity—Luis disbelieved an awful lot of things).

I don't mean to imply that Luis never lost a game of cards in his life. Even pinball machines could beat him eventually, for all his perfect timing and magnificent butterfly-flipping. He was a joy to watch playing pinball (it was said), because he was practically in there with the ball, with the circuits and the clickety-click of the score. But the machines always got the better of him in the end, because that's what they were designed to do. They just kept boosting up the replay score until it needed a miracle to make it. Luis didn't deal in miracles, only in practicalities. He was no wonder worker.

And so it was with packs of cards and racehorses. You can never know it all. The ultimate judgment and control is always beyond you. That's what keeps a poker player playing. No man has a God-given right to win; he can only come out so far ahead relative to the cards. It was that theory of relativity that kept Luis in the game, getting better and better, without end.

Luis made some small fortunes in his time, but he was only a player, never a hustler. The game isn't life—it's an excerpt from life. After the game, win or lose, you have to come back to living. Luis was a master strategist at that, too; but, as everyone in the world knows, the human race is fixed—the deck is well and truly stacked. Not only can't you win them all, you can't win, period. Dalquier had the talent to clean out the world, but that in itself was self-defeating, because his talent told him he couldn't do it.

He made competition for himself simply by telling the truth about how good he was. People hated him for that, and they longed to see him proved wrong. Crowds rejoiced every time Dalquier lost a play. They had a warped idea about what sort of thing constituted proof (and wrongness). Most great artists can win themselves any amount of respect and admiration, but Luis went a little short of that, and made himself more enemies than another man (with a different temperament) might have done. Luis was always one to put the screws on a bit too hard. He didn't just beat a man; he beat him *good*. He didn't go around rubbing people's faces in the dirt and stomping them, nor did he sneer and laugh. But he was a hard, cold man, not a hustler—he was too clear-sighted, too great a player, for that.

He was an alienated man, was Luis. The world was on the other side of the fence. A lot of men would have paid good money to watch Dalquier crawl, but he never did. Even when he was beaten through and through, one way or another he'd always walk away. No one ever saw him crucified. They all loved to see his money slide across a table. They all hungered for his blood to follow it. Many men were so hungry for that blood money that they convinced themselves God and luck were going to give it to them. That kind of man always gave Luis his money back and a lot more besides. They were the easy ones in the game. They were absolute hell outside of it.

Dalquier won, if anything, too much on the table. He left himself without sufficient cards to play outside of the games. That was Dalquier's problem—he loved the game too much. He played the game so well that he gave himself too many handicaps once the game was over. The chips he couldn't cash were the ones he put on too many men's shoulders.

He was immovable. But the world is irresistible, and we all know what happens when the irresistible force launches itself at the immovable object. The object simply disappears. Gone—into another world. Canaan.

I concede to the people who sent Luis to his present resting place that for once they were right. He is mad. Raving mad. Somewhere along the line, he came apart.

The thing that his madness did to him was the worst thing imaginable. It left him his talent, his skill, his feel. All it did was take away his need to win.

Luis Dalquier is the greatest gambler I know. One of *the* greatest. But he doesn't care whether he wins or loses. It just doesn't matter a damn to him.

So what is he?

Nothing.

He's a paradox, a human vacuum.

He's taught me all I need to know about strategy and survival. He's taught us all. He's given to us everything that he can't use himself. He's been broken by the crooked wheel we call the world, slapped out by a hand that came from a stacked deck. He was cheated.

But he was never proved wrong.

We probably owe what we are to Luis Dalquier more than to ourselves. All of us.

We never win, because in the game of cat and mouse you play with us there is no winning in the rules. There is no provision made for us to win.

But you can't prove us wrong. You can't diminish us at all.

MADMAN'S DANCE

CHAPTER 16

You Can Drive a Horse to Water, but a Pencil Must Be Lead

Snow is falling in thick white flakes from a dark gray sky. It is crisp and deep in the ground, smothering the frozen soil. There are tall evergreens all around—their trunks are straight and vertical, like the bars of a cage. No tracks are visible in the snow, but wet black patches on the lower branches of the white-cloaked trees testify to the recent passage of some fairly large creature. I think I can see it, not far off, standing stock-still amid the shadows, but my vision is confused by the diagonally sweeping snow, and I cannot be sure.

As I strive to determine which of several shadows might possibly be alive, other living beings tramp into view from the opposite direction. They are men, wrapped up tightly in thick woolen clothes, wearing tight-fitting caps and earmuffs. At each step their furry, knee-length boots sink several inches into the snow. There are five of them, marching in single file. Four are carrying guns; the fifth has a stout wooden pole some seven feet long.

All are looking quickly from side to side as they walk, as if they think each shadow might be a man or monster in disguise. At a signal from their leader they stop. Silently, he motions one man to the right, another to the left, urgently indicating a spot where he has—or thinks he has—seen something.

The leader raises his hand and pauses to wait for his men to reach their positions. The men raise their guns and aim them. Still there is nothing I can see that I can be sure of. But their quarry, realizing that he/it is discovered, bursts like a black thunderbolt from its hiding place in the crowd of shadows.

At first glance I think that it is a man, unclothed above the waist despite the bitter cold. Then I perceive that the creature is naked below the waist as well, but unhuman. His abdomen sweeps from pale flesh to thick bay fur, short and straight. Where a man would have possessed stocky, heavily muscled legs, he had long, graceful ones tapering to small hooves. Behind, there is a second abdomen, supported by powerful hind legs. A long tail swirls out at the base of the spine.

It is a *centaur.*

Soundlessly, the guns go off, their operation betrayed only by the livid splashes of color accompanying the explosions. The centaur zigzags madly through the trees, apparently unhurt by the first blast. It finds a lone human blocking its way and careers away to its right, charging straight into the sights of the main party of three. The leader aims his rifle, but it is kicked away by flying hooves as the centaur rears to an awesome height. The gun flies

away, and the hunter falls back, his arms protecting his
face. The second gunman drops to his knees, and the man
with the staff thrusts it fiercely into the human solar
plexus. The man-beast collapses to one knee, and the
kneeling man lets loose a blast of fire. The pole is raised to
strike again, but the creature, blood pouring from a
shoulder wound, stumbles away from the men.

The other two draw in, firing twice each, quickly. The
centaur falls, its skull shattered and its body bleeding from
two or three more wounds.

The leader staggers to his feet, brushing off the snow,
while the others tie the centaur's feet together and thread
the pole under the knots so that it can be carried. They set
off clumsily, boots sinking deep into the soft surface, four
supporting the pole and the dead beast, the erstwhile
leader bringing up the rear, carrying two of the guns.
Their faces are averted from the direction of the driving
snow, and for a moment I think they will not see me.

But one looks up, and they stop. Sudden shock registers
on their faces. Their eyes grow wide, and their foreheads
crease, with surprise, disbelief, and fear . . . and something else. I think it must be guilt. I watch the shock die
away, and all that remains is the savage hunger and
perhaps a hint, no more, of guilt.

The leader opens his mouth to speak to me.

THIS IS TITAN BASE CALLING HARKER LEE. COME IN HARKER
LEE. ACKNOWLEDGE PLEASE. ACKNOWLEDGE, HARKER LEE.

But no sound comes out.

As I pass by a rock-surrounded pool, which is replen-
ished at every tide by gray salt water, I hear the voices of
the Medusae. I pause to listen, but I do not dare look over
the rocks to taste the horror of their snake-limbed features.

HARKER LEE

"Sister," wail the two who guide the third (for she is blind, with eyes of black jet), "do not look into our faces. Already they are frozen into terrible masks."

"Where are you

HARKER LEE

?" asks the blind one, and I can imagine her head turning as her black eyes wander in their futile quest.

"Sister," they implore, "turn not your head."

"I cannot see you," she complains in anguish.

ACKNOWLEDGE

"Sister, look out

HARKER LEE

to sea!"

"I am

HARKER LEE

lonely," says the blind one, and she weeps. As the sea waves beat around her crab-clawed feet, her tears dissolve the jagged spurs of stone around the pool and envenom the sea.

THIS IS TITAN BASE

and envenom the sea.

THIS IS TITAN BASE

and envenom the sea. . . .

CALLING

CALLING

CALLING

Titan Nine

CHAPTER 14

Where No Man Has Gone Before, Beyond the Split Infinitive

I said something, but it wasn't words.

There was silence. Shock silence. More silence than shock.

Then . . .

"Is that you? Harker, is that you? We hear you, Harker. This is TITAN base. We hear you, Harker."

My throat was dry. I felt as though I had a king-sized hangover. I could hear burbling from the speaker. It was panic. Rushing about. Disbelief. Anguish.

"I heard him. I tell you I heard him. He didn't say anything, but I heard him. I heard him."

Silly bastard.

"Ta . . . ke it . . . ea . . sy," I said. It was difficult. I coughed.

"There! That's him. You heard him. Never mind me.

Talk to him. Give it to me. Harker! Harker! We hear you. Take it easy yourself, Harker. Just take it easy. You made it, Harker. You made it."
    I didn't say anything. For the moment. I didn't have anything else to say. I waited. I could hear the action still drifting wordlessly over the radio as people moved beyond the microphone at the other end. They sounded right next door. They *were* right next door, there was hardly any lag. Where was I? I didn't like to ask. What a line! I must be late. I'm too close. The ship must be almost home.
    "Hello, Harker."
    "Not so loud," I told him, almost before he started.
    "Sorry, Harker. This is Fred Jacobson. Are you all right?"
    "As well as can be expected."
    I heard him exhale noisily. "Am I glad to hear your voice," he said. "Am I just glad?"
    "Didn't you think I was coming?"
    "Man, you been away a long time. You're late, do you realize that? You're *very* late. You been out there for days without a peep. You had us all very worried, you know that?"
    "If I'd known about it I'd have been very worried myself," I told him. "I just now woke up with a head like a furry teacup."
    "You're days late," said Jacobson, repeating himself like a parrot.
    "Yeah," I said, quietly. "Doesn't time fly when you're enjoying yourself?" And I laughed. Weakly.
    "Take it easy, man," said Jacobson. "No rush. Take your time."
    I found to my surprise that I could flex my fingers and wriggle a bit inside the clamps. I did, and it felt terrible.

Painful. I really was back. All the way. I was cold-sweating something terrible, and I felt as though I'd left my legs behind.

"What's my pulse rate?" I asked.

Pause.

"Sixty-nine, Harker. Your pulse is sixty-nine."

"Stop saying everything twice," I told him. "That's great. Sixty-nine. I'm almost healthy."

"You're okay," Jacobson confirmed, as if it were a miracle. "The important thing is how you feel."

"Ugly," I said. "Just a bit. How long do I have to stay in this thing?"

"Till touchdown."

"I know *that*. How long?"

"Two hours and eleven minutes."

"Two hours!"

"I told you you were late."

"Dammitall, I could have had a couple of hours' sleep." I laughed too long and too loud. I sounded hysterical. "Reception committee all gone home, have they?" I said. "President back in the White House, Hurst in the doghouse, crowds gone back to rent-a-crowd? The band didn't have to learn the Stars and Stripes after all?"

"You're so right, Harker," he said, entering into the silly spirit of the thing. "It's like a wet Sunday in Beverly Hills down here. But we've got the phones jammed right now. The news is spreading."

"Lucky old Hurst," I said. "This is the moment he's always dreamed of."

Silence.

"What time is it?" I asked.

"Four-twenty. Afternoon."

"I didn't get you out of bed, then."

"Nobody sleeps these days."

"Really? You can get good pills, you know."

He sighed. "You sound really great," he said. He sounded really paternal. "Just like you never went away."

"I've been right by the phone all the way," I said. "Never even stepped outside to take à look at the view. No postcards from Proxima this trip."

"What happened, Harker?"

"Just a little trip."

"Bad?"

"Not good."

"You remember?"

"Like it was yesterday."

"Why were you late?"

"My alarm clock didn't go off."

"We've been calling virtually nonstop throughout the time since you came back to normal space. A signal went out every four minutes. We've had a man here every second. There was never a sound, no matter how hard we shouted. Your medical checkout was fine. As soon as Dr. Segal saw your monitor trace she said you'd be fine, but when we couldn't raise you . . . Well, I guess even she had her doubts. She's on her way here now. Henneker's been chewing the carpet. I've lost hair."

"How about Mike?"

Silence. Not pregnant silence, but the kind I was more used to. Deflated silence. Have you ever killed a good conversation by saying exactly the wrong thing?

He must have figured the silence had already told me, because when he spoke, it was only to confirm what I knew.

"He's dead, Harker."

"Poor bastard," I said, all but under my breath. "He shouldn't have done that. He should have waited."

Silence.

"When?" I asked.

More silence.

"He died about an hour before you took off, Harker. We didn't tell you."

"You didn't think it was worth mentioning," I said, dryly. "All those days of small talk. I sent messages back to him. Any kind of stupid crap, just to keep me from being pig-sick and fed up. But you couldn't tell me. Not you, not anybody. Whose idea was it?"

"We didn't dare," said Jacobson.

"You thought it might upset me."

"Yes."

"Well it damn well has. And you reckon I was late. What the hell did you think? That if I knew the old man had died I'd die myself of despair? *Did* you?"

"No," he said. "But it couldn't help. We wanted to help. We couldn't tell you."

"Thanks a lot," I said. "It's nice to know that people really *feel* for me."

"I run a Project, Harker."

"So do I, friend. So do I. The same damn Project, if you want to know. You know, I like to know these little details."

It was a good time to be quiet. He was saved by the appearance of someone I'd much rather talk to. He passed over the microphone.

"Hi, Jenny," I said.

There was a shuffle.

"Hello, Harker," she said. The warmth that came a

thousand miles to meet me had to be felt to be believed.

"You were right," I told her.

"I know," she replied.

I was temporarily at a loss. The radio was about as private as a World Heavyweight Boxing Championship fight. It was a great opportunity for insulting enemies, pushing our PR department copy, and being a big bore. It wasn't actually the right place and time for talking to Jenny, saying things I wanted to say.

"Do I go into quarantine?" I asked her.

"Yes," she said.

"You be there?" I asked.

"Yes."

"I want a cigarette, a drink—not beer—and some food. Mush, I guess. All I can stand is mush. I want to be human enough to take a shower."

"I'll get it."

"You don't have to prepare the mush. Light the cigarette yourself, okay?"

"I will."

"How's everything?"

"Running smoothly."

"You miss me?"

"Yes."

"You still expecting me back?"

"Are you late?" she asked, sounding infinitely tired and infinitely relaxed. "There's been so much to do. I hadn't really noticed."

"Never a dull moment in the secondhand marble business."

"My time's all taken up," she said.

"I know how you feel," I said.

"No you don't."

"I hope you can fit me in."

"I'll manage."

"I'll see you," I promised.

"I'll put the routine boys back on," she said. "I'll be here. But posterity is listening. Take it easy."

"Hello, routine," I said. "Happy New Year from the stars."

"It's July," said somebody.

"Forget it," I said.

* * *

"Hi," she said.

"No crowds," I said.

"No crowds."

"No cameras, no microphones? Off the record for once? They owe me that."

"No cameras and no microphones. Medical privilege."

"Damn. Alone at last."

"It sure as hell didn't do you any harm did it?" she said, and I could see that she was in tears. Happy tears, which didn't affect her voice, but just oozed and crept down her cheeks.

"No," I said. "It didn't do me any harm. No worse than a big drunk or having a tooth out with gas. I've seen bigger space monsters sitting up trees."

"I'm glad," she said. Simple as that.

It *was* as simple as that.

"I'm the same," I said. "You weren't looking for a miracle?"

"After all that time," she said, "wouldn't *you* be looking for miracles?"

"Sorry about that. I guess I just couldn't tear myself away."

"You did it, though."

"I did it, though."

She put a hand on my forehead. The cold sweats were finished. The hangover was dwindling.

"Am I here?" I asked her. "Am I here and not laid out in the bed next to Lindquist?"

"You're here," she told me.

"You could be just saying that."

"Then you'll never know."

"I want to be here," I said. "Not in the bed next to Lindquist. I couldn't stand that."

"It's real," she told me.

"Back in the cage."

"Aren't we all? Did you ever leave it?"

"I left it. I think. So what? One cage, another cage . . ."

"Stop it," she said.

"Poor Johnny Lindquist," I said. "He'd have made a great hero. A really first-class hero. Hurst won't. Not really."

"You're the hero."

"Mike Sobieski is the hero. He died before I came back, before I even went up. It doesn't matter. It's his triumph. He's the hero."

"Maybe."

"So we reached that great big asylum in the sky," I said to her. "A ray of light in a cage of darkness . . . no, that's silly. We reached the stars. There might be a way, you know. There might be a way for you, and for them, and for Lindquist. Even for Mike. You could be wrong, you know."

"I hope I am," she said.

The tears had all dried up.

I hope she is, too.

MADMAN'S DANCE

CHAPTER 17
Adeste Fidelis,
Laete Triumphantes

Adrift in a crystal ball.

All that is visible in a maelstrom of shadows and specters and colored chaos is a dendritic cloud: a mighty silver oak whose acorns are drops of golden starshine, whose leaves are burnished copper shades of sunset, whose buds are shafts of light, whose *fleurs du mal* are sandstorms.

It stretches unattainably into the unimaginable distance. I am one with its network of roots, its web gleaming from the soil of shadows. It grows away from me in all directions like a crystal lattice, like a *reta mirabile*, like tangled silken hair, like great staring eyes mirroring love and fire.

The sinuous twisting of its leaves in a nonexistent breeze tantalizes my blind mind. They twirl themselves into my skull like corkscrews and stir the emptiness of my brain.

The buds, like navels, stark in the sheaths of the growing points, radiate light and a sound which penetrates deep into my bowels. A voice from the dark, into the dark again. A voice from beyond the grave and beyond the stars. A voice from seven hells aflame, a voice which strikes deep into my frozen being, denying, defying the soul which looks on, unafraid and without understanding.

The blooming flowers like the eyes of hell's gate. The twin pools of blurred heaven that meet in love and kindness, and might almost manage to communicate. The spring of existence. Dead eyes. Mine. No reply. In the dream of deathlessness, they reject everything. Utterly and absolutely. Renounce the whole universe. Forbid even laughter. No understanding.

The seed of the tree, like blind, swimming sperm, singing in the lacework branches, falling slowly so slowly so slowly so . . .

HARKER, THIS IS JENNY.

They turn in flight, head over heels, changing shape like drops of water on a hot plate. And to the soul, they *are* water—immaterial. And slowly still they fly. Down deep into the heart of heartless mind, a brokenhearted mind, a broken-minded heart. Diving for the cool calm cool calm cool . . .

HARKER, I KNOW YOU CAN HEAR ME. ALL YOU HAVE TO DO IS LISTEN, HARKER. YOU CAN HEAR ME. YOU'RE ALIVE. LISTEN TO ME, HARKER.

ocean of emotion. And never reaching. Always a little further on, dreaming in the dankness of absolute nothing. The emotions are a cipher, a zero, a nonmeaning. Their stillness is a perfection.

And they land, in the dry dusty dry dusty dry . . .

THIS IS JENNY, HARKER. SAY SOMETHING. SAY ANYTHING. JUST MAKE A NOISE. SHOW US SOME WAY THAT YOU KNOW WHAT'S HAPPENING, THAT YOU KNOW WHAT'S GOING ON. LET US KNOW THAT YOU'RE COMING BACK, HARKER. THIS IS JENNY, HARKER. ANSWER ME, HARKER. PLEASE ANSWER ME.

desert of the emptiness, where only the soul lives in a

cave, coming out to pick the bones of consciousness at dawn and evening.

Smash. Like a broken crystal ball. Crush an eyeball in a fist. Splash. Tear a heart out in sacrifice.

The soul lives in a cave. It comes out at dawn and evening, to pick the bleached bones of consciousness.

HARKER
  HARKER
    HARKER
      HARKER
        HARKER
          HARKER

At the end of a journey in aeonic time, hungry and thirsty, with faint heart and fading vision, I am an old man holding a jug, sitting beside myself. The shade of an oak tree protects both of me from the furious sun.

I am tired. I am tired.

I the old man pours something from my urn into a china cup and offers it to me. I reach for it and find my arm too heavy to lift. All of me is very heavy, especially the old bones and the young head. I press the cup to my (other) eager lips, and I drink as deeply as I am able. As I tilt the cup, liquid runs from the corners of my mouth to stain my shirt and moisten the earth which feeds the oak tree.

"What is it?" I ask, for the draft is very sweet.

"Water," I say, my voice like an echo from far, far away,

HARKER
HARKER
HARKER

"only water."

And the cup in the crumbling hand recedes from me into a giant funnel of forgetfulness.

Jenny
Harker

All around me the magnificent dark, empty and infinite. My kingdom and my joy. A curtain of hungry darkness, ready to take me in its fond embrace, to hug me, to cradle me, to love me. A deep, pregnant silence—a silence of waiting—a silence of anticipation. My empire and my pleasure.

I wait with patience, resplendent in the glory of my halo of light. The light is golden. I am a fly suspended in amber. A firefly, all around me the almighty night.

Afar off, the night splits to divulge a second glow. Tiny as a pinprick at first, it grows. Proxima Centauri.

Within its mute red halo is another man—taller than I and stronger. He is assured and arrogant. He wears red and yellow, whereas I wear gray and blue.

He is
Harker
and he hates me.

"

Harker

" he says to me. "You grow older each time we meet. I will win what you have, and one day soon I will drain you of existence."

"*One day!*" I say, scathingly. "One day, and a sooner day than yours, I will succeed. I *learn*, in my between-times. What have you learned since last we met? What have you in real profit? Nothing. You have spent and you have wasted. You have not saved; you have not speculated. Your one day is a distant dream. Mine is numbered among the tomorrows."

"You are mad," accused
Harker

He comes forward, his chest heaving, his tongue between his teeth, his halo growing hot. But he moves *so* slowly. His eyes are like plates of glass. He is suspended for an eternity. He is afraid, and he is at my mercy.

"One day," I say, mocking him.

"Tell me," he says, recovering himself. "What next? What now, little man?"

"Look around you," I say to him. "All around you is the dark. We alone, you and I, have light. The light defines the reason for our being. We are the light. We exist to scatter the light. And light we shall have, great blazing worlds of fire to flood the dark and force the blackness away. Turbulence. Chaos. Fight."

"Chaos," my
HARKER
whispers, hating even the sound of the word. I can still remember him screaming.

"Your dreams can never come true," he tells me. "You are mad."

The bubbles of light pull themselves apart. My son recedes into the darkness.

He smiles at me as he goes, and says, "Good-bye,
HARKER
We will meet when your lights go out."

"My stars will never go out," I tell him.

I stare defiantly into the lovely, maternal dark. I ignore the small voice which whispers within my skull and says, "You are insane. This whole universe, the dark, you,
HARKER
your dimensions, they are your imagination. You created
HARKER
in your mind. You make mad worlds, and justify them in defeating

HARKER

And even then, who wins? Could you hold and humiliate a real

HARKER

? Do you win your arguments only in your twisted mind?"

The dark is waiting yet. Still and placid. Welcoming and loving.

"Why?" I say, and I cover my eyes with my tired hands. And the sky is full of the dust of distant stars.

Forever?

HARKER THIS IS JENNY

Is there an

ANSWER

answer . . . ?

PLEASE